Perilous Promises

"You cannot leave this house," Lord Temple said with a smile. "Not until you satisfy your bargain with the woman in white."

"But what more can she want of me?" Julia demanded. She was searching her mind for a solution when she found her chin firmly held by Lord Temple's fingers. "What?" she whispered. How had he managed to get to her side so quickly?

"I made a promise, too," he whispered back. Then he kissed her, and it was not the hasty touch of his first kiss. Julia was enveloped in an embrace of the sort dreams were made of: warm, satisfying, and infinitely demanding.

How easy to yield to temptation, she reflected . . . as his hands performed magic . . . as his lips brought forth all the yearnings she had sought to repress . . . as she felt all her virtue mocked by ghostly laughter. . . .

Julia's Spirit

by

Emily Hendrickson

Ⓢ
A SIGNET BOOK

SIGNET
Published by the Penguin Group
Penguin Books USA Inc., 375 Hudson Street,
New York, New York 10014, U.S.A.
Penguin Books Ltd, 27 Wrights Lane,
London W8 5TZ, England
Penguin Books Australia Ltd, Ringwood,
Victoria, Australia
Penguin Books Canada Ltd, 10 Alcorn Avenue,
Toronto, Ontario, Canada M4V 3B2
Penguin Books (N.Z.) Ltd, 182–190 Wairau Road,
Auckland 10, New Zealand

Penguin Books Ltd, Registered Offices:
Harmondsworth, Middlesex, England

First published by Signet,
an imprint of Dutton Signet,
a division of Penguin Books USA Inc.

First Printing, October, 1993
10 9 8 7 6 5 4 3 2 1

1

S HE had arrived.

Julia's heart fluttered within her as the elegant burgundy traveling coach slowed, then turned through an imposing gateway. Great stone pillars guarded the avenue leading to the house beyond, and the iron tracery of the gate itself displayed the griffin that had symbolized the Blackford family through the years.

She leaned forward, eager to catch sight of the manor home where she was to spend the coming weeks. Ignoring the babbling of her twins, the soft-voiced urgings of their nursemaid, and her own abigail, Hibbett, she lowered the window to put out her head, just like any ordinary traveler in strange parts.

"Milady," Hibbett remonstrated, scandalized at her lady's behavior. The abigail had been with the Dancy family since girlhood, and took liberties denied to a newcomer. After all, she had known Lady Winton since her infancy, when she was merely Miss Julia Dancy. Hibbett had long administered reproaches along with brushing soft ash brown curls, quite ignoring the looks from limpid green eyes charmingly set in an oval face. Now, away from home, Hibbett meant to guard her young lady well.

"I want to see, Hibbett. I have read much of this house and its antiquity." Julia's gasp of delight when she espied the Italianate gem set on a velvety green lawn against the wooded hills brought the abigail to the coach window as well.

"Most impressive, would you not agree?" Julia shared a glance with her maid before settling back on the comfortable seat for the remainder of the drive, for it would not do for anyone in the house to see her gawking from the coach window. The soft autumn breeze that had swept into the coach from the open window now ceased when Hibbett closed it.

The traveling coach sent to bring her to this estate had proven superb, and she had been extended all the consideration she might wish by his lordship's servants while on the journey of several days. It seemed that his lordship, at any rate, thought well enough of her to accord her the finest of treatment.

Her feelings regarding this trip had seesawed from anxiety to anticipation. She wondered how the viscount's mother would receive her, never mind that the gentleman had assured Julia his mother awaited her coming with eagerness. Julia had been about society too much to believe that any mother welcomed a young widow to her home when her widower son might well be hanging out for a wife. Uneasy, suspicious, cautious might be more applicable emotions rather than welcoming. The passing days would tell.

The traveling coach bowled down the long avenue to the house after crossing a meandering stream. As they neared the structure, Julia could see details missed from a distance. Sun struck the tall, sparkling, many-paned windows, setting them ablaze. The honey-colored stone building with a taste of the Renaissance was beautifully situated in a Capability Brown landscape. Numerous domed turrets dotted the roof, lending an exotic touch to the otherwise simple structure. To the rear of the house could be seen a rose garden with an orangery in the distance. Julia had looked up the history of the family, and the estate as well. Viscount Temple appeared to be an excellent guardian of the family home.

"The house was built at the time of Queen Elizabeth, you know," Julia informed the others. "I do hope it is not one of those haunted old places one hears about. You know, the sort with a wailing lady who carries her head tucked underneath her arm, or the ghost who lingers in the gallery." Julia chuckled.

Violet, the nursemaid, gave a small worried frown.

"While there are those who devoutly claim ghosts exist, I do not," Julia stated in a firm voice.

"You do not think there will be such here?" Violet asked timidly, not easily convinced.

"Nonsense. That sort of thing exists only in novels like *The Castle of Otranto*." Julia smiled kindly at the girl, then beamed a delighted look at the three-year-old twins, who appeared as fine as fivepence, not upset by the pace of their travel in the least. "We shall be there in a moment, darlings."

Julia gathered her reticule and smoothed her gloves as the coach drew to a halt before one of the flight of steps.

In a short time, a stiff-looking butler had marched across the terrace, then down the steps to greet the arriving guests in the process of being assisted from the traveling coach by the groom.

Julia, her five-foot-five-inch figure drawn properly erect, surveyed the haughty man, then in her most gracious manner said, "I am Lady Winton. I believe we are expected."

Shortly, she was following the butler, who identified himself as Biggins, into the house, her children and servants right behind her.

In the wood-paneled and flagstone entry hall a proper-looking housekeeper, dressed in black bombazine with her chatelaine dangling from a plumb waist, awaited them.

"I am Mrs. Crumpton, milady. If you will be so good as to wait in the great hall, I shall take your children to their room, ma'am." She dipped a proper curtsy, then motioned the little group who had entered with Julia to follow her.

Exchanging a speaking look with Hibbett, Julia signaled her maid to shepherd the children and Violet on their way upstairs. Then Julia followed the sour-looking Biggins across the hall to a severely austere room.

She slowly entered the large room designated as the great hall and strolled to the center of it, looking about her with curious eyes.

"Supposed to intimidate one, I fancy," she murmured to the magnificent marble fireplace surround. On the far side of the room, which was indeed great in size, she saw a shuffleboard table that looked nearly as old as the house.

The Dancy country home, while quite nice, did not run to such antiquities. Carpets of great beauty and age splashed gentle color across the floor, and the tapestry-covered and elegantly carved oak chairs set near the fireplace were stiff relics of bygone years. But, as lovely as they were, they appeared somewhat lost in the large room.

A soft, scraping noise brought her attention to the Minstrel's gallery. Through the elaborately carved railing, she could make out the piquant face of a young girl. This must be Anne, the daughter of Viscount Temple, one of those whose face Julia was expected to paint in the coming weeks. About to call out to her, Julia was forestalled by the entry of an elderly lady dressed in pale gray challis, striped in black and violet, and an exquisite white lace cap.

"Lady Winton? I am Lady Temple. Welcome to Blackford Hall. I trust you are not done in by your journey. But then, perhaps you are accustomed to jauntering about the countryside in your pursuits? I suppose one can become accustomed to most anything if needs be. I think it admirable that you resort to painting miniatures to augment your income. It is so tiresome when husbands die and fail to adequately provide for their widows." Lady Temple sighed as though put-upon. She did not appear encouraging in the least, much to Julia's dismay.

Intrigued by the odd manner of welcome, Julia stepped forward to politely acknowledge the greeting. "My trip went well, thank you. The coach your son sent to convey us was all we might desire in comfort. May I say that I look forward to doing your portrait. And Miss Anne's as well," she added with a flicker of a glance at the Minstrels' gallery. As to the oblique reference to her late husband, Julia said not a word, but firmed her lips at the thought of him.

A stir to her left caught Julia's attention. The man who entered brought a guarded smile to her lips. It was evident from her initial confrontation with Lady Temple that her path while in this house was not to be smooth. How he would handle the matter remained to be seen.

"My Lord, it is pleasant to see you again," she said in the most polite and somewhat distant of manners following an exceedingly proper curtsy. With things being what they were, she had no desire to further annoy anyone.

His black hair was neatly brushed back from a smooth brow above those incredible, meltingly dark eyes Julia had painted while in London. He captured total attention when in a room. Dangerously handsome, she reluctantly admitted.

"Lady Winton. I am glad to see you have arrived without injury, and looking as fresh as a rose. The roads being what they are in these parts, one never knows." Noel Blackford, Viscount Temple crossed the room with swift steps to reach Julia's side. He bowed over her hand most correctly, then turned to his mother. "I am pleased you were here to greet Lady Winton on my behalf, mother. I had requested to be notified at once." That Lord Temple was not best pleased at his butler's neglect seemed evident.

Julia decided she would not wish to be Biggins. The lapse of one who is usually devoted to his master also offered her a clue as to the butler's loyalty. One had best learn these things if one were to visit for a time. She wondered if Mrs. Crumpton was also in Lady Temple's pocket.

"But why are we in this room?" Lord Temple looked about him with a puzzled air. "Come, Lady Winton, join us in the drawing room, where"—he tossed a mystified glance at his mother—"we usually gather."

Julia accepted his arm, then walked at his side up an elegant flight of stairs while wondering what manner of bumblebroth she had tumbled into. The undercurrents were such that one would easily be swept along in them.

The drawing room was a spacious, comfortable-looking room with many windows overlooking the countryside. Commodious chairs Julia knew to be eighteenth-century French were scattered about, with interesting tables, magnificent paintings, and a cozy fire to take the chill off the early autumn day.

Two young women were seated on a cream damask sofa to the far side of the room, and rose as Julia entered with Lord Temple and his mother. They were exquisite creatures, gowned in the highest fashion, groomed to within the

inch, and most likely possessed of a fine pedigree, Julia
concluded with amusement.

Lady Temple drifted across to join the beautiful girls,
then faced Julia and her son with a gracious—and somewhat defiant—look on her face.

"May I present Lady Pamela Kenyard and Miss Edythe
Sanders, Lady Winton." She turned to them and added,
"Lady Winton is to paint my face, if you can fancy such a
thing. She did a miniature of Noel's eyes for me not long
ago."

Miss Edythe Sanders was a petite blonde with baby blue
eyes and dressed in a white muslin that had a profusion of
delicate blue ribbons decorating it. The slender and somewhat taller Lady Pamela had magnificent chestnut hair
dressed *à la Sappho* and wore a gown of the palest peach
jaconet trimmed in deep russet. Neither girl seemed pleased
to see Julia.

Miss Sanders tittered behind a dainty hand. "I cannot
imagine staring at another's face so long. Do you paint
many gentlemen? That seems excessively improper for a
lady." She exchanged a sly look with Lady Pamela.

Annoyed at the little barb directed her way—not to mention the narrow look from Lady Pamela—Julia stiffened,
then replied with a smile, "I am fascinated with the faces I
paint. No two are identical. One can learn much about the
character of a person while studying their visage. Young
girls are particularly pleasing, for they reveal such charm. I
shall enjoy doing the portrait of Miss Anne. I have painted
quite a few children as of late."

Then she smiled at Lady Temple and said, "You have the
same excellent bones your son has. I believe you shall
transfer to ivory very well. Most elegantly, in fact."

Her glance strayed back to the other guests. Lady Pamela
and Miss Sanders both gazed at his lordship as though he
were a particularly succulent dish, and they were starved
for food. Ah, so that was the lay of the land. Julia was not
the least surprised that Lady Temple sought to nudge her
son's steps in a particular direction. It was done all the
time. Which girl might end up with the prize?

Lady Temple gestured to the cluster of chairs, and they

all arranged themselves with varying degrees of grace. Julia made no attempt to appear artful. She found the coy glances and darted admiration of Miss Sanders and Lady Pamela rather amusing. Actually, Julia ought to feel flattered, she decided. Apparently those "Diamonds of the First Water" believed that Julia was competition. There could be no other reason for such silly behavior.

"Mother thought you might enjoy the company of other young ladies while you are here," Lord Temple said, capturing Julia's attention.

So that was the excuse the velvet dragon had given her son for the house party. There was no doubt in Julia's mind that Lady Temple intended to guard her son well from any dangerous dalliance, particularly with a widow of undistinguished background. It really was not the thing for Julia, even if she was Lady Winton, to be painting, and for a fee. Julia bestowed a serene smile on Lady Temple.

"How very gracious of you, my lady. However, I would wish to concentrate on my painting. I shall have no time for socializing. I could not permit myself to impose upon you a moment longer than necessary." Julia could not miss the flicker of elation in Lady Temple's eyes. Quite as Julia had suspected, the dowager had plans.

"Lady Temple said you are widowed," Lady Pamela remarked. "How tragic for such a young woman. And with children as well. So very sad," she concluded with just the proper degree of sympathy.

"Indeed," Miss Sanders agreed. "You must miss your husband very much." She darted a look at Lord Temple, then appeared assured by the bland expression she saw on his face. "What a pity you did not have a son to carry on the line, then you might have remained at your home." Miss Sanders made it subtly evident that she, for one, would welcome Julia's absence.

"Actually, my husband and I were not together for long. I married Giles shortly before he left for the Peninsular War. He never returned." Julia's face concealed her opinion of her loss quite admirably.

"Yet you did not remain with his family?" Lady Pamela queried, a look of avid curiosity crossing her face.

"No. I preferred to reside with my sisters, for they had need of me." Julia well knew that it was customary for a widow to live with her husband's family, particularly if there were children. That had proved impossible when she failed to produce the requisite heir, but she had no intention of making her marriage tea table conversation. She caught a glimpse of the tea tray being carried in by Biggins, and welcomed the interruption.

"Well, I must say that you are very courageous to venture out, painting portraits. How businesslike of you, I daresay," Lady Pamela concluded.

Julia suppressed a grin with great difficulty. If this young—and exceedingly pretty—chit thought she was going to discommode Julia by making her seem like the veriest cit, she missed her mark by a long chalk. Julia had been about in the highest Society, and had observed presumptuous young girls set down by masters of the art. Instead, Julia patiently smiled at Miss Sanders, one of the famous Dancy smiles that had left more than a score of young men dazzled by its beauty. By her sudden blink, it was clear that the beauteous Miss Sanders had not expected such an amiable response.

"I hardly think one might consider Lady Winton as a merchant," Lord Temple chided ever so gently, unexpectedly coming to Julia's defense.

"Goodness me, no!" Julia laughed softly in agreement. "No self-appreciating businessman would keep records like I do. I fear I would make a shockingly bad person of business."

"Artistic temperament?" Edythe Sanders suggested in her soft, sweet voice that bordered on a lisp.

"Perhaps," Julia replied, growing bored with this silly sparing.

"Your little girls traveled well?" Lady Temple inserted, possibly not wishing her protégées to reveal themselves as unworthy of her dear son.

"Quite well, thank you. I am an odiously doting mama, I fear," Julia revealed with a fond smile. "You were most kind to suggest that I bring them with me, for I am most reluctant to part with them for any length of time."

Lady Temple smiled thinly at this disclosure of Julia's excellent example of mother love, then set about pouring tea while Lady Pamela assisted her with the milk, sugar, and paper-thin slices of lemon.

Lord Temple had shifted uneasily in his chair a number of times, reminding Julia of her younger brother when he was about to reveal something he suspected would annoy his parent.

"Whatever is it, Noel, that has you so edgy?" his mother inquired at long last, when the social nothings that so frequently are heard over the tea table dwindled away.

"I trust you do not mind that I invited a couple of particular friends to join us," he said at last.

Julia thought it odd that the head of the household would be reluctant to invite anyone he wished, but then, not every home had a velvet dragon guarding its doors.

"I am sure you may ask anyone you please, my son," Lady Temple declared with a slight softening in her eyes.

Julia smiled to herself. Evidently Lady Temple truly cared for her son, and only sought the best for him. Julia could understand this, being a mother herself. But it was to be hoped that Lady Temple would not resort to drastic lengths to nudge her son into a marriage that might prove distasteful to him. Julia tried to imagine either Miss Sanders or Lady Pamela as fond mothers, and failed utterly. And, after all, was that not the prime reason for marriage? To produce the required heir?

A stir in the hallway caught the attention of those assembled before the tea table. A dashing dandy entered the drawing room with the familiarity of an old friend sure of his welcome.

Julia thought his waistcoat admirable, although most colorful, with its puce and gold stripes on a cream background. It certainly complemented his corbeau coat and the fawn pantaloons tucked into shining boots.

"Reggie," Lady Temple exclaimed, but whether in fondness or not Julia couldn't decide.

The newcomer sauntered forward, making an elegant leg to the group, Lady Temple in particular. He raised a highly fashionable quizzing glass that had dangled from a simple gold chain to view the ladies.

Julia thought his pretensions amusing, if perhaps a trifle overmuch. She had glimpsed the dandy here and there while in London, but he did not often frequent the same sphere that she did.

"Allow me to present Reginald Fothingay to you, ladies. Better known as Reggie to his friends. Lady Pamela Kenyard, Lady Winton, and Miss Edythe Sanders are visiting with us, Reggie."

"Charmed, I'm sure," the elegant dandy replied, then turned his gaze upon his friend. "Jolly glad you wrote, Temple. Always enjoy a stay at your little place. A bit of shooting coming up, perhaps? Partridge are said to be excellent this year." The dandy dangled his quizzing glass from his fingers, his keen gaze now flicking from one lady to the next in a most assessing look.

"Perhaps," Lord Temple replied. The shortness of his answer was belied by the warmth of his smile when he greeted his good friend.

Julia repressed a smile. Reggie Fothingay out shooting? But then, it was an acceptable sport to a gentleman. The beaters did the work, the gentleman walking through the woodland to shoot the partridge that fluttered to the sky in alarm. Or did the elegant Reggie have a different sort of pursuit in mind?

Reggie declined to settle in a chair, most likely to afford the ladies a better view of his elegance. Instead, he politely took his cup and saucer, then lounged against the fireplace mantel, sipping and surveying the others. If he might have preferred something a bit stronger than tea, he gave no indication.

"Anyone else due?" Reggie lazily inquired during the next lull.

"Dick Vansittart wrote he'd be stopping by, but for how long, he couldn't say. His sister Constance has demanded his presence at the upcoming baptism of a little niece or nephew, as the case may be."

"Quite so," Reggie mused. "Family very important to

Dicky. Good lad," he declared with a touch of condescension.

Lord Temple gave a bark of laughter. "Not fair, Reggie, old fellow. Dick would have your hide if he heard you call him a good lad."

"Aye, that I would, if I thought it might do me any good" came a comment from the doorway.

Whereas the dandy had tousled sandy hair and piercing gray eyes, Mr. Vansittart possessed kindly brown eyes and rather nice brown hair with a tendency to curl. He had not the pretensions of a dandy, but was rather like Lord Temple in his dress. Neat but not gaudy, thought Julia with appreciation.

Dick Vansittart strolled across the room, his neat blue coat fitting him with elegant ease over gray pantaloons. His waistcoat, Julia noted, was a simple affair of plum cassimere. Restrained style, indeed. She felt more warmly toward this gentleman, with his easy charm and ready smile.

"We are complete?" Reggie inquired of his host in a soft side.

"But for a couple my mother has invited to keep her company. Lord and Lady Lacey."

Reggie darted a look at the dowager, then nodded. "I suspect she intends to seal your fate, old fellow." He spoke in a voice that just barely reached Julia where she sat a trifle apart from the other ladies.

Lord Temple shrugged, then turned to Dick. "Tolerable trip?"

"Tolerable, barely. My carriage lost a wheel on the way, or I'd have been here before."

The gentlemen fell to a discussion of the road conditions, wondering when the improvements on the main roads out of London would reach the more remote communities.

Julia tore her attention, albeit strained, from the men to concentrate on the ladies. It seemed they had given up enticing the men with their charms and had turned to more familiar topics. Fashions.

"Do you have a favorite mantua-maker in London, Lady Winton?" Lady Pamela inquired with an appraising study of Julia's very modish traveling gown.

Julia blessed her decision to take the time to pause for refreshments, and change from the rumpled carriage gown she had been wearing before arriving at the house. Anticipating trouble was good for something, especially one's self-esteem.

Serene that she looked well, Julia nodded. "My sisters and I patronize Madame Clotilde. I find her designs so original and always in good taste. Have you heard of her?" Julia concluded in dulcet tones.

Since the madame was among the premier mantua makers of Town, it was unlikely that Lady Pamela had failed to hear of her, unless she had not entered Society.

"Or are you not out?" Julia added with a motherly smile.

"Of course. My mother presented me at court, then gave me a lovely ball. What a pity I did not know you then." Lady Pamela said with sly politeness.

"I fear I tend to indulge in Lady Tichbourne's conversaziones rather than come-out balls," Julia said with commendable ruefulness.

Perhaps slightly intimidated by the knowledge that here was a lady who was accepted by the highest sticklers of Society, for only the most interesting people were invited to such doings, Lady Pamela fell into uncertain silence.

Lady Temple asserted herself by suggesting that dear Lady Winton must be exhausted from her journey and would most likely wish to have a quiet lie-down in her room. She abruptly rose, then shepherded the three young women from the drawing room with remarkable speed.

The two other girls were swept along down the stairs with Lady Temple. Julia could hear their clear high voices floating up as they drifted to the lower floor, away from the gentlemen.

Julia remained in the hall, awaiting the attention of the housekeeper and wondering what sort of room she was to occupy. Would she be placed next to the nursery and have a governess type of room far from the guest suites? Or might she be near the others? She must have presented Lady Temple a dilemma. As Lady Winton, Julia deserved a room of quality. As a painter of portraits, she rated a lesser accommodation. How interesting to see the solution Lady Temple had reached.

Mrs. Crumpton bustled up, motioning to the stairs. "Follow me, milady."

As she walked slowly up the stairs behind the housekeeper, Julia heard the sound of additional voices down in the entry hall. No doubt the remaining couple in the house party had arrived, the Laceys.

In a way, Julia found it comforting that there would be people about, and things to do. Her feelings for the elegant Lord Temple were too hazy, and most likely exceedingly foolish, for her to desire the intimacy of just his family, not to mention his frequent company.

Lord Temple was a most intriguing man, rather uncommunicative, even abrupt in his speech, although his voice was rich, and what he did say was usually of interest. He possessed beautiful eyes. When Julia had painted a miniature of one of his eyes—a ridiculously popular rage at the moment—for Lady Temple, she had become an expert on the color, depth, expression, and utter beauty of Lord Temple's eyes. The emotions stirred within her when she had touched his face while adjusting his position during the painting sessions had not faded from her memory. It was best she set aside such impossible sensations.

At the absurdity of her thoughts, she smiled to herself at the moment the housekeeper paused before a door, then opened it. The charming room quite put an end to her evaluation of Lord Temple for the moment.

Julia politely thanked the housekeeper following that woman's kind explanations, then shut the door, grateful to be alone for a moment.

The bedroom appeared exquisite, with handpainted wallpaper of a delicate Oriental pattern. The twins would adore looking at the multitude of birds and flowers, not to mention the quaint figures of Chinese here and there along the border just above the cream wainscoting.

Drifting to the chaise longue, nicely done up in blue print to match the chairs and pelmet above the window, Julia settled down to rest a bit. Surprising elegance, for the artist. So Lady Temple decided she belonged here. Most interesting. Would the lady lend her cooperation in regards to the painting? Julia wondered, considering the thinly veiled hostility observed.

As to Miss Anne Blackford, his lordship's seven-year-old daughter, Julia would wait to assess her chances with her.

The door of her dressing room opened, and Hibbett entered with Tansy clasped in her arms.

"She wants to see you," the abigail declared.

"Let them join me for a while. I fear the days to come will be busy ones, and I shan't have as much time for them as I might wish." Julia exchanged a rueful look with Hibbett, then sat up on the chaise.

Putting aside her fatigue, Julia welcomed her precious Tansy with open arms, and smiled at the sounds of an imperious Rosemary in the next room.

Although the twins had yet to speak an intelligible word, they made their wants known with amazing clarity.

One of these days something would happen, and they would speak. Julia knew they would. She just wished it would be sooner than later. It frustrated her that they remained silent.

Perhaps while here . . . ? She sensed that this might be a far different visit than she had anticipated, and wondered what was coming her way.

Turning thoughts to the practical, she considered that nice Mr. Vansittart of the lovely brown eyes. Not the entrancing black pools Lord Temple possessed, but warm, friendly . . . eager? Perhaps. The coming days would reveal whether or not he might prove to have potential. Julia was tired of living alone, and when her younger brother returned from the war, she might well marry. Julia had no desire to share a house with newlyweds. She needed a husband. Someday, before too long.

A rustle of skirts in the doorway, and Violet entered the bedroom. "Miss, I surely do hope this house will be a welcoming one. I like to tell you that I feel vibrations already." The young nursemaid's eyes were huge in her pointed little face.

"Pooh," Julia said, chuckling at the nursemaid's imagination. "Nothing in the world is going to go wrong."

"But what about the otherworld?" Violet whispered just loud enough for Julia to overhear.

It vexed her to think the nursemaid might frighten the girls by foolish talk. They might not speak, but they could hear well enough. Julia ought not to have mentioned the possibility when in the coach.

"Violet, listen to me. Everything will be fine. Do you hear?"

"Yes, mum," the nursemaid mumbled dutifully. But she sounded far from convinced.

2

JULIA was not convinced of her reassurances the following morning when Violet reported that the servants had
filled her ears with tales of a ghostly White Lady who had
appeared from time to time over the years. It had required a
great deal of patience to calm the nursemaid before going
off to hunt for the elusive Anne Blackford.

To add to the problem, Hibbett reported that the hierar-
chy belowstairs was extremely rigid.

"I do hope that my evening dress will prove suitable, for
I have no desire to eat in the servants' hall," she murmured
just loud enough for Julia to hear. "That Biggins is most
starched up. Although Mrs. Crumpton is all that is amiable.
Lady Temple's dresser goes in on the arm of the steward,
while Lady Charlotte Lacey's maid is escorted by the butler. I come next, ahead of Lady Pamela's." It was obvious
this turn of events suited Hibbett to a tee.

Julia tossed her maid a frustrated look while heading toward the door. The intricacies of life belowstairs in a great
house was quite as complicated as above.

Julia intended to begin her painting immediately, and set
about finding her model. Only, Anne could not be found. A
trip to the nursery wing did not prove successful. The
schoolroom not only was deserted, but looked as though it
had been rarely occupied with no sign of instruction of any
sort. Odd, indeed.

While Julia searched the likely rooms after inquiring of
Biggins where Miss Blackford might be found, and receiv-
ing little help, she considered the situation in which she had
landed.

Last evening had been a struggle between holding her

tongue and laughing at the inanities of Miss Sanders. Lady
Pamela had held herself aloof from the others, when she
wasn't casting lures at Lord Temple. Gracious, how did the
man stand such nonsense?

Lady Charlotte Lacey, who had arrived with her husband, Thomas, Lord Lacey, to round out the house party,
had shared several looks of amusement with Julia as the
evening progressed. Julia felt drawn to the older woman,
and thought she might very well turn out to be the only lady
who might prove agreeable during the stay at Blackford
Hall. At least, they both found the flirtations of the young
girls entertaining.

How wonderful to be independent and not desperate for
a husband, she thought. It had been decided that Julia
would join her younger sister, Elizabeth, in a pretty cottage
in Kensington in the event that the Dancy home was required for a newly married Geoffrey. The only trouble with
this plan was that from Elizabeth's letters, it seemed she
was highly enamored of her aunt's neighbor, Lord
Leighton. Julia wagered a marriage would soon result. And
that would leave her on her own, for she utterly refused to
intrude upon her newly married sister, Victoria.

Well, other widows had managed before, most likely she
would, too. She tilted her head in an engaging manner, then
continued her hunt.

"Miss Anne? Try the billiard room," Mrs. Crumpton
whispered as Julia paused in the hall.

Taking due note of the raised eyebrows and knowing
look, Julia quietly walked to said room to discover the
young lady ensconced on the window seat, staring out at
the rain-splashed scene beyond. She had soft, curling blond
hair that clung to her head in pretty ringlets, and when she
turned, she revealed a heart-shaped face with lovely blue
eyes. Her simple white dress edged with two frills boasted
a wide blue ribbon that matched her eyes perfectly. Anne
did not resemble her father in the least.

"Tiresome, is it not?" Julia said pleasantly. "Yet, where
would we be without the rain to nourish the crops, keep our
grass a lovely green, and provide lakes for boating and the
like."

"Papa will not allow me to go boating. He says it is dangerous," Anne replied, turning a hostile gaze on this intruder.

"What a pity. I believe that if one behaves in a proper manner, it is safe enough. But you must obey your papa, for his word is law here." Julia's eyes held sympathy for the motherless girl protected by proper prohibitions.

Anne's face became speculative, as though she examined all facets of this interesting thought. "Are you going to paint me?"

"Gracious! You make it sound as though I shall do something exceedingly painful and not at all nice. Actually, you may get a bit tired. That is why I wish to do a sketch of you first, and save you a sitting or two. May I?" Julia produced a tablet and pencil from behind her, offering Anne a coaxing smile.

"I do not wish to be painted. Nanny Gray says it is nonsense," Anne said with a mulish expression on her pretty face. She hunched her thin shoulders, bestowing a obstinate look on Julia that promised trouble.

Julia drew up a chair while hoping that the gentlemen would forget about billiards this morning, at least for a time.

"Well," she temporized, "this is to please your father, you know. We had best humor him. Who knows what might happen if he were to become angry. Does he cast spells on you if you misbehave?"

This notion truly captured Anne's attention, and she settled herself firmly on the cushions, hands folded neatly in her lap, to demand an explanation.

"Well," Julia said in her best story-telling way, "there are father's who do cast spells, you know." She proceeded to weave the most outrageous tale she could think of about a bumbling father whose wishes were transformed into ill-chosen reality with disastrous results, all the while sketching the pretty little face before her.

Anne was enchanted and reluctantly laughed a good many times, thawing considerably over the next hour. Julia could see that the girl had intended to stand aloof, or possibly refuse to sit for her altogether. Why? A portrait was harmless enough, for certain.

At the hilarious conclusion of the story, Julia rose from her chair, turning to leave the room after thanking Anne politely for her attention.

"Stop." Anne demanded with an imperious lift of her hand. "Will you tell me another story the next time I sit for you?" There was a wary look on Anne's face. It was compounded of caginess and a sort of fear, although Julia couldn't think what Anne would have to fear from a mere artist, and a woman at that.

"Indeed." Julia paused near the door, then smiled at Anne. "Until you get tired of my offerings."

"So this is where you hide yourself!" an older woman declared from the doorway, giving young Anne an awesome frown that even made Julia flinch. Garbed in a white apron over a gray challis print dress, with a severe white cap primly tied beneath her chins, her plump figure fairly quivered with her indignation. Snapping black eyes peered out from a lined face with a mouth deeply carved in a downward curve. Not a very inspiring person, nor one to delight a child.

Anne visibly shrank into the fat cushions piled behind her, her smile completely disappearing as her brief pleasure crumbled before her nurse's vexation. "Papa wishes me to be painted, therefore I must, Nanny Gray." Anne's faint voice seemed to plead with her nurse, in contrast to the autocratic conduct of previous moments when she had strongly resembled her grandmother right to the tone of her voice.

The hostile, freezing gaze that Nanny Gray turned on Julia caused that young lady to edge away in consternation.

"Indeed?" Nanny Gray intoned in an awesome manner.

"That is why I am here at Viscount Temple's request," Julia reminded in what she hoped was a kindly, and mollifying way. "And to paint the portrait of Lady Temple as well."

Nanny Gray's piercing stare seemed to strip all veneer from Julia, penetrating right to her heart. What an extremely uncomfortable woman to have about the house,

Julia concluded. Little doubt but what she was the origin of Anne's reluctance to be painted. Although what possible difference it might make was more than Julia could see.

"Come along with Nanny, Miss Anne. I shall take care of you proper." Nanny Gray gathered her chick within her wing, and bustled off to the nursery rooms on the top floor.

Julia watched from the central hall as they disappeared up the stairs and around the bend before she turned away.

"What a wretched woman," she murmured, relieved to be free of the older woman's depressing company. Young Anne most assuredly needed to be removed from the influence of Nanny Gray. And why did the girl still have a nanny at an age where she ought to be taught proper accomplishments by a governess? While Julia knew that a few people still retained the idea of a nursery ruled over by a nurse until the adolescent years were reached, most of the women she knew hired a governess once the eldest child reached the age of six. Surely Lady Temple must have suggested that one be employed to direct the education of her granddaughter.

Concerned, Julia marched down the hall, wishing to find an answer or two. Although it really was none of her affair, being a tenderhearted mother made her long to see little Anne happy. It certainly seemed Nanny Gray was not the one to do so.

Turning a corner, Julia crashed into Lord Temple. He caught her arm to prevent her from losing her balance, then left his hand there as he studied her face.

"Why the frown?" He glanced at the sketchbook in her hand. "Have you been working with Anne? You must tell me if she misbehaves. She has developed some trying manners as of late." He sighed, as any bewildered father might.

"Little girls will do things like that, you know," Julia replied with care. "I suspect it is a part of growing up, and she is nearly eight, or so you said." Julia spoke such ordinary words, yet felt the oddest breathlessness steal over her at his touch on her arm. Really, she was not some green girl, close to a man for the first time. Silly. She stared up at him with confused eyes. Then, as she took a step back, her earlier thoughts returned and she plunged ahead into what she supposed she ought not say, yet must.

"I confess that I wonder why your daughter still has a nanny at an age when most girls would be under the guidance of a governess." She searched his face for a clue, thus saw the hardening of his dark eyes and faint frown that creased his brow before he replied.

He gave her a cool look, his hand dropping to his side. "Anne is a very delicate child. She needs a great deal of care. I'm assured that Nanny Gray is utterly devoted to her."

Julia stiffened at the rebuke in his voice. While she had possibly overstepped herself in expressing an interest, she had nevertheless spoken honest truth. The child's education was likely shamefully neglected. If Julia's glance about the schoolroom revealed the truth, Nanny Gray did nothing but cosset or scold the child.

"Forgive me for my concern, but her nurse appears to have a very *un*healthy control over Anne. Nor does she support the portrait sitting. Perhaps someone less severe. . . . " Julia's gentle voice grew stern as she recalled the recent scene. She tried to remain calm, remembering she sought to assist a girl who, from the fear Julia saw in her eyes, needed help.

"I believe I commissioned you to paint my daughter, not advise me on her parenting or education. I am quite satisfied with the way things are at present." With that succinct observation, he bowed slightly, then strode off down the hall.

"Abominable man," Julia whispered in frustration. Why had he not taken the trouble to learn the proper age for a girl to acquire a governess? And, why had she expected him to immediately see what appeared so obvious to an outsider? Julia feared that by her hasty words, she might have made matters worse. It had been most unlike her to interfere like this, and she could only put it to the frightened look in Anne's eyes as Nanny Gray had led the girl away.

Aware there was nothing she might do about the problem, and wanting very much to see the joy light up in

Anne's eyes again, Julia wandered deep in thought down the hall to the stairs.

"Ah, Lady Winton, can you spare me a moment or two?"

Julia turned to discover the smiling and most agreeable person of Mr. Vansittart bearing down upon her.

"What may I do for you, sir?" she replied with modest charm.

"What a dreadful dreary day. I was wondering if you might join me for a stroll, perhaps along the gallery? I could tell you tales about Temple's ancestors to amuse you." He bestowed an engaging grin that soothed Julia's esteem.

"That sounds like a lovely notion." A delighted smile lit up her face. She decided that the charming Mr. Vansittart would be highly welcome company, especially after the confrontation she just experienced.

She accepted his arm, and they strolled to the gallery, so beloved by Elizabethan ladies on tedious winter days. The ceiling of the room contained small pictures that resembled work done by Wedgwood, appearing like cameos and looking terribly classical. The room also held comfortable chairs in small groupings here and there, so one might have a comfortable coze, if one wished. It could not be said that the house had been neglected over the years.

"Here is a dandy ancestor," said Mr. Vansittart, pausing before the first in the line of portraits. An Elizabethan gentleman in an imposing black coat over a slashed ivory doublet, dated 1566, stared back. "Sir Henry Blackford was the one who commissioned the house. Made his own fortune, mostly buying land, taking chances. This house is built on the site of a priory that he'd acquired after the dissolution. He married well, as have most of the Blackfords." They moved along to view the painting next to the builder of Blackford Hall.

"His wife?" Julia suggested, admiring the exquisite late Tudor-style gown decorated with a profusion of bows and the requisite lace ruff at the neck.

"*Second* wife, Catherine—they had not acquired the present title as yet. The portrait of Mary, the first wife, has been destroyed—most likely by this one. At least, no one has seen it. From all accounts Catherine was a wicked woman, and an even more wicked stepmother to the young lad who was to inherit this estate. Rumors abound among the servants that Mary yet haunts the place."

Recalling the tale Violet had told, Julia gave an involuntary shiver. "Dreadful story." Catherine's faintly malicious and cold eyes gazed down upon Julia with a superior mien.

"I am sorry," he said with a rueful chuckle. "I promise you the rest of the relatives are a harmless lot."

They strolled on down through the beautiful room, Julia enjoying the magnificent portraits of the family while Mr. Vansittart told amusing anecdotes about each.

What must it be like to reside amid this splendor and wealth? She could not fail to observe the high quality of the portraits. Nor could she miss the little priceless pieces of art on tables scattered here and there in the room. Previous Blackfords had been an acquisitive type.

One thing for certain, the dark, brooding eyes were an inherited characteristic, for the men of the family stared down from their frames with a black-eyed gaze that was all too familiar. The final pair of portraits were the present viscount and his departed wife. Anne strongly resembled her, especially her eyes. About the dead viscountess, Julia heard not a word, and she wondered about that omission.

When they had completed their tour, Mr. Vansittart drew Julia along to the hall, then said, "Why do we not join those in the drawing room? I believe they intend to get up a game of cranbo to amuse the time away."

"Allow me to check on the girls for a moment, then I shall be happy to join you." Julia beamed a pleased smile at him, the brilliance of which seemed to leave him bemused.

"Might I meet your cherubs, perhaps?" the appealing gentleman inquired.

"If you wish," Julia replied, then darted a quizzical glance at him as they walked up the stairs to the floor where she and the girls were housed.

At her suite of rooms, she paused after a cautioning rap, then opened the door. Not daring to flout convention, for she was far too proper, even if there were not a soul to be seen, she remained there with Mr. Vansittart, requesting Violet to bring the twins.

"How are Tansy and Rosemary? I have a visitor who would like to meet them." Julia gestured to the gentleman she could not invite within.

"They be a real angels, milady," Violet said, peeping at the gentleman with shy eyes.

"Da," Tansy declared at that moment, toddling over to where Mr. Vansittart stood at ease watching the scene.

"Da," Rosemary echoed, following her twin.

Julia froze, wondering if they might make another intelligible sound.

"Da?" Tansy demanded. Rosemary repeated that intriguing syllable.

Julia exchanged a wordless look with Violet just as Hibbett entered the room in time to also hear the twin's venture into speech.

"Do you suppose?" Julia whispered with hope in her voice.

"Quite possible," Hibbett said quietly.

"Oh, mum," Violet declared with a smile.

Sensing that poor Mr. Vansittart was quite in the dark, Julia turned to him. "The girls have yet to speak, and it seems you have broken their silence. I must thank you for your company, sir," Julia concluded with a heartwarming smile that brought an arrested expression to Dick Vansittart's kind brown eyes.

"I take it the children's father is no longer among us?" He bent to hold out a finger to the delighted Tansy.

Assuring herself that her darlings were happy and entertained, Julia left, with Mr. Vansittart at her side.

"He never saw them, for he was killed while in Spain."

"Nasty business, war. You must miss your husband a great deal, ma'am. Those little babies ought to have a papa to look after them. You need someone as well, unless I miss my guess," he said with commendable consideration.

Julia paused at the top of the stairs, giving Mr. Vansittart an assessing look. His kindly face held nothing more than polite interest. She let out a breath she suddenly realized she'd been holding.

"Let me assure you that they are well-nurtured by a cluster of doting females." As to missing her husband, Julia said nothing. How could one miss an insensitive bore? She also noted that although Mr. Vansittart courteously assisted her down the stairs, she felt none of the emotions that had overcome her when she was close to Lord Temple. Perhaps with time she might feel an interest in this nice man. And quite forget that wretched Lord Temple.

"Forgive me if I seem intrusive. I believe two parents to be ideal. See how they responded to a man? Surely that must tell you something?" he persisted.

"Nothing more than you are highly appealing to young females, sir," Julia said, chuckling lightly as they reached the bottom of the stairs, then turned toward the drawing room.

She entered what she tolerantly considered to be enemy territory with a delighted smile on her face and her arm complacently tucked close to Mr. Vansittart's manly side.

Her pleased expression faded a little as she observed Lady Temple's frown. Julia stepped away from her escort's side, withdrawing her arm.

"Good morning, Lady Temple, Lady Pamela, Miss Sanders," Julia said most properly. "Mr. Fothingay, you appear in good spirits today, in spite of the weather. Mr. Vansittart has graciously been showing the gallery to me."

"Reggie and Dick can always be depended upon to charm the ladies of the household, Lady Winton" came a deep, rich voice from behind Julia.

She turned, puzzled at the viscount's cold tone. Where had the charming gentleman she had first met in London gone? She, for a brief foolish time, had nurtured silly hopes. It seemed obvious that she had best stay out of his lordship's path as much as possible if this continued to be his manner.

"Good morning, Lord Temple," Julia said with deliberate care. She decided to behave as though their earlier altercation had not occurred. "Mr. Vansittart has persuaded me to join in the game of cranbo."

Lord Temple tossed an unfathomable look at his friend, then smiled, albeit rather coolly, Julia thought.

"I feel certain you have more important things to attend than participate in drawing room games. Did you not mention you wished to transfer Anne's likeness to the piece of ivory today?"

Julia had said nothing of the kind. But Lord Temple clearly did *not* wish her in the drawing room with his friends. Although normally of the most calm disposition, Julia straightened her spine more than usual and fearlessly met his eyes, her own snapping with irritation.

"I had momentarily forgotten, my lord." She executed an exquisite curtsy, then said, "Excuse me. Perhaps some other time, Mr. Vansittart." She turned to sweep from the room only to be detained near the door by the touch of a hand on her arm.

"I should like a word with you, if I may?" Lord Temple spoke in a casual way, but there was nothing detached about the look in his eyes. They blazed with anger that made Julia tremble slightly.

"But, of course," she managed to reply. Head bent, back stiff, she marched down the hall to the bottom of the stairs that led up to the bedrooms.

"You may behave in any way you like elsewhere, but you shall not entertain gentlemen in your rooms while in this house." There was subtle menace in his voice.

It took a moment before she realized to what he referred. The softly spoken words shocked Julia to her core. That she, as proper a lady as might exist, should be accused of such scandalous behavior was unthinkable.

"It was not what you imagine, sirrah," she protested softly. "Mr. Vansittart wished to make the acquaintance of my twins. I scarcely believe you might think ill of so innocent an intention." Of the difficulty with the twins' speech and joy in those few syllables, she said nothing.

The look she received was dubious to say the best.

"I have no wish to husband hunt, Lord Temple," Julia added with a rare flash of temper. "I have known the so-called pleasures of marriage once, and I am not eager to repeat them. Nor do I wish to give up my independence." She moved away from him and placed a foot upon the first step, then turned again. She omitted her logical alibi, that Mr. Vansittart had not been *in* her room.

"I shall not forget myself—or my place—again, you may

be certain." Head raised, her pride proclaimed in every graceful line of her body, she marched up the stairs with all the dignity of a duchess.

Noel watched the lovely, charming—and decidedly annoyed—Lady Winton disappear, and cursed himself for being the worst of fools. What had possessed him to accuse her of improper conduct when he knew full well that she would most likely have a reasonable explanation for what he had seen minutes ago. As well, he knew that Dick would not seek to take advantage of a lady while under this roof. He was far too good a chap.

Strolling slowly back to the drawing room, Noel considered the words that Lady Winton had flung at him in her quiet, yet impassioned, outrage. She had not known a happy marriage. She as much as said so. He had the notion that her love, *if* she had known such, had withered. This meant that she did not cling to the past, sighing over one now gone. Feeling absurdly cheered by this thought, Noel entered the drawing room, prepared to join the group. Upon seeing Dick, Noel made a mental note to meet the twins soon.

"What an ogre you are, Temple. Surely Lady Winton could work at her drawing later in the day?" Dick Vansittart chided quietly, yet watching Temple with an assessing gaze.

"She said something about morning light being the best," Noel replied blandly by way of explanation.

"Well, let us begin. Do join us, Lady Temple," Lady Pamela urged in the most demure of voices. She fluttered her fan in a manner she had no doubt been taught by an expert.

Her ladyship gave a faint nod, followed by the faintest of sighs, then moved to another chair so as to be closer to the restless group of young people.

Lady Charlotte entered the room with a jolly smile, offering to enter the game.

Shortly thereafter Lady Pamela put forth a line of verse. Much hilarity followed when each person sought to give an appropriate rhyme.

* * *

Upstairs, Julia fumed as she stalked down the hall until she reached her rooms. Entering, she snapped the door shut behind her, then paced across to stare out of the window at the drizzle.

"Oh," she declared to the drops that trickled down the pane of glass, "I cannot recall when I have been so angry. That he could think such things of me! What a wretched man." She whirled around and began to stride about the room, clenching her hands in her agitation. "Do I give that kind of impression? A hussy, or a trollop who would entice a gentleman to her rooms? And with my girls here?"

Provoked more than she could remember, she sank down upon the chaise longue to decide what she must do. She had agreed to paint the portraits, so she must do those. But never would she work so hard, nor complete the miniatures as quickly as she did these.

Could he have been retaliating for her remarks about the lack of governess made earlier? That seemed unlikely. Yet the charges appeared so incongruous with the amiable gentleman she had come to respect while in London. A reluctant smile came to her lips as she recalled the clever way he had handled his lofty sister, the elegant Lady Chatterton, dispatching her with ease.

Nothing made much sense at the moment. Sighing over the peculiar change in the man who had hired her, she went to the desk where she had placed her sketch and the painting equipment. She located the five-inch-long oval of ivory she intended to use, then took it to the window and lost herself while she transferred the sketch she had done earlier of Anne Blackford. Ivory made such a satisfactory surface to paint upon. It gave a luminous quality to the miniature that could not be found in any other medium.

For some time, Julia was able to forget the aggravating gentleman who had begged her to travel to his home. But as she set aside her pencil, she recalled everything, and wondered how she could face him. What would she do about dinner, which soon approached?

A gentle rap on the door stirred her from her desk. Rather then blindly welcome the caller, she cautiously went to see who might be there. She wished no further trouble.

3

"EXCUSE ME, Lady Winton, but I thought we might become better acquainted on our own, so to speak." Lady Charlotte Lacey stood in the doorway, her pleasant face lit with a smile, her shrewd eyes assessing Julia's face. "They tired of cranbo when Lady Temple proved too clever at finding a hard-to-rhyme line."

"Do come in," Julia urged, glancing about the hall, and noting there wasn't a soul in sight.

The slender lady, her brown hair in a fluffy, somewhat disordered halo about her head, entered the room, looking about her with a frank curiosity.

"I hope I may see your twins. My maid says your Hibbett talks about their clever doings with obvious relish." The sharp gaze returned to study Julia, much to her confusion.

Why this pleasant stranger sought her out to become better acquainted was indeed puzzling, although nice. Somehow, the notion that she was here merely to view the twins did not strike Julia as logical. But then, there were women who couldn't resist infants, quite a contrast from those who viewed them only when absolutely necessary. Lady Charlotte seemed to be the doting type, and that Julia must approve.

"Yes, the servants do seem to gossip about us frightfully." She was about to fetch the girls when Lady Charlotte raised a hand, gesturing to the chairs by the window.

"In a moment. Let us chat for a bit." She led the way, then plumped herself down with a pleased air, smiling at Julia with a twinkle in her faded blue eyes. "We are privileged to see some delightful plotting and flirting, are we not?"

The lady believed in coming directly to the point, whatever that might be. Julia nodded with caution.

"Goodness," Lady Charlotte said followed by a sigh, "were we ever that young, or frightfully obvious?" She stared out of the window for a moment before turning again to face Julia, her eyes alive with mirth.

"Hard to fathom, is it not?" Julia relaxed a trifle, refusing to be piqued at having her twenty-four years linked with the older woman.

"I was very sorry to see you leave earlier today. Forgive me for being a nosy old lady, but did you really wish to transfer that sketch? It is such a dreary day, that the light cannot have been all that good for your eyes."

Torn between loyalty to her employer and the desire to confide in an older woman, Julia's good manners won, and she shook her head. "The light proved acceptable by the window, and the sooner I complete the paintings, the sooner I may leave."

"Is it so important that you depart from this house?"

Julia studied her clasped hands, then nodded, confiding, "His lordship has made it clear that he does not desire my presence."

"And after going to such trouble to bring you here, complete with your little family? Not to mention dragging Thomas and I away from town, and I suspect coaxing those dreadful young ladies to visit. His gentlemen friends appeared with amazing promptness, I think."

Julia repressed a smile, then said, "Lady Temple invited Miss Sanders and Lady Pamela."

"Did she, now? I had thought better of her. Young Vansittart is a pleasant gentleman, is he not?" This remark was accompanied by a shrewd smile.

"True," Julia said. She swiftly rose, then crossed the room to open the door to where the twins played with their toys on the carpet of the adjoining room. "I should like to introduce you to my girls. Tansy and Rosemary?"

"Da?" Tansy inquired with a dimpled smile as she toddled over to where Lady Charlotte stood in the doorway.

Julia laughed, picking up her girl to give her a hug. "She may be a trifle confused, but it is a greeting of sorts."

"I suspect she is not the only one who is confused, my dear. I should hate to see the most worthy opponent I have yet to observe abandon the field to rank beginners. Promise me you will stay and not run off before the battle begins?"

Julia thought her guest had everything all wrong. No contest loomed in which Julia wished to vie. However, she really had not been eager to leave this lovely home.

"I promise to remain, although I shall not compete for anything."

"That will do for the moment. Now I wish to know what Noel said to you to bring that hurt look to your eyes. Then we may begin to make our own plans. For once, Hermoine is not going to get her way. She was responsible for Noel's first marriage, and that was a disaster."

Julia did not know what to say. She placed Tansy on the carpet, then left the twins, closing their door firmly behind her. She studied the lady who faced her with such complacency from her resumed seat.

"I do not like to speak ill of anyone, Lady Charlotte."

"Rubbish." She smiled reminiscently, then continued, "I read your fortune in the cards last evening. It is a pastime I enjoy. According to the cards, you are to remain at this house, but not until you are tested. There is danger afoot, but of what kind, I cannot say. We had best prepare for anything."

Julia sank down on the small chair that sat close to her caller, her mouth slightly ajar at the outlandish revelations. "Gracious!"

"Come, come," Lady Charlotte said impatiently. "I must know what Noel said to you."

"He accused me of entertaining Mr. Vansittart in my rooms," Julia responded reluctantly. "Lord Temple knows the children are here, and surely any woman of sensibility would scarcely lure a man to her rooms with anything naughty in mind, what with children, maids, and all that entails close about." Considering her words, Julia chuckled, then added, "Besides, Mr. Vansittart remained in the hall. He certainly never came in farther than the doorway. Truly, 'tis absurd." She gave Lady Charlotte an incensed look, then waited.

Lady Charlotte rubbed her chin, then said, "Perhaps it does reveal an interest, however. Now, listen to an older and wiser head, my girl. You will remain, and participate in everything offered. Your painting may be done early in the morning. It will not harm Hermoine to rise before noon for once when you come to doing hers. Tell her she will look younger in the soft morning light, that will bring her 'round."

"Dare I command Lady Temple? She is more than a bit intimidating." Julia gave Lady Charlotte a concerned and rather doubtful look.

"Only human, and more vulnerable than you think," Lady Charlotte said with a knowing expression in her eyes.

"Lord Temple permitted her to select his first wife, however," Julia reminded.

"He was young and foolish. I doubt very much that would happen again." Lady Charlotte wore a look of "knowing" that gave Julia the oddest sensation.

"I must say, this all seems fantastical." Julia did not accept what Lady Charlotte claimed to have "seen" in her cards, but she decided it best to humor the lady.

"I once read that passion often turns the cleverest men into idiots and makes the greatest blockheads clever. Some Frenchman wrote that, I believe. Noel is a very *clever* man." Lady Charlotte toyed with her reticule while eyeing Julia as though to gage the impact of her softly spoken words.

"No doubt he was an idiot to accuse me of improper conduct with Mr. Vansittart, but it hardly seems likely that he has acquired a passion for anyone, least of all me." Julia smiled at the preposterous notion.

"Just promise me that you will do as I have suggested." Lady Charlotte rose from her chair, then walked to the door, pausing again to face Julia. "And abandon any notion of eating your dinner in your room. Greet the assembled guests as though you actually sought your room to transfer the sketch. If anyone comments on your work, simply admit that it goes slowly. Remember, you know the truth of the matter, and you may work at any speed you like." She gave an emphatic nod of her head, then slipped from the room. Julia watched in wonder from the doorway as Lady Charlotte crossed the hall to enter her room.

Closing the door with a gentle click, Julia leaned against it a moment, frowning in bewilderment. Had she just heard what she thought she had? That slightly dotty woman had more than implied that Julia would remain in this house.

Strolling to the window to gaze at the grounds without, Julia smiled wryly. The only way she could see that she remained was if she took the position of governess. That brought a chuckle and a rueful shake of her head. Now who was an idiot?

Following the sound of the dinner gong, Julia left her room dressed in a deceptively simple gown of morone red satinet designed to enhance her slender form. In London, she had selected the gown thinking the combination of silk and wool would be needed in a country house, for they were notoriously ill heated. Now, she felt a deal of pleasure that the soft sleeves draped becomingly on her arms, and the satin stripe emphasized her slim figure. Although the neckline didn't dip low, the bodice was most cleverly cut to more than hint at her nicely full bosom.

At the bottom of the stairs, she discovered Lord Temple waiting for her. As she had not caught sight of him while descending, she could only assume that he had been lurking in the shadows. The absurdity of that thought brought an amused curve to her gentle lips.

"Please. I should like to speak with you." He gestured toward the left, and Julia nodded regally. She walked at his side while wildly speculating what on earth he would accuse her of this time. That he wished to do anything else never occurred to her.

Once inside a large library, she crossed her arms before her and stood waiting. "Well, sir?"

"I do not know quite how to say this, but I best be direct." More than ever he resembled her brother Geoffrey when he had committed an utterly dreadful deed. "I am sorry for my earlier remarks. All reports I had of you, your character, were of a woman who is most proper. I heard you not only are artistic, but devoted to your family and a patient, gentle woman. Not the sort to flirt, as I accused, and would not wish around Anne. I feel certain you would have had a logical explanation for what I saw, and I ought to have asked first."

Taken aback at this handsome apology, Julia could only give him a hesitant smile, then nod.

"I hope that you will stay on here, forget this incident happened, and try to enjoy what must be a welcome respite from the city." He faced her from some distance, leaning against the massive desk in the room, arms folded across his chest. Elegantly garbed in biscuit pantaloons, with a white marcella waistcoat topped by a deep gray coat, he placed most men in the shade.

"I shall." She discounted the rare trip to the country to visit Aunt Bel, or the Dancy country home, for they were exceedingly brief. "I ought not have chided you about Anne and her lack of a governess," she confessed in a rush. "It is none of my affair whether she has a governess or not."

"But you would procure one for your girls by her age?"

"Indeed, I would. Anne seems such a sweet girl, really, not frail or invalidish in the least. I must say that I cannot care for Nanny Gray."

"How fortunate you do not have to, then."

"Oh, dear, now I have done it again." Julia blushed the peony color of her gown when she realized she had again implied criticism of his lordship in an area that truly was none of her concern. Where had all her propriety gone?

"Come, we had best join the others, for the gong has sounded, and my mother believes in being punctual. Good cooks are difficult to keep in the country."

Pleased that relations between her and the man who had commissioned her were more tolerable, and that he seemed inclined to overlook her latest faux pas, Julia proceeded to the door, pausing when his voice reached her from over her shoulder.

"About the painting. I am persuaded that it would be best if you use a small salon to the rear of the ground floor. It has north light, a suitable table, and comfortable chairs, and you shan't be disturbed while at work. I doubt if the smell of your paints and solutions would be welcome in your bedroom," he concluded as he moved toward the door.

She stiffened a moment, then decided she had imagined that intimate note in his voice when he mentioned her bedroom. Really, how silly of her to allow her mind such invention.

"That seems most agreeable, my lord." He opened the door for her, and she slipped quickly along the hall to join Lady Charlotte and her husband.

Lord Lacey possessed a beaky nose, a high forehead surrounded by improbably wild white hair, and most understanding gray eyes. His height wasn't nearly as impressive as Lord Temple's, yet because of his thin frame, he gave the illusion of being tall. Julia liked him at once.

Lady Temple did not seem best pleased that Julia appeared in such good graces with her son, and Julia found her pique most amusing. Why that woman thought for a moment that Julia had designs on him was utterly absurd.

Looking around at those seated at the table, Julia could see Miss Sanders flirting with Reggie Fothingay, while Lady Pamela tried her wiles on Lord Temple.

Julia had to admit that Lady Pamela used all her considerable skills to advantage. Languid glances, agreeable conversation mostly given to inquiring about his estate, and a dainty appetite that implied she scarcely ever touched food, could only be designed to capture a husband.

With a disgustingly healthy liking for her meals, and preferring to listen rather than prattle, Julia decided she couldn't match up to Lady Pamela's enticement. Not that she particularly cared to compete.

At her side, Mr. Vansittart sipped his excellent claret, then inquired, "You completed transferring your sketch?"

"As a matter of fact, I did not. Interruptions from one thing or another prevented me. The children, you know. Lord Temple has offered me the use of a small salon in which to work. Perhaps I shall be able to concentrate better while in there."

"Then Temple spoke the truth. I had the oddest notion that you had been sent to your room like a schoolgirl over something." He glanced at Julia before returning to his meal.

"I had a most agreeable chat with Lady Charlotte this afternoon. She is, er, most remarkable. Do you know her, or Lord Lacey at all?"

Accepting that Julia prudently wished to change the topic, Dick followed her lead. "Unconventional is the best word to describe them both. I have heard that she reads the tarot cards."

"Truly? Like a Gypsy? How fascinating." That explained what Lady Charlotte had meant when she said she had seen Julia's future in the cards. "I should like to watch her at it, I think. Not that I believe that nonsense."

Julia glanced at the lady under discussion to find that she in turn was observing Julia with a benign smile. It gave Julia a queer feeling, and she hastily changed the subject to something else. Lady Temple was to Julia's right, and there was little point in trying to converse with her when the time came to alternate conversation as the others all did when the next course was brought to the table. Lady Temple had other ideas, carrying on a polite chitchat with Lord Lacey at her right, ignoring Julia.

When she signaled the ladies to leave the table and the gentlemen to their port, Julia strolled along at the side of Lady Charlotte. She wondered if she ought to be pleased at being included with the older women, rather than Miss Sanders and Lady Pamela, who couldn't be more than a few years younger than Julia. She decided she really didn't care. Lady Charlotte was far more amusing.

"Lady Winton," Miss Sanders said with hesitation, "would you consider doing sketches of us this evening." She blushed a fiery red, then plodded on. "I do not mean finished ones such as you would use for a portrait, but just sketches. I think it would be vastly diverting."

Knowing that evenings could drag, particularly if the men took their time over their port, Julia smiled. "Allow me to fetch my drawing pad, and I shall be happy to try to put your faces to paper. However, if I am to use my talent, I think it only fair that Lady Charlotte use hers. Would it not be intriguing to have her read our fortunes?"

A sniff from Lady Temple revealed her opinion of the scheme, but Lady Pamela seized the moment from her.

"Oh, I do hope she would. I had a friend, Susan Willowby, whose fortune Lady Charlotte read and it came true, every bit of it. Please say you will, dear ma'am."

A dagger glance from her ladyship was the closest Julia came to a scold. "Well, remember that things interfere with the cards, and at times it is a matter of interpretation."

Tantalized by her obscure words, the girls begged her ladyship to oblige them all. Consequently, Lady Charlotte joined Julia in a trip up the stairs to their respective rooms.

"I trust that you are aware things may not go as you wish?" Lady Charlotte said.

Julia glanced at her in some confusion, but said nothing, as she'd not the least notion of what the woman meant by that obscure remark, then entered the room.

It took but moments for Julia to locate her drawing pad and a few pencils. In the hall Lady Charlotte waited for her, holding a pack of large cards in her hands.

"That was a naughty suggestion, my dear girl." Lady Charlotte swished along down the stairs at Julia's side.

"I thought it fair. Sketching can be so boring. This will provide an additional diversion."

Cognizant of the lady's pensive expression, Julia led the way into the drawing room.

Julia elected to start with the demure countenance of Miss Sanders. She began to sketch the piquant little face while listening to the words from Lady Charlotte, who attempted to "read" the future of Lady Pamela.

The silence that followed the placement of the cards upon the card table stretched until Julia looked up from her drawing pad to see what had occurred.

Lady Pamela sat opposite Lady Charlotte, while Lady Temple watched with a distinctly vexed expression.

Lady Charlotte pointed to one of the cards, then another. "This is a favorable time for you. Do not lose any time." Then she pointed at two other cards, then added, "You shall have a wonderful journey by ship."

"But, how splendid!" Lady Pamela exclaimed, pink color staining her cheeks.

Julia wondered if a person might not interpret that fortune in a number of ways. Obviously, Lady Pamela would take it to mean that the moment was propitious for her to gain what she sought—an alliance with Lord Temple, and soon. But, could those words not mean other things as well? Julia could think of several possible interpretations.

Since the sketch was precisely that, not polished, Julia completed her rendering of Miss Sanders not long after Lady Charlotte finished the fortune reading for Lady Pamela.

"Now, we shall change places," Miss Sanders declared, "and I shall learn of my future." She fluttered across the room to take the chair vacated by Lady Pamela.

That delighted girl drifted over to where Julia waited, a victorious expression upon her beautiful face. Julia reflected that the girl's beauty made it far easier to draw her, as loveliness could be portrayed with less time than it took to improve one who appeared truly homely.

"Well," Lady Charlotte mused aloud after shuffling the cards, then laying them out on the table. "I see a change for you. You will have a meeting that will lead to marriage. Financial uncertainties will plague you, but they will be overcome. Beware of one you believe a friend, for she could prove false."

Miss Sander's hand crept up to her throat as she considered the words uttered by Lady Charlotte. A hesitant smile hovered on her pretty mouth. "Oh, my."

"She shall be married? Will it be soon?" demanded Lady Pamela of Lady Charlotte.

"That all depends on whether she trusts herself or another," Lady Charlotte replied enigmatically.

"Gracious, whatever shall I do?" Miss Sanders picked up the sketch Julia had done, ostensibly studying it while most likely considering the ominous words just heard.

Julia tore the sheet of paper that bore the drawing of Lady Pamela from her pad, then handed it to her as the men entered the drawing room.

"What ho?" Mr. Fothingay said, catching sight of the cards on the drawing pad.

"Lady Winton has been kind enough to do little sketches of us," Lady Pamela explained.

"And Lady Charlotte has been telling these girls a deal of

nonsense," muttered Lady Temple, most unlike her usual polite self.

Lord Lacey looked down his beak of a nose at Lady Temple, then strolled over to join his wife.

Lord Temple sauntered across the room to take a peek at the sketch done of Lady Pamela and nodded. "Very lovely, as are you, my lady."

"And what did Lady Charlotte predict for you, Miss Sanders?" Reggie Fothingay inquired with a smile.

"Oh, I shan't tell, I think. I suppose it is good."

"You only suppose? Come now, I am all agog with curiosity," inserted Lord Lacey with a tolerant look at his wife.

"She will meet someone soon whom she will marry. There will be financial problems, but if she trusts herself rather than one she regards a friend, she will come out all right in the end," Lady Pamela said with a snap. She quite ignored the reproachful stare from Miss Sanders.

"I think it unfair that the ladies are to be drawn, but we are left out. Fortunes, for that matter, as well." Mr. Vansittart crossed the room to sit opposite Julia, saying in an amused way, "It is my turn, now."

"Only if she does me next," Reggie said from behind him.

"Oh, do go away, or I shan't draw either of you," Julia murmured with a smile.

"Then I shall insist on my fortune." Reggie gave Lady Charlotte an insouciant grin, then plopped himself on the chair the girls had used, and awaited his reading.

With surprising patience, Lady Charlotte again shuffled and placed the cards before her, surveying the figures with a shrewd gaze.

"Well?" Reggie asked at long last, a trace of nervousness in his voice.

"You will come into money when you least expect it, but need it. This card tells me that you will have a happy time after a communication." She pointed to the king of cups, then said, "You are a good friend, and no doubt will be a most devoted husband."

"Leg-shackled? I suppose we all must go sometime."

This observation drew chuckles from the men and a frown from Lady Temple.

"You have not read my fortune, Lady Charlotte," Lord Temple said, taking the place Reggie had quickly vacated.

"Do you wish it, Noel?" Lady Charlotte asked with a darting glance at his mother.

"Please." He ignored his mother's frown, leaning forward to watch as the cards were placed, then turned faceup.

"You will find a fair solution to a difficult matter. But, I see hesitation regarding your love. There is danger . . . "

After which words Lady Charlotte gathered up the cards and prepared to put them away. Although her expression revealed nothing, Julia had the impression more could have been said, but the lady chose to be silent.

At her move, Dick Vansittart left the chair where he had sat while Julia did a quick drawing of him and walked to stand by Lady Charlotte's side. "You cannot stop until you do me. Has Lady Winton heard her future?"

Julia wondered if Lady Charlotte would tell the group about her morning reading, and the results. She didn't.

"If you truly wish it." With the cards spread before her, Lady Charlotte gave Dick a fond look. "You certainly are a fortunate one. You shall have a journey, and you shall know progress in what you pursue. The cards also tell me that when you truly love, that love will be returned."

"Aha!" Reggie exclaimed. "She don't say marriage, but I'll wager you will be there, too."

Vansittart gave Lady Charlotte a questioning look, then glanced at the beautiful young ladies by Lady Temple. "Perhaps."

"Now, Julia, my dear, Mr. Vansittart insists I must read your cards as well. Do you mind?"

Wondering if she was to hear the same words, Julia nodded cautiously even as the cards were set out on the table.

"You are to remain in this house until you are tested. There will be danger, my dear," Lady Charlotte said in a low voice repeating her earlier words. "But I foresee a great love," she concluded, dropping to a whisper that only Julia heard.

"I say, that doesn't sound like a very jolly future," Reggie protested.

"She had the queen of swords before her, a widow, and a positive force. The ace of cups symbolizes perfect unconditional love. Joy, abundance, and perfection in love and friendship, as well. I should say that Julia will have a future many will envy once she survives her time of testing."

"Nonsense," Lady Temple declared, rising from her chair by the fireplace from which she had been silently watching the evening's entertainment. "Forgive me for saying it, Charlotte, but that is utter poppycock. You might as well read tea leaves, or the placement of sticks."

"Oh, but my lady," Miss Sanders dared to say, "I believe all will come true." She turned a troubled face to Julia, her concern plain on her lovely face. "I wonder what Lady Winton is to endure?"

"Cold tea and porridge, I expect," Julia said briskly, gathering up her pencils and pad. She bestowed a sympathetic smile on Miss Sanders, then turned to Lady Temple. "I believe I shall retire to my room now, if that is agreeable. I should like to look in on my girls."

"You all must meet her little darlings tomorrow," Lady Charlotte declared, not at all put out at the reception of her fortune reading.

Julia left the room amid speculation about those fortunes, and how they might be interpreted. Swiftly walking up the stairs, she turned the corner, then halted.

Down the corridor drifted a misty white shape that strongly resembled a lady. A white lady in a Tudor dress. And she appeared to beckon to Julia.

Clutching her pad and pencils to her chest, quite ignoring the stabbing of one of them, Julia's eyes grew huge, and her mouth opened as though to cry out. She took a step forward, and the figure grew more distant, gesturing, inviting Julia to follow it. What did the lady want? Dare she follow her?

4

CURIOSITY won over prudence. Fascinated with the spectral shape, Julia slowly began to walk down the hall, one foot cautiously after the other. She eased away the pencils that had stabbed into her, yet continued to hold the items close to her, as though to ward off evil.

Did she hear the word "come"? A wispy white sleeve wafted upward, then gestured again as the ghost floated farther away, teasing Julia to pursue. It was utterly impossible for her to resist the lure.

The hall stretched off into deep shadows that danced about in a most alarming manner, and one lone candle flickered in the wall sconce as though close to guttering out. It did not appear the sort of thing to cheer a body, Julia concluded.

"Well," she said somewhat prosaically, "I cannot go through walls, you know. But I shall attempt to follow you." Just why she felt the White Lady needed reassurance, she didn't know, but Julia experienced a sense of urgency, compulsion.

"I do believe you wish my assistance." Where that notion had come from, Julia didn't know, but it had popped into her mind, as though planted there. She proceeded along the hall, wondering where her path might end. Could this be the ghost of Mary Blackford? It seemed incredible, and yet, Julia knew full well that she was awake, not asleep and dreaming.

"What a pity you cannot simply tell me what it is that troubles you," Julia murmured. "Or perhaps what omen you bring. From what I have heard, there usually is something of import about to happen."

The ghostly figure merely continued to entice Julia to follow. Once her heart steadied, and her breathing resumed a more normal rate, Julia found the specter intriguing. What would she find? What lurked down the corridor, or around the corner, or . . . through the walls! Whatever it might be, Julia determined she would uncover it.

The door to her room suddenly opened, and, after glancing around to see an empty hall, Hibbett stared at her mistress with astonished eyes. "Milady, did I hear you speak? There seems to be no one about."

Julia threw a frustrated glance at her abigail, then looked down the passageway. The White Lady had vanished.

"Merely muttering to myself, Hibbett. Are the girls all right?" Julia resigned herself to a mystery of an appearing and disappearing specter, right out of a book by Mrs. Radcliffe.

Giving her mistress a wary look, the maid nodded, then stood back so that Julia might enter the room. "They are sound asleep this age, milady."

Watching Julia stand uncertainly in the center of the room, bemused still from what she had seen, the maid said nothing more. Hibbett busied herself helping her mistress undress, then left the room at Julia's impatient urging.

Once alone, Julia peeked from her room down the empty hall. A light could be seen from under the Lacey's door. Murmurs from approaching voices floated up the stairs. But no White Lady beckoned to her from the distant shadows.

"Why?" Julia wondered aloud. "The ghost doesn't appear for many years, but not *I* see it." She closed her door, then leaned against it with a sigh, wrapping her arms about her, drawing the folds of her cambric nightgown comfortingly close.

She supposed she ought to have been frightened. At first, she had been. Then, a feeling of peace had crept over her, and somehow she knew that the White Lady meant her no harm. No words had actually been spoken, but they might have. She felt them.

Was this part of the test Julia was to endure? The test that had to come before that supposed great love? And what of that great love? There was no sign of a lover, great or otherwise, on the horizon. Personally, while she would never wish to say anything to offend Lady Charlotte, Julia thought the entire business about the card reading a pack of nonsense.

She frowned, then wandered to the window to stare out into the darkness. Dare she report this ghostly sighting to Lord Temple? He might think her daft in the head, or imagining things, particularly after the card reading Lady Charlotte had done earlier. He had not, Julia recalled, seemed enamored of the idea. All in all, it had proved quite an evening to remember.

No spectral figure could be seen hovering outside of her window, nor peering from the woods on the grounds. Nothing beckoned to her to drift over the countryside in a midnight ramble. The stars glimmered from a dark velvety sky. A thin sliver of a new moon promised brightness to come as the nights progressed. Silence reigned.

What of the words Lady Charlotte spoke to the effect that Julia would remain in this house? Did she mean that literally? That Julia must be confined to within these walls until the testing time concluded? Absurd. Utter foolishness.

This bizarre thought made Julia smile, and she scolded herself for being fanciful and silly. After taking another searching look, she crossed to the twin's room, checked to see that all was well, then crawled beneath the covers of her most comfortable bed.

Sleep did not come immediately, which really did not surprise her a great deal. Considering that one did not encounter enticing ghosts every day, she believed she had done rather well not to have violent hysterics. She tried to recall what she knew of the family ghost, and realized she would have to discreetly ask Lord Temple about the White Lady in the Tudor dress come morning. Nothing concrete about the ghost had been offered.

Her last reflections were of that puzzling gentleman. Why had he laced into her with furious dispatch, then most handsomely apologized to her not long after? It seemed to her that Lady Charlotte wasn't the only muddled soul around this house.

* * *

Following a bracing breakfast, Julia sought out his lordship in the library where he appeared to have taken refuge. Alone and looking quite meditative, Lord Temple gave Julia an impatient frown from where he sat at his desk when she tapped on the slightly open door, then entered at his command.

"What is it, Lady Winton? If you are seeking Anne, best ask Nanny Gray. She is usually not far from Anne's side." He did not rise from his desk, but behaved in a way that led her to surmise he expected Julia to depart immediately.

Repressing a comment on the subject of hovering nannies, Julia shook her head, then nearly closed the door behind her, advancing on his desk—a magnificent piece of polished mahogany—with caution, while deciding how best to approach the subject.

"It is the family ghost I should like to ask you a question or two about," Julia declared at last with blunt directness.

Clearly startled, he rose from his desk, then gestured to the chairs drawn up before the fireplace where a modest coal fire burned, offering a surprising amount of heat.

Julia moved along with him, taking note of the gracious, but austere, harmony of the room. It held richly colored rugs on a highly polished oak floor, with muted red velvet draperies hung over tall, elegant windows revealing a superb view of the gardens and fields beyond. The aroma of leather-bound books, a whisper of cigar smoke, and the faint, but intriguing, scent of a spicy cologne teased her nose.

"Did I tell you about her? I cannot recall." His lordship not only looked puzzled, he appeared rather apprehensive. What did he think Julia might do, or had done, for that matter?

"No one, other than Mr. Vansittart, has said a word to me," Julia offered as she paused before the chair. "The servants have frightened poor Violet half out of her wits with tales of a family ghost, a White Lady, that comes now and again." Julia gingerly eased herself onto the mate to the chair Lord Temple selected, giving him a frankly questioning look.

"What did Dick tell you?" Lord Temple shifted back in

his chair, giving Julia a curious look from beneath frowning brows.

"He took me to see the gallery, you know. When we viewed the paintings there, he happened to mention some story regarding the Blackford who built this house, and his two wives. Little seems known about the first wife, Mary. But Catherine is reputed to be a somewhat menacing woman." Julia gave Lord Temple an apologetic look. "Does the ghost of Mary Blackford roam these halls?"

Julia clasped her hands lest they betray her slight nervousness regarding the subject of the ghost. She had yet to reveal her encounter to anyone, and wasn't quite sure how it might be received.

He met her frank, curious gaze, rubbing his chin as though deciding what he ought to tell her, then cleared his throat.

"Over the years the most visible ghost has been that of the woman in white, not an uncommon sighting in old homes, you must admit." He tapped his fingers on the arm of his chair, turning his gaze to the flickering fire.

Julia nodded agreement, for she had heard of more than one similar tale. However, this was the first time she had actually *seen* a ghost.

"Whether or not she is really the ghost of Mary Blackford, I cannot say. The tale carried down through the years is that she appears for a reason. I should have to search the records, for it has been a long time since anyone has seen her. Why?"

"Well," Julia said, swallowing before proceeding with her amazing story, "I believe I encountered her last evening in the upstairs hall. At least, I saw a White Lady in a Tudor-style dress floating down the passageway before me." Seeing that this did not bring instant denial or probing, she forged ahead. "It was dreadfully frightening for a moment or two, to see that wispy figure beckoning me to follow her down the hallway, but I trailed it for a brief time."

The tense figure across from Julia now shot up from his chair, then began to pace before the fireplace. "I can scarce believe that you, an outsider, have really seen her!"

Affronted, Julia snapped back, "I am not in the habit of making up tales, sirrah."

He waved his hand, "No, no. 'Tis that she is, as I recall, usually seen by a member of the family, not someone beyond the family circle. Even I have not seen her."

"Perhaps she sensed one who is sympathetic?" Julia replied in a tentative voice.

"You found the story of the wicked stepmother shocking? I assume that is what Dick told you?" Lord Temple paused before the fireplace, hands placed behind his back while he studied Julia where she sat so demurely in her chair.

"It would appear she proved an unpleasant stepmother. I wonder what really happened to Mary? Would the family records indicate, do you suppose? I confess that I am vastly curious." Julia unclasped her hands, then smoothed her gown of plum-colored India mull over her knees.

Lord Temple's figure stood out against the unpretentious fireplace surround with dramatic clarity. While he pondered over the matter of the ghost, Julia studied his elegance, from the superb claret coat of well-cut Bath cloth and a tasteful waistcoat, to neat buff pantaloons tucked into shining boots that reflected the light of the fireplace. Those dark, hauntingly beautiful eyes turned on Julia were full of speculation. She met his gaze, locked in wordless communication.

"Vastly curious about what, pray tell?" Dick Vansittart entered the room after a tap on the door with a ready smile, totally ignoring the dark look tossed at him by his host.

"You ought to be more careful what stories you tell the guests, Dick," Lord Temple scolded. "Lady Winton believes she saw the long-departed Mary Blackford in the hallway last evening."

"No!" Mr. Vansittart, clearly fascinated by the very notion of a ghost said, "What did she look like? Did she say anything? Whatever did you do? Not faint away, I trust?"

Annoyed that another had been included in what she felt to be a rather private matter, Julia rose from her chair, slowly crossing to the door with the intention of fleeing to the top of the house.

"A beautiful wisp of sheer white Tudor drapery drifted down the hall in a rather fetching manner, beckoning me to follow her. Oddly enough, I did not feel threatened, nor apprehensive once I recovered from the shock of seeing an apparition. I began to follow her." Julia paused, then wryly concluded, "My abigail opened my bedroom door, spoke to me, and when I turned to look once again, the ghost had vanished."

From behind her Reggie Fothingay gave a low whistle.

Julia backed away from him, dismayed that yet another had heard her tale. No doubt the entire household would know before long.

"I say we ought to dig out the old records of the house, have a look-see at what is there," Dick stated, giving a concerned look at Noel Blackford, the current Lord Temple, and descendant of the involved parties.

"Yes, well, I suppose we might at that. Poor day for shooting, anyway." Lord Temple gave Julia an unfathomable look, then gestured to his gentlemen friends. "You may as well come along, for who knows how long it would take me by myself. Best thing is to consult with Dimbleby." At the questioning glance from Julia, he added, "He's my steward, and ought to be able to at least show us where best to investigate."

Accepting that she was not to be included in the hunt, even if she was the one who had viewed the specter, Julia bowed her head briefly, murmured something about finding Miss Anne, disappeared down the hall, then went up the stairs before Noel could suggest that she might join them.

"Rum happening, what?" Reggie muttered as they ambled from the room.

"Good morning, gentlemen," Lady Charlotte said from the bottom of the stairs, her eyes making note of the varied expression. "Has something gone amiss?"

Noel had not intended to make known the ghostly event until he'd had a chance to do a little investigation of his own. Not so Reggie.

"Why, ma'am, Lady Winton encountered the Blackford ghost last evening after she left the drawing room. Dashed brave of her, too. Didn't turn a hair, by the sound of it,"

Reggie declared proudly, quite as if he had engineered the whole event.

"At least, we did not hear a scream," Noel amended, deciding that were any other lady of his acquaintance to suddenly come upon a ghost who beckoned her to give chase, not one would be as tranquil about it as Lady Winton. "Our charming young artist definitely possesses a sturdy set of nerves and a strong backbone. Rather pretty one, too, come to think of it." He had found Julia Winton quite attractive, if puzzling at times. "We are off to the muniment room now for a bit of a hunt."

"How interesting. I should like to ask her about it. Do you know where I might find Julia?" The older lady smiled at Noel with a seemingly calm face, but her eyes held a lively curiosity that Noel suspected longed to be satisfied. He gave Lady Charlotte a sharp look, wondering when the two women had come to such an informal status. From what he knew of his mother's friend, she might be a shade eccentric, but she insisted upon convention and manners.

"I believe she went to the nursery, ma'am," Noel replied with civility, wondering what Nanny Gray would make of the matter. He hoped that the nurse would have the good sense not to frighten Anne with outrageous horror stories.

The men straggled down the hall to the rear of the house where the muniment room was located. Once there, Noel explained to the man in charge what was wanted.

"Oh, dear," the bespectacled Mr. Dimbleby exclaimed, running suddenly nervous fingers through a crop of thinning blond hair. His esteemed employer did not show up in his rooms every day. "Oh, my. Gracious me," he mumbled as he searched the shelves for what he wanted.

The chest containing the muniments, that is, the title deeds, the papers detailing the acquisition of the peerage, and all other records of importance, sat on a low shelf to one side of the room. On the upper shelves stood boxes of accumulated letters, bills and receipts, and ledgers from over the years. It was in one of these that Noel hoped to find the history of the Blackford ghost, the White Lady, as Lady Winton called her.

"Ah, here we are, gentlemen. These are the earliest

records of the family." From the top-most shelf, Mr. Dimbleby removed a ledger and a speckled cardboard box. He
blew off the dust, then placed them on the narrow wooden
table, opening the box to reveal faded and yellowed letters,
other documents, the bills and receipts from the late 1500's.

The three gentlemen drew up stools to the high table,
Reggie and Dick looking to Noel for guidance.

"I say," Reggie muttered, "gives a fellow a turn to think
when these were written."

"Quite so," Noel replied softly. "I need not say these
must be handled with care. Reggie, page through that
ledger, not that I anticipate much there, but one never
knows. Dick and I will divide this stack of papers between
us, and see what can be found."

Oddly silent after all the chatting and laughing they had
done on the way to the muniment room, the three began
their work.

Upstairs in the nursery, Julia faced a stubborn nanny
with determination and what she hoped was cool hauteur.
She refused to allow this termagant to get the better of her.

"I wish Anne to come with me for another sitting. Or
should I say that Lord Temple will be most displeased
when he hears that you refuse to cooperate."

"You dassent!" the nanny replied, her gray-print gown
rustling with starch while crossing the room to stand defen-
sively before her precious Miss Anne.

"Oh, indeed, you would be surprised at what I dare."
Julia faced her adversary with resolve. What possible dif-
ference a painting might make to Nanny Gray was beyond
Julia to fathom.

From the doorway another voice was heard. "She is quite
the bravest of women. I should be loathe to cross her."
Lady Charlotte entered the nursery, looking about the drab
room with an expression of distaste.

It seemed clear that Lady Charlotte was not more impressed with the bleak atmosphere of the nursery than Julia.
Why the schoolroom had not been furbished to suit a growing girl was beyond Julia. There were delightful bits and
scraps to enliven a dreary room, and even colors and pretty

papers could make it more cheerful. Instead, Anne remained cooped up in a chilly, gloomy room as dreary as her nurse.

Nanny Gray moved back a step, giving the newcomer a hard stare before bowing her head in recognition of a lady of quality.

"Brave, milady?" the nurse queried as her curiosity obviously overcame her reluctance to talk.

"Now, Lady Charlotte," Julia said in dismay.

"I merely wondered what our good nanny knows of the Blackford ghost that haunts this house. I expect you have heard tales over the years, have you not?" Lady Charlotte said in a coaxing way.

"Indeed, I have," the nurse replied. "Why? If I may ask?" she concluded sullenly.

"Lady Winton saw the ghost last evening. We are consumed with curiosity, and so far have not learned the whole of the story."

The nurse had paled greatly with the knowledge of the ghost's appearance. She darted a concerned look at Julia, then said, "As to what it means, I can't say. Most likely a parcel of nonsense, anyway." With that, she motioned to Anne to follow Lady Winton, forgetting to admonish her to be a good girl as was her custom.

Out in the passageway, Julia and Lady Charlotte watched as Anne sedately walked before them. When the child paused, looking at them with enormous guilt in her eyes, Julia placed a hand on Lady Charlotte's arm in dismay.

"Whatever?" she whispered, more than a little curious.

"Please," Anne demanded in no more than a whisper, "may I have Wiggles with me? I promise that he will not cause you a moment of trouble."

"Wiggles?" Julia inquired faintly.

Anne beckoned with the crook of a finger. They followed her to the door next to the stairs, just beyond the unused schoolroom. Here they found a homely King Charles puppy peering up at them with large, hopeful eyes from a nest of tattered but clean rags.

Her heart melting at once at the sight of Anne on her

knees with the puppy licking a finger, Julia said, "Why do you hide it here?"

"Nanny Gray does not approve of animals in the bedroom. She says they are dreadful things and not to be trusted."

"Mercy!" Lady Charlotte exclaimed, meeting Julia's eyes with perfect accord.

"May I take him with me while I sit to be painted?" Anne persisted.

"I should think so, love," Julia replied with a martial light in her eyes. If things continued at this rate, the elegant and wildly handsome Lord Temple was going to receive something he did not in the slightest desire—a piece of Julia's mind she was quite certain he would not like in the least.

Leaving a sympathizing and still curious Lady Charlotte in the central hall, Julia guided Anne and Wiggles along to the small salon where Lord Temple had arranged for her to paint.

Everything was as it ought to be; oils, thinners, the ivory, and a comfortable chair for Anne. Wiggles appeared to think it great fun to toy with a bit of crumpled paper while Julia placed Anne so the autumn sun would light up her face in a charming manner.

The girl at first remained silent as Julia worked, washing in the underlying colors with care. Then she spoke, startling Julia with her words.

"Did you truly see a ghost? What did she look like?" Not waiting for an answer, Anne continued, "I think it vastly unfair that you saw her when I have never. And I live here!"

Smiling a little at the indignant note on the girls' voice, Julia replied, "Yes, I believe I did actually see a ghost. Really and truly. I have heard of such things, but never thought to see such."

"Were you frightened? I would be terrified to death. I shouldn't think even Wiggles could manage that," the girl replied sagaciously, with an air of maturity far beyond her years.

Julia threw Anne a concerned glance before returning her

attention to the portrait. Gracious! The child sounded like an old woman.

"I most assuredly felt afraid. 'Tis a good thing no one spoke to me when I first sighted her, for I might have fainted dead away. Odd, though, I doubt she intended me any harm. One usually believes a ghost to be bad. I do not believe this one is evil, more like sad."

"I wonder if my papa shall discover anything about her? Lady Charlotte said he was in the muniment room, and that is where all the papers are kept. I heard papa say so."

"Why do I not tell you a story of a ghost I once heard about? He was a dreadfully little ghost, and longed to grow truly large so he might frighten every one he saw. But he failed to increase his size, and he became horridly sad."

Anne settled in her chair with that charmingly delightful look in her eyes once again. Julia wove her story with less skill than an intent to enthrall her listener. And retain that lovely expression.

Wiggles played with the crumpled paper until exhausted. Disappointed that his mistress neglected him, yet seeming content to merely be at her feet, he snuggled down on the rug and fell asleep.

When the tale of the little ghost drew to its ridiculous end, with Anne giggling as a child of nearly eight ought, Julia concluded the session for the day. And not a moment too soon.

Nanny Gray appeared at the doorway like a gray wraith, inducing a shiver in Julia that she could not prevent.

"Come along, Miss Anne," the dour nanny ordered. "And leave that pup here. He'll not darken the door of the nursery as long as I am there." She gave the dog an annoyed glance, then nudged the young Anne from the room.

Julia watched silently, nodding ever so slightly as Anne tossed her a beseeching look after gazing at Wiggles with longing eyes.

Utterly furious that his miserable, handsome, aloof, and quite uncaring lordship would permit such heartrending misery in his only child, Julia resolved to do something about it.

Cleaning her brushes, then putting the room in order so

that nothing need be touched by the maids, Julia then left the little salon to which she had been assigned, with Wiggles tucked carefully in her arms. Marching down the hall, she sought, and at last found, his elegant lordship.

Lord Temple hunched over a table in the muniment room, seated on a stool like some clerk. Only, Julia knew there wasn't a clerk in the country who had the confidence and self-possession that his lordship knew. A musty old box crammed with papers sat at his side, a frayed journal next to it. Lord Temple appeared to be going through a stack of old bills. From the looks of it, they had been around for a time.

"I would speak with you, sir," Julia ventured at last, when he failed to look up.

"By the sound of your voice, it isn't anything very good," he replied with a wary eye in her direction.

"I fail to see how you can be so heartless as to deny your only child, that dear little Anne, her adored puppy." Julia held up the animal, pleased it gave an eager little bark. "Did you never have a pet? I knew the joys of a puppy, and I treasure the happy memories of those days. I fully intend to allow my girls the delight to be found in a pet, you may be sure," she concluded with a certain amount of relish. His lordship stared at her with wide eyes, and so he should.

"What did you say!" he said with an awful note in his voice. "No. Never mind repeating yourself. I believe I heard what I think I heard. I know nothing about a puppy. I gather this creature is it?" He gestured to the animal in Julia's hands.

"Well," an affronted Julia declared, more incensed than ever, "your daughter has this perfectly dear," she ignored the dog's ugliness, "and most well-mannered little King Charles spaniel appropriately named 'Wiggles.' I cannot know which is worse—that you fail to know of it, or do not care enough to see she has a pet."

"I assure you, Lady Winton, that I shall look into this immediately. I have nothing against a puppy, especially one such as you describe. My only reply to your charge is that I truly knew nothing about it. But I shall."

Julia took a step back at his grim tone. She would not

relish being in Nanny Gray's place at the moment. Not that the woman didn't deserve a scold, and more, keeping that poor, lonely girl from her pet.

He left the desk where he had been pouring over the history of his home, carrying with him a thin and somewhat ragged-looking volume. Dick and Reggie had given up some time before, sauntering off to the billiard room with Noel's blessings.

Catching her curious glance at the book, Lord Temple said, "Dimbleby found a journal kept by my illustrious ancestor, the one who built this house. I intend to spend a number of hours in the hopes of finding a clue to our ghost. Later. But first I shall go up to the nursery."

5

NOEL approached the nursery suite with mixed feelings. While reluctant to confront the nurse, who had been with the family these many years and chosen by his mother with great care, he had been stung by Lady Winton's charges.

Had he been neglectful of his daughter? She looked so much like his departed and unlamented late wife that he confessed he did not often seek Anne's company. But truly, he had not intended to be cruel to the child.

His knock unanswered, Noel opened the door to the first of the rooms, the schoolroom, then paused. Chill, damp air rushed forth to greet him. No evidence of a fire in the grate could be seen. Bare windows revealed nothing more than a cloudy sky beyond, the roof being extended here so that the grounds were hidden from view. Not precisely an enchanting view for a child.

Just inside the door to the room he looked about him, trying to see the place as a stranger might. He was not pleased with what he beheld. Hadn't someone requested a sum to refurbish the nursery not too long ago? Last year? He furrowed his brow as he considered the vacant schoolroom. Dusty shelves and lack of interesting materials with which to instruct brought to mind Lady Winton's charges.

It seemed that the charming, if militant, lady knew whereof she spoke. A girl might not require knowledge of history and Latin, but a small competence of the globe, a smattering of culture, plus the ability to do simple sums were deemed proper. Noel sniffed with derision. Not a sign of embroidery, nor music, nor watercolors could be seen, either. These were most certainly accomplishments his daughter ought to be learning.

Casting a disparaging glance over the meager contents of the schoolroom, he proceeded to the nursery, throwing open the door with little regard for the hinges. The door crashed against the wall. This room appeared little better to his eyes.

Blotchy gray could best describe the walls. Anne's cot looked lumpy and uncomfortable, not what the daughter of a viscount ought to enjoy. This must be the same wretched bed he had slept in as a child and hated every moment of it. How could his mother allow his little daughter the same misery?

Of toys he saw few—a pathetic-looking doll, a tattered primer he recalled from his youth, a pile of wooden blocks. He kicked at one with the toe of his boot. He knew that he had ordered a variety of playthings from a London toy shop. Where were they?

The door to his left opened and Nanny Gray entered, considerably taken aback to discover his lordship in her domain. Clearly flustered, she straightened and advanced upon Noel with a grim travesty of a smile.

"'Tis a pleasure to see you, your lordship," she whined. "Miss Anne shall be in directly. I made certain she washed herself after playing with that nasty puppy. I'm sure I don't know how she got 'hold of it, sir." Nanny's air of meek apology was marred by the hint of malevolence in her eyes.

"I should like to know who gave him to Anne." Noel tried to keep his voice carefully neutral. He had found if his view wasn't known, he learned more.

The nanny turned, then went to the door of the small room adjacent, instructing Anne all the while. "Now hurry up, child. Your father is here, and you shall hear what he has to say about that dog, I'll wager."

Noel compressed his lips with anger. In her voice could be heard a hint of intimidation, an unkind desire to punish, the threat of reprisal. For what? A puppy?

Anne entered the room with timid steps, her face pale and eyes enormous with apprehension. It seemed to Noel that she looked at him like he was some sort of monster.

Had she always been so afraid of him? He feared he couldn't answer that question.

"Who gave you the puppy?" It seemed that even his attempt to sound neutrally pleasant failed.

Anne appeared to shrink against the wall, as though she wished to be far on the other side of it. Obedient, however, she replied, "Cousin Harriet sent him to me with her groom. She knew how much I wanted a puppy."

It was more than Noel had known, although he ought to have suspected such a thing of a child her age.

"It was kept from me?"

"Cousin Harriet said you'd not approve. It was our secret." Anne's voice faded away to a whisper, and she looked white enough to faint.

"Well, now I know about the secret, and I think it a fine thing." Noel knew he sounded grim, but the entire situation was an intolerable predicament.

With a frightened glance at her nanny, Anne looked at Noel with sudden hope shining in her eyes. "I may keep Wiggles, Papa? Truly?" A faint hint of pink began to steal into her cheeks.

Bestowing a wry smile that was more than a little chagrined on his daughter, Noel nodded. "That you may." He turned his attention to the nurse, who stood dour and sullen at Anne's side.

"I am most displeased, Nanny Gray. These rooms were to have been refurbished. Where are the toys I ordered from London? The doll?" He looked about him, wondering just what Lady Winton had thought of this place. Very little, most likely. "Or, perhaps you wish to seek a position elsewhere?" he suggested.

A pale Anne rushed to her nanny, clutching at the gray-print skirts with tears in her eyes. "Oh, pray don't send Nanny Gray away, Papa. I should be quite l . . . lost without her. I should have no one, then."

Faced with a dilemma like this, Noel was at an impasse. Instinct told him to discharge the nanny immediately, ship her away as fast as possible. But he had just made a notable discovery about his daughter, and he scarcely felt that this was the time to break the fragile bond growing between them.

"If matters can be improved here, I shall give your nanny a second chance. But," he turned a cold gaze upon Nanny Gray, "I expect changes. The first shall be the painters. I desire this room to be a pretty color." Inspiration struck, and he turned to a wide-eyed Anne.

"What color should you wish, Anne?" he asked gently.

"Pink?" she said in a soft hesitant voice.

"Pink, it shall be," he informed Nanny Gray with a firm voice. "And that doll I ordered from London will be found as well, no doubt. I paid the bill, so it must be somewhere about."

With that, he turned to leave the room. Pausing by the door, he added with a smile for Anne, "Lady Winton has your puppy for the moment. You may fetch him now if you wish." With that, Noel turned and marched down the stairs to the ground floor, feeling quite virtuous.

An anxious Lady Winton lurked in the central hall, not far from the stairway. She clutched Wiggles to her, ignoring his obvious desire to scamper away. "Well?"

"My daughter will be down shortly to take possession of her pet. Her Cousin Harriet sent him to her. It was a great secret, although I really would not have forbidden the animal." He looked at the little spaniel, adding, "For the life of me, I cannot imagine why anyone would think I should mind if Anne had a puppy. Not even one as ugly as that."

"Perhaps her nanny does not care for dogs?"

"Her nanny has nothing to say in the matter."

Remembrance of the scene in the nursery returned. He wished he had yielded to his impulse, and sent the nanny away from here and Anne.

Julia compressed her lips at the instant withdrawal of his lordship. She had no business intruding as she had. His voice was that of the lord of the manor who did not expect anyone to cross his will.

"I am sorry. I trespassed again. Truly, my sisters would be most amazed at me." Her eyes sent him an apology.

Not bothering to inquire why her sisters would be surprised at Julia's behavior, Lord Temple bowed politely, then strode off down the hall to the rear of the house, the thin, ancient journal still underneath his arm.

Julia carried the puppy up the stairs, thankful that his lordship had been fair about the matter, and that Anne would have her pet.

At the second floor landing, she met Anne. The girl looked at her with happy eyes, as she did when enchanted with one of Julia's stories. While still too solemn, Anne's shy smile more than compensated for any uneasiness Julia might have felt.

She knew a tug of worry, recalling the animosity the nanny held toward the puppy and most likely Julia, as well. How would the unsympathetic nanny deal with this challenge to her authority, even if from Anne's father?

"Would you like to introduce your puppy to my little girls? They are not old enough to have a doggy as yet. But since you are more grown-up, you could teach them how to pet him and play with him. If you would not mind, that is?"

Julia bestowed a wiggling little dog on his mistress, and the child followed Julia down the hall to her rooms with a self-important air.

While the three girls played on the floor of Julia's bedroom under her benevolent gaze, she considered the situation. Unless she missed her guess, Lord Temple had sustained a shock when he visited the nursery. A gentle question to Anne brought forth the description of the scene. Julia thought she concealed her reaction admirably.

What a lesson for Lord Temple. Her wry smile might have been for the sight before her of the three little girls fussing over a homely puppy.

Julia could only hope the dog improved with age. However, she was not quite so sanguine about it's temperament. The puppy had acquired a nasty habit of biting that would have to be gently, but firmly, broken. The pup nipped at Tansy, bringing forth tears.

"Yes, love, you shall be fine," Julia said, soothing Tansy with a loving hug.

Tansy held out a wounded finger, sniffing. Tear-drenched eyes looked at Wiggles with gentle reproach.

Before long Anne left with her puppy, and the twins returned to Violet for their nap.

Julia decided to stroll about the house with the hope of discovering something more of her ghost. Although it wasn't precisely her own, it was near enough. No one else had seen it, not even Lord Temple. And this bit of history Julia found most intriguing. Surely one would think the owner of a house would see the family ghost.

At the central stairs she encountered Lady Charlotte, intent upon an errand of her own. They both paused to look while Nanny Gray marched down, stopping on the bottom step as she eyed Julia with a cold stare.

"The ghost you have summoned to this house will bring disaster. You ought to leave here now, lest you bring trouble on us all!" The nanny's eyes snapped with her conviction of catastrophe.

Quite taken aback, Julia exchanged glances with Lady Charlotte, then turned her attention to the nanny again.

"How could a gentle ghost cause trouble for any of us? I should think I am most likely the one to be anxious, and I doubt it means me any harm."

"Many's the tale I have heard of cruel and savage ghosts who'd done away with people, and aye, pets as well. She appeared to you." The nanny pointed an accusing finger at Julia. "You ought to be the one to go," Nanny Gray declared in a most venomous tone, her little black beady eyes sunk above the round curves of her cheeks.

"It is for his lordship to decide, I believe," Julia replied, striving for tranquility in her voice. "However, I should suggest you do what his lordship has requested." Not knowing precisely all that had been said, only what little Anne had revealed, Julia could not say more.

"Aye." A grim smile crept across the nanny's face. "I shall do all as is proper."

Julia watched as the nanny returned to the upper regions of the house, then slowly walked down the stairs with Lady Charlotte.

"I would say offhand that she was not best pleased with you. I wonder why? Have you threatened her in any way?" Lady Charlotte said in her gentle manner.

"Not that I know about. Pray forget all that was said in that exchange. I shall as well." Julia stood aside to permit Lady Charlotte to enter the drawing room ahead of her.

"Hm. I shan't, you know. This is all too intriguing," Lady Charlotte murmured. "I had not expected such excitement when we set forth from our home."

"Lady Winton, is it true you saw a real ghost?" Miss Sanders lisped in a breathy whisper, glancing about her with wide, frightened eyes.

"Well," Julia replied, "I am not certain if one may call a ghost 'real' or not, but I did see something."

"Tell us all about it," Lady Pamela demanded.

"I say," Reggie declared as he charged into the room, "is there some way you can summon her up? I should dashed well like to see a genuine ghost."

Behind him, Dick Vansittart strolled into the drawing room, a grin on his nice face. "I doubt if ghosts are very biddable, Reggie."

"Nanny Gray claims the White Lady brings death," Lady Charlotte said sweetly.

Julia could have shaken Lady Charlotte. Talk about putting the cat among the pigeons! Miss Sanders looked about to swoon, Lady Pamela rushed to meet Lord Temple with a cry of distress. In the background Lady Temple groped for her vinaigrette and handkerchief.

"What is going on now?" Lord Lacey said from behind Lord Temple, his manner more indulgent. Living with Lady Charlotte obviously prepared him for anything.

"Nothing much, unless you want to try to call forth the ghost. Only, I understand she's a murderous one," replied his wife with her customary placidity.

Reggie, apparently seeing he had begun an uproar that threatened to get out of hand, sought to change the subject. "Learn anything from that book you found, Noel?"

"Not as yet," Lord Temple said, then returned to the matter at hand. "Surely you do not believe that the wisp of white that Lady Winton claims to have seen would do anyone harm."

Annoyed that he appeared to doubt her assertion, Julia tilted her chin up and declared, "I fear I very much did see that ghost. And none of us actually believe that a ghost could do injury, sirrah, but Nanny Gray insists the ghost does not care for outsiders."

"Oh, I cannot accept that," he said thoughtfully, "for we have had visitors often over the years, and she has never bothered anyone before."

"Did you do anything in particular before you saw the ghost?" Lady Pamela inquired, leaning against Lord Temple as though she might faint if he failed to support her.

"Nothing I deem out of the ordinary," Julia replied, wishing she might send the ghost to Lady Pamela, for she certainly deserved something out of the usual as a reward for her acting ability. Also, Julia was forced to admit to herself that the sight of this elegant lordship with his arm about the beautiful Lady Pamela proved annoying. Even if he did but support the girl.

"Well, I can scarce believe that the ghost appeared after all these years without a reason," Miss Sanders declared, retreating until she might gain Reggie as a prop should she need him.

"One never knows about these things," Julia murmured, perversely delighted with their wide-eyed stares while scolding herself for planting such notions in the heads of these ninnyhammers. "Nanny Gray declares that the ghost means disaster."

"Enough of such silliness," Lady Temple asserted in the momentary hush that followed Julia's injudicious remark. "The ghost was last seen about thirty-odd years ago. My husband observed her. Surely we can think and talk of something else besides something Lady Winton believes she saw? It may have been nothing more than a vivid fantasy. After all," Lady Temple concluded with a faintly waspish note, "she is an artist, and artists are known for vivid imaginations, are they not?"

Julia felt utterly dreadful at Lady Temple's words, every syllable chastening like a whip. How stupid of Julia to speak out as she had, merely to tease the two beauties. It had been unworthy of her, and quite unlike her, for Julia, while possessed of a slight temper, tried to be patient and loving toward others. As a rule. She had not decided what she wished to be toward his elegant lordship. While those perfectly beautiful eyes might set her heart quivering, his attitude left much to be desired.

"Shall we go for a stroll in the gardens now that it has stopped raining?" Lady Pamela said, casting a coy glance at Lord Temple, clearly expecting him to escort her.

"By Jove," Reggie declared, "why do we not all walk down to see if the shooting will be good on the morrow, then we could go along the ornamental pond?" He fixed his gaze on the pretty Edythe Sanders. No fool she, Miss Sanders eagerly accepted his suggestion. After all, a wealthy man on the arm was worth two at the assembly.

This plan appeared acceptable to all. The young ladies hurried upstairs to don their pelisses, pretty bonnets, and gloves. Lady Pamela and Miss Sanders had rooms at the opposite end of the floor from where Julia was housed. She left them at the landing to pursue her own room and clothing.

Julia found herself downstairs again before a hint of the others returning could be heard. She pulled on her gloves, then went to the door Biggins opened for her to peek outside. It would be well to take the weather's measure.

Biggins looked down upon her with a quizzical expression on his usually sour countenance.

When Julia sought to slip through the open doorway, she found herself unable to do so. It was as though an invisible hand reached out to stop her, preventing her from going to the terrace.

"Problems, Lady Winton?" Lord Temple crossed the hall in hurried steps to join her while he pulled on his gloves.

"This is absurd," she whispered with an impatient wave of her hand. "I wished to take a look at the weather from the terrace while awaiting the others." She glanced at him, giving an uneasy shake of her head, knowing full well how preposterous she must sound. "I know this sounds foolish, but I cannot walk out. It is as though there is a barrier, a very chilly barrier, preventing me from doing so."

She gave him an uncomfortable laugh, then turned a vexed look at the opening through which she seemed unable to pass. Was there ever such a coil?

"You must be imagining things. I feel certain no one has experienced anything of the sort here before." He walked to stand squarely in the doorway, a teasing grin curving his lips. "See? I have no problem. Come," he commanded, holding out a well-gloved hand to her.

Julia took note of the indulgent smile, the sort one gives a silly child, then grimaced. Something tugged at her memory, but she concentrated on what might be stopping her from leaving the house.

"Come," he urged again, walking to her side, "allow me to escort you to the terrace. From there we should have an excellent view of the woods and meadows where we mean to walk." He offered his arm, and Julia accepted his suggestion with no hesitation. Surely if she found it difficult by herself, the obstacle ought to disappear when her host wished to go out?

His superior smile faded when he found himself able to walk through the doorway, and Julia halted in her tracks, her hand clinging to his arm at the center of the threshold. She gave Biggins an annoyed look when he uttered a faint gasp of horror.

Hastily, she pulled her arm back, not liking the sensation of cold that draped itself over her hand.

Lady Charlotte elected to walk out into the hallway at this point, pausing in her intention to retreat elsewhere at the sight of Julia standing before the open door. Julia supposed her exasperated expression must have conveyed more than intended. The lady marched over to join her, exchanging a look with Lord Temple.

That he was clearly puzzled needed no saying. Not so Lady Charlotte.

"I did tell you that you would be staying in this house, did I not?" Her sweet smile and merry eyes prevented Julia from total exasperation.

Julia sighed, then stepped away from the door. Lord Temple followed, nudging both women across and into the great hall with more haste than gentleness.

"We need not provide more fare for the servants to gossip about," he murmured while closing the door behind him, although he supposed a deal of damage had already been done, what with Biggins standing there all ears. Once the door was securely shut, he studied Lady Charlotte. "I trust you have an explanation for what you just said?"

"When I read Julia's cards," the lady replied with patience, "they quite clearly said that she would be tested, and that she would remain in this house until her time of testing was past."

"Surely," Julia objected, "that could not mean that I may not cross the threshold until this supposed testing is complete! Why, I could be here for ages. Years!"

"Besides," Lord Temple added, "she really could not cross the threshold. I should swear that she tried, and it was as though an obstacle prevented her." He gave Julia a bewildered look.

Feeling like some freak in a raree-show, Julia clasped her hands together for a few moments while she considered the matter.

"I neglected to say that she is also to be subject to danger, Lord Temple," Lady Charlotte concluded mildly.

"For the time being, it is best if I return to my room or remain hidden from view. I scarcely wish to alarm the others about this peculiar happening. Perhaps . . . " Julia snapped her mouth shut, giving Lord Temple a resolute look.

"Yes?" he inquired, sharing a concerned glance with Lady Charlotte.

"Never you mind, sir. I have a bit of thinking to do. Please join the others and make some excuse for me. I shall have to consider the matter, then decide what to do." She retreated, removing her bonnet as a clear indication she no longer wished to leave the house at this time.

The look he gave her in return let her know what he thought of her reply. Still, he didn't argue with her. He escorted Lady Charlotte from the great hall, leaving Julia alone to sort out her speculations.

Once the front door had slammed shut behind the chattering group of strollers, Julia placed her bonnet on a table, then removed her gloves, looking about her at the antique furnishings and room. She strolled around the room, deep in meditation, mulling over her problem from as many angles as possible all the while. It would have been lovely to wander along the garden paths on this beautiful October day. She resented being detained by a ghost. It clearly was the outside of enough, and she intended to get to the bottom of the issue as soon as possible.

"Are you here?" she whispered.

Silence.

"I believe we should reach some sort of accord," Julia continued firmly. "I really ought to be allowed to leave the house when I please, as long as it is not to go away any distance. Perhaps the village could be the boundary? Otherwise, there will be uncomfortable questions, you know. I fancy you would rather avoid those."

Julia searched the shadowed corners of the room, feeling very much the fool. Although she had not actually seen the White Lady at the door, she suspected that the sensation of cold that had draped itself across her when she attempted to leave the house was none other than the family ghost.

"I shan't attempt to go out again today, but I expect that tomorrow I shall not find a chilly barrier at the door again," Julia said in a gentle scold. "I will try to help you, my lady. But I think I may do so without being confined to the actual building."

Julia's whispers died away, and she waited. In the deep recesses of the room, a glimmer of white slowly evolved into a misty figure.

"Is that acceptable?" Julia said softly.

Since the ghost refused to speak, it proved difficult to discover her reaction. Yet, Julia sensed that an agreement of sorts had been reached.

"The next thing to do is decide what you wish of me," Julia declared firmly. That she was conversing with an insubstantial white wisp that hadn't appeared for nearly thirty years impressed her as being completely mad. But then, strange things had been happening since she arrived at this house.

The white wisp wafted across the room, and through the door. Julia followed, hastily grabbing her bonnet and gloves before dashing up the stairs behind her ghost after opening the door. The ghost had a distinct advantage over

Julia in being able to move about at will, ignoring such mundane things as doors and walls. An excitement gripped her, and she wished Lord Temple might be here to actually see what was going to happen.

On the second floor, they paused before the door to the attics. Julia was about to enter when Lady Temple rounded the corner from the stairs.

"Lady Winton," she declared with surprise. "I felt sure you had gone with the others. I must say Miss Sanders and Lady Pamela looked most charming in their lovely pelisses and bonnets. Is something amiss?"

Her tone and manner were more friendly than since Julia had arrived. While it offered hope for more amicable relations, it also frustrated Julia in her pursuit of the ghost's secret.

"I decided that I would wait until tomorrow. It seemed a trifle damp out yet."

"Very wise. A mother must take care of her health. I should like to see your twins, if I might. Charlotte declares they are quite delightful."

At such a handsome peace offering, Julia could scarcely inform Lady Temple that she had planned to tag along after a ghost. Hoping the White Lady would understand, Julia smiled, then meekly walked over to join Lady Temple, casting only one backward look at the door to the attics. Did she imagine the drooping wisp of white?

When they reached the door leading to Julia's rooms, she ushered Lady Temple inside, then paused long enough to toss a second look at the door to the attics. "Later," she promised the wisp of white, closing the door when the White Lady appeared to bow in return.

Inside her room, Julia shut her eyes a moment. Clearly she had gone quite, quite mad.

6

"AH, your little darlings," Lady Temple said with what appeared to be genuine enthusiasm.

Unprepared for such an animated reception of her twins, Julia blinked before offering a hesitant smile in return. "Thank you, my lady. I am partial to them, but then, I am their mother so it is to be expected."

Resigned to a chat over the difficulties involved in rearing children, or something similar, Julia was most surprised when Lady Temple arranged herself on a chair, studying the girls with a thoughtful expression on her face.

Suddenly aware of the silence, she glanced up at Julia, then said, "My maid mentioned something to the effect that the girls did not talk. But they appear normal in every way that I can see."

With that, Rosemary toddled over to Lady Temple, leaning against the chair, but not touching the elegant silk velvet skirt of Lady Temple's gown. In her simple white cambric dress tied with a blue sash, Rosemary was a miniature version of her mother, as was her twin. Clutching a wooden dog, the child stared up at the visitor, then offered her toy, saying, "Dog."

Hope welled up within Julia at the word, for it made sense. It had sounded like "dog" to her ears, but it might have been the "da" that the girls had been testing for a few days.

"Why, she said dog as clear as a bell," Lady Temple exclaimed. "There is not a thing wrong with those girls, in my opinion." Then casually rising, she strolled to the door, pausing to add, "Does Anne play with them often?"

Wondering why Lady Temple did not have a report on her

granddaughter's actions each day, for she seemed remarkably aware of all that went on in the house, Julia nodded.

"I have invited her to show her puppy, and talk to the twins. They enjoy her company, and I believe she likes to be with them, a role of elder sister, you might say." Julia smiled with the hope that Lady Temple would not forbid the little playtimes.

"Did you think to make that a reality when you accepted the commission to paint her portrait, mine as well?" The erect figure by the door looked unruffled, not as though she had just made an offensive charge against Julia.

Taken aback at the sharp words, Julia hoped she concealed her inward dismay at the pointed remark.

"My lady, I intend to execute the paintings to the best of my ability as quickly as I may. Then I shall leave here." Julia firmly met that challenging gaze with a nod that acknowledged that she quite understood her ladyship's intent.

Julia thought it prudent not to mention that she couldn't at present manage to cross the main threshold. What good would it serve? She could see it now, Lady Temple standing by the front entry with Julia crashing against the invisible barrier, her ladyship ordering Julia to try just a bit harder. Julia doubted if she might even creep out of a window.

Perhaps by the time it became necessary to leave, her testing would be over and Julia could disappear without a trace. She didn't accept the prediction from the cards Lady Charlotte had read. While it was lovely to dream that she might live here with Lord Temple, who had to be the most handsome gentleman Julia had ever encountered, it seemed best to face reality.

Besides, her previous experience with matrimony had not endeared that state to her. Yet her memories were becoming blurred, past grievances were fading from her mind. Could it possibly be that she might forget the past, live for the future? But not with Lord Temple. The viscountess had a different bride picked out for him. Perhaps Lady Temple would select more carefully this time.

Besides, that gentleman had a good deal to learn about women and children. Not that Julia would object to being his teacher, mind you. But, she knew insurmountable odds when she faced them.

An odd smile crossed Lady Temple's face as she caught the purpose of Julia's words. She studied the twins, then looked back to Julia.

"I shall order Cook to send up a plate of gingerbread for the girls. How fortunate you are that they resemble you," she declared fervently.

With that most peculiar observation, Lady Temple quit the room.

Stunned, Julia stood near her bed for several moments while she considered those words. The existence of a grand-daughter who did not in the least resemble her son, nor her-self apparently bothered Lady Temple a great deal. Perhaps that explained why she paid so little heed to Anne. She had found what appeared to be an acceptable nanny and left Anne to her.

Sinking down on the edge of her bed, Julia mulled over the implications of her theory. If she was correct, little Anne had grown up shamefully neglected while given every care, if one believed clothing and food, and a venerable roof over one's head to be of top importance.

However, this belief failed to explain why Anne seemed afraid of Nanny Gray. Although, as awesomely grim as the nanny seemed to be, it was small wonder Anne trembled in her slippers when that frown was turned against her.

Nevertheless, Julia had the absurd notion that something else prompted that reaction of blind fear glimpsed on more than one occasion.

Then the idea that the reason Lord Temple had ignored his daughter could be due to her resemblance to her unfortu-nate mother brought Julia to her feet. While she knew it ut-terly reprehensible of her to poke her nose into another's affairs, she was consumed with curiosity. Lady Charlotte appeared to know a great deal about the Blackford family history. Who better to question?

Later.

First, Julia resolved to climb to the attics, possibly dis-cover what it was that the White Lady wished her to know. No one else seemed convinced the Tudor ghost was that of

Mary Blackford. *But*, if Catherine had murdered Mary to get her out of the way so that Catherine could marry Sir Henry, might she not linger about to avenge herself? Or could there be something else, some other reason, that caused the ghost to continue to haunt this house instead of disappearing into the mists of time, as she ought? Something was distinctly havey-cavey around this place.

Adjusting a lovely morning cap of net and Brussels lace, Julia murmured a few words to the twins, then left instructions with Violet before leaving her rooms.

Glancing up and down the beautifully paneled corridor, she could see not a soul, not even Biggins, who seemed to pop up when least expected. But then, perhaps the butler would keep his distance after that slightly ridiculous tug-of-war at the front door when Lord Temple tried to draw her out and the ghost kept her in.

Julia paused before the door to the attics, then bracing herself for whatever might happen, she opened it, noting with approval that it didn't squeak one bit.

The narrow stairs had been dusted lately, leastways Julia did not find the hem of her kerseymere skirt picking up much soil. At the top of the flight of steps she paused, searching the shadows for a glimmer of white.

The attic contained the usual assortment of odd bits and pieces. There were chairs with a too-short leg, or tattered and old-fashioned coverings. Assorted pictures had been propped up against the wall in the shadows at one end of the room. Trunks stood scattered here and there. Boxes were piled higgledy-piggledy in no proper stack. Whoever was responsible for the arrangement of the attics had been most remiss, Julia decided. It was nowhere as tidy as the attics at Dancy Court, which she had made her province when at home.

Off to a corner, a mist began to materialize into the now-familiar form.

"Hello, again," Julia began, wondering if she ought to record her conversations with a ghost. Rather one-sided, they most likely would be dull reading.

The white form became more distinct than previously, and Julia could see that her garb appeared to be definitely late Tudor. Leastways, there was a ruff at her neck, and the skirt seemed to float in soft folds. Not court dress, but the loose gown that hung straight to the floor. Soon her features became more definite, revealing firm resolve carved into a pleasant face framed by a prim cap.

"I do not suppose you are able to speak to me," Julia continued calmly. "However, it would be a help if you could. This is rather tiresome, if you think about it, trying to guess what you wish, and then being interrupted every time it becomes interesting." A slight grin hovered on Julia's pretty mouth for a moment.

The White Lady bowed, then drifted across the floor to stand by a trunk. Julia sighed.

"I gather there is some significance to that particular trunk." Julia surveyed the article with growing curiosity. It was one of the few things that had absolutely no dust on it. How odd.

"How odd," she repeated out loud, although she had the idea it was not necessary. The ghost appeared to sense what was in Julia's mind. However, it made more sense to Julia to speak out loud.

"It is polished clean." Since the White Lady waited patiently beside the trunk, Julia decided that she had better open it up.

The lid lifted easily, contrary to most attic trunks Julia had encountered. Inside were to be found the usual assortment of tumbled clothes. What was so different about this? Then Julia realized that they ought to have been neatly folded away, not an untidy jumble.

"Does Anne come up here to play?" It would explain the disarray.

A negative shake of the head confirmed Julia's suspicion that Anne would not be permitted anywhere outside the nursery if Nanny had her way.

"Hmm." Julia poked about the trunk at the gesture from the White Lady, who, Julia was certain, had once been Mary Blackford. At the bottom of the trunk Julia espied a number of neatly rolled bundles, quite a contrast to the chaos of the rest of the contents. Swiftly kneeling beside the trunk, she unrolled the closest at hand, then gasped at the object within.

"Mercy me!" she whispered. A ruby necklace of incredible beauty lay draped across Julia's palm. With trembling fingers, she rolled it up again, then opened the next bundle. Sapphires sparkled from a pendant of exquisite design. Taking care to return the pendant to its previous spot, Julia searched each bundle in turn, feeling almost faint with the riches revealed. Diamonds, rubies, sapphires, topaz, beautifully wrought gold and silver, jewelry of inconceivable value all in an orderly row.

"What can this mean?" Julia raised her gaze from the unexpected cache to where the misty figure lingered not far away. "If you could only speak," Julia murmured, quite frustrated as to what the fabulous collection of jewelry might be doing hidden in the trunk.

Why did the viscount not keep it all safely in a vault? Or was this his version of a vault? She'd have to confess that she would never think to look for such wealth in the bottom of a very ordinary-looking trunk.

Tossing the articles of clothing again on top of the neat rolls containing the jewelry, Julia then closed the trunk lid, sitting down upon it, thinking wildly that it had to be the most valuable resting place she had ever been near.

"I dare not say anything, I suppose. I doubt it would be well received if I, a mere artist and barely tolerated guest, were to make it known that I had uncovered the Blackford jewels. I have heard no hint of lost possessions, which might account for their concealment. But, I wish I knew more. One could not think that these splendid things might be simply tucked away, then forgotten. One does *NOT* overlook such things," Julia concluded, sensing that there had been a reason the jewels had been shown to her.

"I shall make a mental note of this, you may be certain," she confided to the White Lady. "Is there something else you wish me to see?"

When the ghost was drifting across the attic, Julia decided to tax her with the barrier business again. "You have decided to permit me to go outside of the house, I take it?

There shall be none of this halt-at-the-door sort of nonsense again? I tell you, it was most embarrassing."

The figure made a regal bow, then gestured to an area in the dark recesses of the attic with a wave of a hand.

Just at that moment, Julia heard the door to the attic open and steps coming up the stairs. "Drat and double drat!" she fumed.

Giving the ghost a cautioning look, Julia called out, "Who is it?"

"Lady Charlotte, my dear. So this is where you are. I searched everywhere for you. Whatever has driven you to seek refuge in the attic? Surely this ghost business is not distressing you to the point you must hide away from us?" At these words, the genial face of the lady appeared, followed by her pleasantly garbed figure.

"Not at all. I fear I came up here out of curiosity. Shameful, I suppose. I admit it had something to do with the ghost, however. But, it is not a simple matter to explain. Shall we return to my rooms for a comfortable coze? I vow I should enjoy a cup of restoring tea, and perhaps some biscuits." Julia decided she had best get Lady Charlotte out of the attic to safer quarters before she observed the polished trunk.

Eyes narrowed momentarily in a considering look, Lady Charlotte nodded. "I do hope you will tell me sometime what has been going on up here. I feel vibrations, you know."

Julia did not have to turn around to know that the White Lady had disappeared. It seemed that she wished to reveal herself to Julia and none other. Which made matters a trifle delicate, as Julia did not like to keep secrets from the owner of this magnificent house, particularly when they were most likely his jewels.

The knowledge that someone had stored costly jewelry in an ordinary trunk had been given to Julia for a reason. Now, to figure out why!

She took a last wistful glance back into the attics before losing sight of the jumbled contents. She knew more secrets awaited her up there, secrets that the late Mary Blackford wanted her to know. Fretful, yet resigned, Julia joined Lady Charlotte in the corridor after a walk down the steep, narrow set of attic stairs.

"Now, dear Julia, I should like to get better acquainted. And perhaps you will consent to confide a few things in my tender ears. I can help you, you know." Lady Charlotte offered Julia a comforting smile, while guiding her along the corridor.

Wondering whether that was a threat or a promise, Julia agreed to tea and a chat. They had reached Julia's door when Lord Temple appeared on the central landing.

"Ah, I was hunting for you, Lady Winton. Will you and Lady Charlotte both join the group for tea? After our invigorating walk, all have declared themselves famished. I trust you have not been idle in our absence?"

He had walked toward them during this speech until at their sides. At this final remark, he reached up to waft a cobweb from the chestnut curls peeking out from beneath Julia's lovely cap.

"Tolerabley, sir," Julia replied as demurely as she might. Tossing a warning glance at Lady Charlotte, she continued, "Lady Charlotte and I are becoming better acquainted, but we should enjoy the promise of a lavish tea, you may be sure." Which was nothing less than the truth. Hunting about with the family ghost was hungry work.

When the trio entered the drawing room, Lord Temple gave Julia a veiled look, while Reggie drifted across the room to draw Lady Charlotte and Julia away from Noel.

"We missed your company," he said to Julia. "I trust that whatever came up to prevent you from joining us on our walk has been solved by now?"

Thinking of her recent chat with the ghost, Julia resisted the urge to chuckle by means of pinching herself rather hard. "I daresay you might draw that conclusion."

"Dearest Julia has more to do with her time than spend it in frivolous walks along a pond," Lady Charlotte asserted, with a playful tap on Reggie's arm.

"Ah, yes, the paintings. I hope Anne is proving a good subject. Perhaps I should have my portrait done for my mother. Do you think you might manage that, Lady Winton?" He preened slightly, fingering the elegant fobs at his waist.

This time Julia permitted a small chuckle to escape. "I

might. But, you know that one must sit perfectly still, and not speak, and that, I should think, would be difficult for you."

"If Noel can manage it, so could I," Reggie snapped back, albeit with a twinkle in his gray eyes.

Biggins approached with a tray bearing biscuits and a steaming pot of tea. Julia gratefully accepted a generous supply of thin, crisp lemon wafers along with her tea, then edged away from the conversation between Lady Charlotte and the irrepressible Reggie regarding portraits.

Lord Temple was at the moment by himself, and Julia hoped to somehow learn something about the trunk of jewels in the attic.

"I must thank you for offering some plausible excuse for my absence, sir," she began.

"It was simple enough. I said you needed to rescue your painting that one of the maids had accidently touched."

"I trust there isn't some poor girl being punished for what did not happen?" Julia slanted a glance at him before focusing her attention on the rug design.

"Not that I know about. As devoted to your artwork as you are reputed to be, I thought it a logical reason."

At the smile in his voice, Julia looked up to meet his gaze. That was most likely a mistake, as she fast became lost in the depths of his beautiful dark eyes. "You, sir, are a complete hand."

"No, am I? I've been accused of many things, but not a tease." His smile widened to a grin, and he was once again the man Julia had met in London.

Julia scoffed at that bit, then decided to plunge into the topic she intended to learn more about. But precisely how did one ask if there were jewels missing? Or whose they might be? She was stumped.

"Have you seen more of our ghost?"

Julia glanced about her with caution. When she observed that none were close enough to hear her reply, she said, "Yes, in the attics. She beckoned me to follow her, but I still do not know what all she means for me to learn, because Lady Charlotte came up to find me, and that was the end of that." Julia still hadn't figured out how Lady Charlotte knew where to find her. Perhaps the dear lady learned it from her infernal cards?

"You can communicate with the ghost?" he said, not concealing his surprise.

"Well," Julia said carefully, "I believe she knows I sympathize with her, and I suspect she seeks my help."

"You are convinced she is Mary Blackford, then." Lord Temple edged Julia along to a window embrasure. It offered a lovely view of the grounds, and Julia was distracted a moment before answering.

"I do."

"Ah, that sounds most promising," Reggie bubbled, charging up behind Julia and Lord Temple with maddening cheerfulness. "And to what have you agreed, fair lady?" His gray eyes twinkled down at her, and a rather droll smile lurked about the corners of his mouth.

"That certain gentlemen ought to be strangled at birth," Lord Temple said with an abrupt laugh.

Catching sight of Lord Temple, Julia took a prudent step back from Lord Temple, turning to Reggie to add, "You ought to see the painting I did of Lord Temple for his mother. Perhaps I might do one like it for you."

"Rubbish! I'll not have you gazing into Reggie's eyes as you did mine," Lord Temple declared with surprising vehemence. Then, aware he had revealed something he perhaps ought not, he smiled at Reggie and added, "You are famous for those wicked eyes and teasing ways. I must protect Lady Winton, you know."

"Dashed if I know whether to be insulted or pleased," Reggie murmured, then wandered off to seek the company of Edythe Sanders.

"Do you go to the attics very often, my lord," Julia dared to ask.

"Never, or at least not more than once a year to hunt about for something or other my mother wants."

Julia frowned. It did not appear he could be the one who frequented the special trunk. She was more than a little aware of his curiosity at her remark and sought to divert him. "Attics are strange places, or so I think. So much history deposited helter-skelter up there."

"You mean the clothing, old furniture, and the like?"

"Paintings as well," Julia added, recalling the stack in the dim recesses of the room.

"Some of those phizes are best left to the wall, as I remember. There once was a grim-faced lady gracing the entry wall years past. We tucked her away, you can be sure."

"Might that have been Mary Blackford?"

"No," Lord Temple said musingly. "I believe this one came later on, around the time of Charles I. You are determined about Mary, aren't you?"

"Perhaps." Julia decided that if she didn't wish to wake up to find herself dead one morning, she had best remove herself from this tantalizing man's company at once. The glare emanating from Lady Temple could put frost on a body at ten paces. Julia simply did not trust the woman.

The notion occurred to her that the viscountess might be stashing away the family jewels in the event her son married against her will. She might take them away with her, a sort of guarantee against deficiency, as it were. Or perhaps punishment. Lady Temple did not seem the type that would allow a small matter of entailment to bother her if she wanted something.

Which brought Julia to the matter of the viscount's first wife. "Excuse me, my lord," Julia said with demure formality, hoping that whoever lurked about could report to the viscountess that her son was quite safe from the widow's attentions. "I wished to ask Lady Charlotte about something."

With that vague remark, Julia sidled away, then crossed the room to sit down by Lady Charlotte.

Noel studied the young widow with curious eyes. What had prompted her questions about the attics? No point in his barging up there if the family ghost wouldn't appear for him. Why Julia?

Nothing had come to light so far in the journal he had been searching. The spidery writing was the very devil to decipher, but it seemed the ghost postdated the man who built the house, which seemed only reasonable if one thought about it.

He caught sight of one of the footmen hovering by the

door, an anxious expression on his face. When the man espied Noel, he wended his way through the assembled guests
to Noel's side.

"Sir, your daughter is most concerned, and begs that you
help her." The footman tried to look untroubled, but his eyes
gave him away.

"I shall come at once." Without bothering to excuse himself, for most of the group were deep in conversation, Noel
hastened from the drawing room and up the stairs.

Anne stood waiting at the tops of the stairs, her thin little
face looking pinched and paler than usual. "Papa, I am so
glad you have come. Perhaps you can wake Wiggles up for
me. He simply will not get up to play."

Offering a trusting hand, Anne led Noel to the small room
off the schoolroom where the puppy stayed, since Nanny refused to permit him in the nursery.

With a strong sense of foreboding, Noel knelt to examine
the puppy. "He cannot play with you, love. Not ever again."

"He's dead? Like mama?"

The fragile whisper tore at Noel's heart, for it held such
despair, such utter hopelessness. Only an adult ought to
know such an emotion, he thought with growing anger.
Whoever murdered the ugly little pup would feel Noel's
wrath, he would make certain of that.

"Oh, Papa. Why!" She welcomed his arms about her,
nestling her face into his shoulder while sobs racked her little body.

Could a ghost vent its hostility on a puppy? Noel wondered. He'd heard someone telling tales about dastardly
things ghosts could do. Or was it done by someone most
human with malicious intent? But who would wish to hurt
Anne? For she was the one most affected, after the puppy,
naturally.

He patted his daughter's back, uttering soothing words,
promising another puppy or a bird, whatever Anne wished.

"What has happened?" a gentle voice said from behind
him. "Forgive me if I intrude, but one of the servants
thought I might be of use."

"Lady Winton. Someone" Noel knew it wasn't the
ghost—"did away with the pup. Anne's a bit upset."

"Oh, you poor little love," the soft-spoken and sweetly scented woman said.

Noel watched as his little girl turned to the very womanly figure kneeling on the floor, disregarding her lovely gown, only concentrating on his unhappy child.

"I shall be very brave," Anne declared between sobs, "but it is not easy at all."

Julia gathered Anne close to her, offering solace as best she could. Over the girl's head, she met his lordship's eyes. "Do you have any idea as to who . . . ?" Her gaze drifted to the still shape of the puppy. She shook her head, forlorn and most perplexed.

Lord Temple rose, then rang for a footman. When the man came, he gave instructions regarding the disposal of the dog. Julia couldn't hear the softly spoken words, but she did insert some of her own before the footman left.

"I do believe it would be a very good thing if Anne could have a little funeral for her puppy. When my dog died we did that, and it was oddly comforting."

At first his lordship shook his head, but that might have been in dismay at her suggestion. Before the footman took the remains away, Lord Temple said, "Take him out behind the stables. I wish one of the carpenters to fix a simple pine box for the pup. We shall be out later on."

"Very good, sir."

The man could not conceal his approval of the gesture, and Lord Temple turned to Julia, a considering expression on his face. "I owe you a debt of gratitude, my lady. I'd not have thought of that." He knelt beside Anne, touching her tear-stained cheek lightly with one finger. "You wish a funeral for your puppy?"

She gave a somber nod. "I do not think we must call the vicar, though. Lady Winton will know what to say," she concluded with that great trust a child sometimes places in an adult they know is sympathetic.

"Lady Winton is a very knowledgeable person, it seems," Lord Temple said softly, gazing into Julia's eyes with something that looked like more than mere appreciation.

7

"I THANK you for all you did yesterday," Lord Temple said to Julia when she entered the breakfast room the following morning. "You seemed to know just the right words to say over that little box before it was placed in the ground. I feel sure that Anne's grief will be far less for the comfort you offered." He exchanged a curious look with her, then added, "How good of the White Lady to permit you out of the house."

"Indeed!" His perusal flustered Julia, usually the more composed member of the Dancy family. Even as she looked away, she could sense his gaze upon her. She didn't know what to make of the warmth in his eyes. Odd, she had never realized that such dark eyes could reveal warmth of expression. His could. And they were quite, quite beautiful.

"I was pleased to help, you know," she said softly at last. "She is a precious child."

Julia walked to where the food was spread in lavish array to select her morning meal. Keeping her back turned to his elegant lordship, she chose buttered eggs and a bit of ham. Gathering her dignity about her, she then turned to join Lord Temple at the table.

"Kind of Dick and Lady Charlotte to join us yesterday," he continued. "Odd, how much that ugly pup had come to mean to Anne." He forked a bite of egg in his mouth, washing it down with coffee.

"Yes, well," Julia replied, quite affected by the sight of Lord Temple in his simple morning garb. Did the man never look less than perfect? "Anne has no little friends with whom to play, so I trust the puppy assumed a place of companionship for her."

"I intend to find another pet for her, you may be sure. Perhaps a little kitten or bird might do for a change? Another puppy could be a painful thing, perhaps." He sounded unsure, hesitant, something simply not associated with Lord Temple, in Julia's experience—which admittedly was limited.

Impressed by his thoughtfulness, Julia nodded, accepting toast from the footman, then carefully buttering it as though she performed an important task. She sought her next words with care, wishing to lure some information from him.

"One day Anne will grow up, be presented to Society. She will not only need to do honor to the family jewels, but show a kind heart to win a worthy husband." If Julia hoped to lead him to comment on the jewels, missing or otherwise, she failed, for he merely gave her a confused glance, then turned his attention to the doorway when Reggie sauntered into the room.

"What a perfectly ghastly thing to happen," Reggie said in dramatic accents, quite obviously referring to yesterday and the death of the puppy. It had been the substance of much of the previous evening's conversation.

"Shocking!" Lady Charlotte declared, seeming much perturbed as she closely followed the young man to where he selected a hearty breakfast. "How is little Anne this morning?"

"The poor dear child," Miss Sanders cried from the doorway, pausing before entering the room. "That some unkind person would do away with her puppy!"

"Beastly," muttered Reggie, while eyeing Miss Sanders as though ready to rush to her aid in the event she looked about to faint.

The young woman in question remained in the doorway, gazing about with an air of sadness that was most affecting. Her dainty heart-shaped face and sweet blue eyes conveyed a sense of the tragic even before she had opened her mouth. "So, so sad," she concluded in a breathless voice.

"Oh, rather," Dick exclaimed as he peered over Miss Sander's shoulder, his attention focused on the food.

Seeing she no longer stood framed alone in the doorway,

but shared the space with a gentleman, Edythe hastily crossed to the table where she requested a cup of hot chocolate.

"You must eat, Miss Sanders," Lady Charlotte declared. "It will not do for Anne to see wan faces about. Poor little mite."

"I declare, the tragedy has quite stolen my appetite away from me." Miss Sanders bestowed an apologetic look on Lady Charlotte, then his lordship. "But I shall try to keep up my strength, if you insist." The tender smile bestowed upon Lord Temple was not missed by Julia.

"Why kill a pup?" Reggie demanded, waving a fork in the air. "It doesn't make any sense."

"Well, if you ask me," Lady Pamela said, having just entered the room, "I believe the ghost had something to do with it."

Julia took note of Miss Sanders sudden pallor, Reggie's look of disquiet, and Lady Charlotte's expression of disgust, and observed to herself that no one had asked Lady Pamela her estimation of the situation. Somehow, it seemed fitting that Lady Pamela should make a stupid statement. However, there was nothing that promised a great beauty should have a mind to match.

"Now, no one is certain there was a ghost about," Dick scolded gently. "Perhaps it was naught but an accident, the pup ate food that had spoiled?"

Lady Pamela turned her limpid gaze upon him, smiling bravely as she did. "How kind you are, sir, to be so thoughtful of a girl's sensibilities. A true gallant."

At this encomium, Mr. Vansittart widened his smile, offering to assist Lady Pamela with her plate, or anything else she might think of that needed doing.

"I should like to see you a moment when you have finished eating, if I may, Lady Winton," Lord Temple said in a soft aside, quite ignoring the inane remark from Lady Pamela. "Please join me in the library."

"Certainly," Julia replied, wishful of leaving the breakfast room and the ghoulish speculation of its inhabitants. She devoutly hoped that the solution offered by Mr. Vansittart would be accepted by the others. Having quickly finished eating her simple meal, Julia rose from the table, catching the eye of Lady Charlotte on the way to the door.

"I should like to chat with you as well, Julia," Lady Charlotte stated. "Later on. May I watch while you paint Anne? That is, if you intend to proceed with her this morning?"

"I think not," Julia replied softly. "I had best let her portrait be for a few days and concentrate on Lady Temple instead. But you are welcome to join us in the little salon placed at my disposal." If Lady Temple was tardy in rising, Julia intended to work on a sketch of someone else, and Lady Charlotte might be of assistance.

Seeing that met with Lady Charlotte's full approval, Julia walked down the hall in the direction Lord Temple had gone with a rapidly beating heart. What next?

A feeling of disquiet seemed to hang over the house. She did not consider herself overly sensitive to things like that, but she could note the change. Biggins looked even more dour than usual, an unnatural silence lingered in the air, maids tiptoes about as though afraid of their own shadows. Lady Pamela and her ghost story!

Not but what a ghost lurked about the place. However, she didn't think anyone but Lord Temple and Lady Charlotte knew just to what extent the ghost existed, if a ghost could be said to exist, that is.

Julia paused in the doorway of the library, catching sight of Lord Temple before he became aware of her presence. Her measure of the man had taken a complete turn yesterday at the little service held for the puppy. His solicitude for his daughter not only deeply touched Julia, it revealed a side of his nature she found much to her liking. It appeared that he was not only the man about town, the handsome gallant, but a person of deep emotions, worthy of great esteem. How unlike her departed husband, who had proven in their short time together to be a gay blade, a fribble, and an aristocratic rowdy.

"Sir?" She took a step forward, entering the room with hesitancy, not certain what to expect.

"Ah, Lady Winton. Come in." His warm smile of greeting did much to allay her apprehension. "Please be seated. I have some information I wish to share with you." He crossed over to the doorway as though checking the hall, closed the heavy oak door, then returned to his desk.

"I very much doubt if anyone will come seeking us considering what was going on when we left the breakfast room, but I prefer privacy for what I have to say." He fiddled with some papers, not meeting her gaze.

"I cannot think that anyone would believe that we have an assignation following your request at breakfast," she said, perching uneasily on the nearest chair. "Recall, if you please, that I am in your employ, and therefore not quite subject to the rigid rules of Society." Julia's heart beat at an erratic pace, and she clasped her hands tightly in her lap, her gaze upon them.

"Nonsense. You are as entitled to respect and consideration as Lady Pamela or Miss Sanders. But, I have information you should know. I found a small vial in the corner of the little closet where the pup slept. It looks suspiciously like it might contain poison."

Julia gasped, one hand flying to her heart. Her gaze flew up to meet his in startled dismay. She had surmised something of the sort, but to have it confirmed frightened her.

"Indeed," he affirmed. "I intend to slip up to London to have it tested. At the same time, I may begin the search for a proper governess for Anne—I insist that Nanny Gray shall go. Also, I shall bring another pet back for Anne. Did I mention a bird? What do you think of the idea? For you must know I value your opinion." At this, he bestowed a charming half smile on her that quite undid Julia, even at her staid age of four and twenty.

Julia did not flatter herself that his remark meant anything more than what was stated. She was a mother, and had successfully coped with a sad situation yesterday. Nothing more could be involved.

"It seems an admirable solution, my lord. As you said before, a puppy might be difficult right now. But a bird, well, it would be different. You do not think that whoever killed the puppy might do the same to a bird?" she said, loath to bring the possibility up, yet it did exist. Just like the ghost.

He seemed to consider the matter, then obviously discarded it, for he shook his head decisively. "No, I doubt it. Fright was all intended. With that achieved, I cannot see what would be gained by killing a bird. No, Lady Winton, I daresay that things will calm down now."

"Very well, sir." Julia did not have the same sanguine feelings as he about that probability, but prudently remained silent. It had been her experience that it was better not to argue with a man over something like this. Better not to argue about anything, for that matter, which rule she had broken time and again since coming to Blackford Hall. And still remained unscathed, wonder of wonders.

"I shouldn't say anything to Nanny Gray about my looking for a governess, nor to Anne either, if I were you. I should like it to be a surprise." He went back to fiddling with the papers on his desk in a manner Julia thought a shield for his true reasons.

"You intend to pension Nanny Gray, of course." It might be well for the woman to know her future was secure. In Julia's limited knowledge, nannies seemed to set strong importance on such.

"She might not take well to the idea of leaving, and I wish to be around in the event she causes Anne any distress."

"Commendable, my lord." Julia believed he was wrong, but he was certainly entitled to be bullheaded about the matter if he chose.

"You frown. I gather you feel otherwise?"

"It is not my place to comment."

"That did not stop you before. Well, out with it."

"We do not know for certain who killed the puppy. I can only trust that the demented soul will not strike again whilst you are away." The shocked expression that touched his face gave her a great deal of satisfaction. She had the distinct feeling that his lordship was not often caught off guard.

"I shall leave Dick and Reggie on guard, you may be sure. I'll make a fast dash to London, take care of my business, and return before you know I have left." He rose, as though intending to depart that moment.

Julia smiled. "I doubt that. You are far too important a person not to be missed."

He paused in his progress around the desk, tossing Julia a quizzical look. "I shall accept that as outright flattery, Lady Winton. And I thought you such a reserved lady." He paused by the door, his hand on the ornate knob. "The ghost . . . you have seen her again?"

"Oh, yes," she admitted rather prosaically. "I expect it is not the last time, either. If I could just be undisturbed! It seems every time things become interesting, some fool interrupts. 'Tis very frustrating." She shared a vexed look with him, knowing he would welcome the solution to the mystery of the family ghost. She rose from her chair, then walked to the door where she faced him, her concern obvious.

"You shall manage. I have no fear of that." He didn't bother to conceal his grin, touching her lightly on her arm, as he reassured her.

There it was again, that sensation of tingling, light-headedness, and a rapid heartbeat that assailed her when his lordship drew too close. She fought a sigh of regret. "I shall do what I may, sir."

Julia wandered back to the small salon where her painting materials lay neatly arrayed for her. Taking a drawing tablet, she began to sketch the face, blurred though it might be, of the ghost, Mary Blackford.

"Hm, that face looks somewhat familiar to me, for some reason," Lady Charlotte said from over Julia's shoulder.

"You mean you know someone who resembles this sketch?" Julia cried with rising interest.

"I may. I repeat, who is it?" Lady Charlotte sought the chair where Anne usually sat when posing, then dropped down on it with a faint sigh.

"If I am correct, it is the face of Mary Blackford," replied Julia quietly. She bent to her task, frowning while trying to recall the details that seemed to elude her.

"Trouble, Lady Winton?" Lord Temple said from the doorway.

"Not in the least," Julia hastily denied. She licked dry

lips, while wishing he would go away. She was not certain she wished him to see the sketch of Mary.

For a moment he did not reply, then nodded after taking a deep breath. "As you say. I am off. Do you have any commissions for me while I am in the city?"

Julia looked down at her hands, then raised her clear green eyes to meet his. "I have not heard from my brother in some time. If it is not too much trouble, perhaps you might send someone to Dancy House to see if there could be word from him?"

"It shall be done." He bowed. "Ladies."

"Such a fine figure of a man," Lady Charlotte said with satisfaction once he left. "Pity there are not more like him about. Good men are rather thin on the ground."

"And everywhere else, as well, I suspect," Julia murmured. "And yet he has not remarried. About his wife . . . what happened? If I am not being overly inquisitive?"

"Margaret ran off with an Italian tenor when Anne was very little. Never seen again." Lady Charlotte ended this bald tale with a sniff of disgust. "Foolish woman."

"Unquestionably," Julia replied, wondering how any woman in her right mind could run away from Lord Temple.

"I should like to know why a lovely young woman like you is still on the shelf," Lady Charlotte stated with her usual forthrightness.

"I am a widow, have been for over two years." Julia reminded gently, "and I have the twins."

"Fiddlesticks. If you think men are blind, think again. Do you send them away? For I suspect you have had offers." Her ladyship scrutinized Julia, and that young woman hoped her heightened color would not be noted.

Disconcerted, Julia chuckled at the memories brought to mind with that remark.

"Aye, I have had offers, two quite disreputable, I'll have you know." She ignored Lady Charlotte's shocked gasp and continued. "And then there was a gentleman who turned out to be most unacceptable." Julia sighed, thinking of her genial but disappointing suitor. "He was followed by a baron of great respectability, but immense girth. I fear that when I discovered a half circle had to be cut from his table so that he might dine with ease, I declined his gracious offer. I feared for his health, and have no wish to be widowed again, at least so soon." Her eyes twinkled with mirth at this tale.

Lady Charlotte shook her head, then gave in to the urge to laugh. "What a complete hand you are, Julia." Sobering, she searched Julia's face. "Or is it true?"

Julia raised her hand as though swearing in court. "It is true, I declare it. As well, the gentleman has grown so fond of his food, I scarce see how he could find time to care for a wife. I should be on my own, much as I am now."

"But," Lady Charlotte said, "you should have no need to paint."

"I truly do not need to do painting to survive, my lady. I value my independence highly, and wish to contribute to my support. I invest my earnings in consols for the time when I might need a nest egg arrives. You see, when my brother returns from the Continent and his service under Lord Wellington, he shall want a wife."

"And you have no wish to intrude upon a newlywed couple? Admirable. Amabel Moseley's sister went with her on her honeymoon, and I cannot imagine what her new husband thought of that! What a silly peagoose. Yet, I know it is a common enough practice."

"You see my point precisely. I wish a few others might as well."

Apparently sensing a topic of deep annoyance, Lady Charlotte glanced at the tablet before Julia, then said, "And this is the face you have seen?"

"Such as I am able to recall. She is misty, you see, and difficult to draw. How peculiar that there is no portrait of her in the gallery. I fancy there must have been one, for the family seemed to delight in having them done. Where might it have gone?" Julia grimaced with perplexity at the missing painting.

"I should wager the second wife could tell you," Lady Charlotte replied with a sage nod.

"Do you think so? Pity *she* doesn't linger about the place, then."

Lord Temple entered the room, and Julia put away the pad with the sketch of the elusive ghost where it could not be seen. Lady Charlotte chatted with her old friend while Julia attempted to capture Lady Temple in a drawing. It proved a difficult task, when she simply could not sit still.

"Ghosts, now the death of that ugly puppy. What shall be next, I wonder? I declare, I cannot recall such goings-on at Blackford Hall before." She darted a glance at Julia. And Julia wondered what she might do about it, for she had been responsible for neither event.

Noel had sent his valet to London the previous afternoon with a number of requests that needed to be en-trained. So, when he cantered down the drive, and onto the London road, he went alone and at a pace to suit none but himself.

He had set his mind somewhat at rest with assurances from Reggie and Dick that they would keep watch over the inhabitants of Blackford Hall while Noel did his investigation in London. Reggie was a good sort, if a bit of a featherhead. Dick was a solid fellow, one a man could depend upon to do what was right.

In return, Noel had a few simple errands to perform for his friends. That plus the favor for Lady Winton.

It would be interesting to see the establishment where she lived when not traveling about the countryside painting. He strongly suspected that she really did not require the sums she received, although with the amount she demanded, she could augment her income quite nicely.

He had not at first contemplated having portraits done of his mother and Anne. However, there was something about Julia Winton that drew him, compelled him to bring her to Blackford Hall so to get to know her better. Pity his mother had kicked up a dust over bringing Lady Winton home. One would think he intended to marry the woman, the way his mother had carried on. This notion struck Noel with a curious effect, and he rode on in reflective silence until it became necessary to stop for a change of horses.

Once in London, he went straight to a friend he knew

dabbled in chemistry. A few simple tests, and Noel knew that the pup's death had been no accident from tainted food.

From there he stopped by his home to collect any messages and the results of the missions on which he had sent his valet. Elstow met him in the entry hall with all the needed information, and Noel was off without pause.

At the Dancy residence, Noel found the butler an odd mixture of impressive stateliness and fond pride when he spoke of his Lady Winton, forgetting her status once to call her Miss Julia. Noel guessed that the older man had been with the family since his youth, from the way he spoke. Discovering that there was no news to be had of "that scamp," the present Baron Dancy, Noel jaunted on his way.

One could tell a fair amount about a family from their retainers. This man—Evenson, he said—clearly held great pride in serving the family. Interesting.

Procuring a proper governess turned out to be another matter entirely. Noel hadn't informed his mother of his mission, wanting for once to have her fingers out of his life. Now, he was all at sea. An old, much-married friend and father of ten children, set him on the right path. Before long, Noel found himself at an agency, informing the imposing woman in charge of his requirements.

Not a simple task, he quickly learned, and fumed all the way back to his town house over the delay this problem would cause while he waited for the various females deemed suitable to call upon him.

He performed one final commission, a quick trip into old London, before settling before his own fire with the stack of mail. Once he found precisely what he wished, he returned to his house, the mail, and excellent food. Not to mention peace and quiet, which he rarely had when his mother was around.

He supposed that was one thing he enjoyed about Lady Winton. She could be silent. All the while she had painted, she was most restfully quiet, speaking only when necessary, and then never simpering or flirting. She spoke as a rational woman, one with brains and common sense.

That his opinion had proven correct over the matter of

the pup gave him satisfaction. Noel liked being right. Still, he had detected a slight show of temper in Julia Winton. But that was all right, no woman should be servile. At least, not in his estimation. He liked a spirited lady.

It took him two days before he found a woman he felt suitable to teach his daughter. Miss Gilpin appeared of good birth—a genteel family of small means, forced to seek her way in the world. Her knowledge adequate, he found she reminded him of Lady Winton in her quiet behavior and polite demeanor. So, he hired her and arranged for her to come to Blackford Hall before long.

"And now to return home to the dilemma of Nanny Gray and her dismissal, the poisoner, the ghost, and Lady Julia Winton of the lovely green eyes," he informed his mirror before leaving the house. His reflection gave him an amused grimace. Who did he fool as to priority?

Elstow would follow with the baggage and other paraphernalia, including the green bird.

"Do you expect to see the ghost again," Edythe Sanders inquired of Julia in a breathless little voice, glancing about her with wide blue eyes as though the specter might pop up behind her.

Julia narrowed her eyes, and they took on a storm-tossed hue that would have told her sisters she was greatly annoyed with this simpering peagoose.

"Oh, do not tell us," Lady Pamela implored. "I vow I should simply die of fright were that ghost to appear before me!"

"Then I shan't say a word, you may be sure," Julia assured her. Whatever did Dick Vansittart see in this woman with such airs? And Reggie, well, he had constituted himself Edythe Sanders's personal guard, rarely leaving her side. A pack of silly cabbage-heads, the lot of them. "What a blessing it is that the two of you are housed in the opposite end of our floor. Since the ghost appears near my door, you need not worry in the least!"

"Mercy," Edythe gasped faintly, sinking upon the sofa while wafting her handkerchief about most delicately.

"See here," Reggie exclaimed, "I daresay, what you say

is the truth, but I cannot see why you should overset Miss Edythe's nerves. A lady of such great sensibilities ought not be troubled by such things as a family ghost."

"Since it is not *my* family ghost, I fear I have no say in the matter," Julia shot back, severely tried.

She left the drawing room after that exchange, feeling somewhat put upon. Lady Temple did not see fit to cooperate in regard to the morning sittings. Julia found that Anne was more than delighted to join her every morning, whether she sat for her portrait or not. But there was a limit as to how long one could insist that a child sit still or keep her from Nanny Gray.

"Problems, Lady Winton?" Lord Lacey inquired. "I trust your ghost is not haunting you overmuch?"

Julia wished most heartily that she had never mentioned the ghost. "No, sir. One becomes a trifle weary of the pea-gooses—or ought it be peageese?"

"I gather your intent. Say no more. I shan't tease you about it, either." He turned at a sound coming up from the front entry and went to peer over the railing. "What ho?"

"Lord Temple has arrived." Julia tried to keep the excitement from her voice when she caught sight of the elegantly trim figure standing below.

With an absent quirk of a smile, Lord Lacy motioned to Julia. "Come down with me to greet our returned host. I feel certain he has news from Town for one of us."

Feeling oddly shy, Julia drifted down the stairs until she was on a level with Lord Temple. "I trust you had a good journey. You were not gone very long." However, Julia privately thought that it had seemed like at least two years.

He turned, bestowing a wide smile for his guests. However, his gaze lingered upon Julia. "Indeed, it was a profitable trip. The new governess, Miss Gilpin, will arrive before long to assume her duties." He exchanged a significant look with Julia.

"And?" she inquired with daring.

He looked to Lacey, then back to Julia, saying in a low voice, "It was definitely poison."

They nodded their heads, silent lest the information be noted by others.

"I stopped by your home, Lady Winton, but I fear there was no news of your brother." Then, for no apparent reason, he added, "I am sorry."

"Thank you." Julia blushed and didn't know where to look at the intimacy in his regard.

"But, I brought what I hope is a consolation. First, there is a parrot for Anne. He's as green as your eyes and twice as saucy."

Lord Lacey chuckled at this, refusing to take the hint that Lord Temple might have wished him gone.

"Indeed," Julia replied, repressing a grin with difficulty.

"And I brought you these, with the hope you will have no reason to mar that pretty brow with a frown while painting ever again." He held out a little packet to Julia, which she accepted with puzzlement.

Upon opening it, she found a dainty pair of magnifying spectacles, cut so she might be able to see over them with no difficulty. It would make transferring her subject to the tiny ivory piece far simpler.

"How very thoughtful of you, sir." Lady Winton's smile curved a delicious pair of lips, lighting up her face and those remarkable green eyes. "I am most grateful to you."

Noel found himself wishing Lacey to Jericho and Lady Winton in his arms.

8

"NOEL, my dear, you are arrived home!" Lady Temple floated down the stairs after a dramatic pause at the top, during which she wafted her fan about with great effect. Her day cap of the most delicate lace and cambric and trimmed with silvery lavender ribbons blended beautifully with the dainty gown of lavender China crepe she wore. She appeared fragile, most worthy of kind indulgence.

"I trust you were not worried, Mother." Lord Temple drew himself to his full six feet of height and assumed a somewhat distant air.

Watching the display, Julia firmed her resolve not to linger in her brother's home once he returned. A man needed to be on his own, if for no other reason than to realize he needed a wife. What he did not need was someone who interfered, no matter how estimable the intent.

Lady Temple stood before her son, a picture of motherly grace. She smiled with forgiveness.

"We have been desolate without you, dear boy. However, Reggie and Dick have attempted to entertain your guests. It is simply not done to go haring off to London while one has a house full of company," she gently chided.

Julia thought that his lordship quite admirably restrained from reminding his mother that the young ladies had been invited by her. However, if they were in the house, they automatically became his guests.

He bowed correctly, then presented his mother and Lord Lacey with a thin smile. "I shall endeavor to remedy the situation. Perhaps we could take advantage of the mild weather and have an outing?"

As the previous days had been dampish, with a nasty

wind, Julia thought it was a praiseworthy suggestion, but remained silent. She guessed that any contribution she might make would be promptly rejected by Lady Temple. Her reticence paid off, for her ladyship apparently saw it as a chance to forward her plans for her son. She beamed a delighted smile up at him.

"The very thing. You may all go nutting while Lady Winton works on my portrait. It has been difficult for me to assume that pose for very long. You must know my sensibilities are so very great." The sigh she affected appeared genuine to Julia, and she gave Lady Temple her just due. The lady knew how to exert control, no doubt about it.

Lord Temple slapped his fine leather gloves against his thigh, giving his mother a brief, but knowing, look.

"Oh, I think Lady Winton may be spared to join us. Otherwise we shall be an odd number. I'll wager she would welcome a spell in the autumn sun." He turned to Julia to add further (although quite unnecessary) persuasion. "You will consent to go with us, I trust?"

"I should be delighted, my lord." After darting a glance at Lady Temple, Julia added, "Could not Anne join us as well? I believe she would welcome a change, and I would be happy to see that she comes to no harm."

Lady Temple narrowed her eyes, staring at Julia as though suddenly discovering a fly in her soup. When her beloved son looked at his mother, she was all gracious smiles and nodding agreement. "The very thing. Poor dear has been rather sad, I am told."

"You have not seen her whilst I was absent?" There was a thread of steel in his voice that Julia promptly decided she'd not wish directed at her.

"Dear boy, children are so fatiguing. Nanny Gray copes with her most admirably." Lady Temple fluttered her fan in a helpless gesture that had Julia's reluctant admiration.

She wondered when Lord Temple intended to spring the news that he had hired Miss Gilpin, and hoped she might not be near when he did. From what Hibbett had learned, her ladyship possessed a fine temper.

"If the weather holds for the morning, we shall make our excursion. By then Nanny Gray ought to be reconciled to

Anne briefly leaving her wing, and Cook may be persuaded to prepare a suitable repast for us. Nutting is hungry business." Lord Temple's wry tones failed to stir his mother in the least.

"As you wish. You know you have but to suggest to have it be." Somewhat ruffled, Lady Temple nodded graciously. After all, it had been her idea in the first place.

Julia was thankful that she wasn't eating anything at that moment, or she would have surely choked.

With that settled, Lord Temple excused himself, and went off to his room to dress for dinner.

Not wishing to receive Lady Temple's tart tongue for any reason, Julia saw fit to disappear up the stairs to her rooms.

That evening, following a somewhat tense dinner hour due to her ladyship's annoyance with the way her plans were proceeding, was spent speculating on the morrow's weather. Over cards Edythe Sanders declared she could not abide dampness were it to mist, while Lady Pamela asserted that she found nutting such a delightfully rustic pastime. London ladies rarely found such opportunities for innocent pleasure, she claimed.

Julia listened and withheld comment, occasionally meeting the enigmatic gaze stemming from Lord Lacey with gleaming eyes. Lady Charlotte declared that it sounded like capitol fun.

"What a pity a lady my age cannot join in such foolery." An air of wistfulness lingered in her voice.

"You never would!" Lady Temple said, quite shocked. "Why, they carry baskets and gather nuts, and they walk!" she concluded with a note of horror in her voice.

Julia was almost sorry she had agreed to go along, for it meant she would be kept from meeting the ghost for another day. Then she decided her best plan was to wait until the others had gone to bed and slip up to the attic.

The party elected to retire early, an arrangement that suited Julia to a tee.

Once in her room, she quickly removed her respectable gown of soft challis. It had been rather lowering to realize that neither of the young ladies had a thing to fear from

Julia's depressingly proper garb. In its place she donned a simple round gown of galatea, figuring that the sturdy fabric might be welcome when prowling around the attic. Rather than taking her soft woolen shawl, she pulled on a spencer, deciding she might be thankful for the extra warmth later on. Also, she wished to avoid tugging at a slipping shawl, what with a candle in one hand, and needing the other to cope with doors and the like.

Hibbett had retired early at Julia's urging, the twins were peacefully settled for the night, and Julia was prepared to face the ghost again.

What a blessing that none of the boards in the corridor squeaked.

She paused by the door to the attic stairs, listening. The rustle she heard was most likely mice somewhere in the woodwork. Few homes this age were without them. The knowledge didn't prevent her from feeling a trifle uncomfortable. Memories of her young brother concealing a mouse in her bed had never quite left Julia. She'd had no fondness for the little gray animal, although she had tried hard to conceal it from Geoffrey.

She opened the door, then shielded her candle from a slight draft while mounting the steep steps. At the top, she paused, looking about her while quelling any tendencies to nervous starts.

"Are you here?" she inquired at last. Did ghosts require sleep? She had no idea, but rather believed they were past that sort of thing.

Julia found the polished trunk, then seated herself, patiently waiting for her ghost to appear. It didn't take very long. Soon the shimmering shape began to form, developing into the now-familiar figure of the Tudor lady.

"Good evening," Julia began politely. "I fear I've not had time to visit you, what with all that has had to be done. Do you have something you wish me to see tonight?"

The figure appeared to nod, then beckon with a wave of her shimmering arm.

Julia arose, following the misty figure across the attic to a neat trunk on the far side, beneath a slit of a window.

Figuring that she was intended to open the trunk, Julia

carefully placed her candle holder on a battered table close by, then attempted the task. She searched about for a key. Then her eyes grew wide as it floated to where her hands could grasp it, held in a vaporous hand. Swallowing with care, she said, "Thank you." One ought to be polite, even if it was a ghost.

The lock had rusted, evidence of lack of recent use. By means of determined pressure, Julia turned the key, then lifted the lid. Inside were neat piles of account books and journals, such as she had observed tucked beneath Lord Temple's arm on one occasion.

"You want me to look through these books?" Julia was somewhat disappointed. It scarcely appeared to be a thrilling occupation.

The figure bowed, then faded from sight. Julia suspected the ghost most likely hovered somewhere beyond her awareness.

Shifting the relict of the table closer, Julia opened the first of the books. Dull figures, at first glance. Then she examined the pages more closely to discover the book contained an account for the household expenses back somewhere in the 1600s written in highly creative English. How fascinating to see what was purchased, and in what quantities.

Yet she sensed this was not the book she was supposed to find, so she set it aside, deciding to investigate all the books before really trying to read a particular one, given the originality of their spelling and the difficult handwriting. She delved into the trunk again, pulling one book after another for perusal.

Had she not been so engrossed in searching the contents of the slim volume, she would have been better prepared for what happened next.

A creak of the floor, a flutter of her candle flame did not alarm her, but when another light joined hers, she near expired from shock. "Oh, dear heaven!"

"Sorry, if I frightened you. I had not realized you were so intent," Lord Temple offered by way of excuse.

"I do wish you had said something," she whispered, not

knowing for certain if there was a person housed in the room beneath them. "My heart may never recover."

His glance fell upon the nicely rounded, decently covered area that concealed that particular organ and he smiled. "Pity, for I suspect it is a rather fine example."

"What are you doing up here?" she demanded, ignoring the rapid beat of said heart.

"I could say the same of you. Actually, I was unable to sleep. Then I felt the strangest urge to come up here. I recalled there were more papers stored somewhere, and I suspect that is what you are looking at now. How did you happen on them?"

"Your family ghost led me to them. Since she does not speak, I do not know for sure why, but there is a reason for all she does." Julia held up a thin account book for him to see.

"Perhaps we ought to take the contents down to the library. It would be more pleasant to sit by a fire, with adequate light, perhaps a plate of biscuits and a pot of coffee at our sides?"

"I vow that does sound appealing. Here, you take part of them, while I shall take the rest." She suited actions to words, dumping a stack of books into his arms. Then, first blowing out his candle, she gathered the remainder of the books in her arms, holding her candle precariously in her hand.

"Are you sure you can manage with that lot and the candle?" He appeared to find it difficult to whisper, and Julia devoutly hoped that no one would hear them.

"Hush," she admonished. Within minutes she had negotiated the stairs to the upper corridor, then followed him along and down to the ground-floor library.

"Good, this door is open. So much easier," she murmured, passing by him into the room. A fire still burned, although down to mostly embers, and the room was cozily warm, intimately lit with her one candle.

He proceeded to stack his volumes in a neat pile, light a brace of candles, and stir up the fire with efficient dispatch.

Julia watched him with mixed emotions. She ought not be here with a man she was so dangerously attracted to, a man most likely to wed another—if his mother had anything to say about it. Julia suspected Lady Temple would do a great deal to get her way.

Her books carefully placed in a ragged stack on his desk, the two then set about finding the promised biscuits and coffee, or whatever might be available for drink.

Biscuits came easy, the coffee did not. They settled for a lovely glass of sherry.

Julia sipped her wine with appreciation, relishing the warmth that seeped through her body, then she set the glass aside to peruse the top of her stack. "Account books. Your ancestors were obsessed with keeping records."

"Fine thing they were." His deep voice was amused, tolerant. "It tells us when repairs were made, furniture purchased, not to mention the scale for wages and the price of oats. They are history, my girl." Those dark eyes twinkled at Julia from over his glass of sherry.

Ignoring her bits of history for the moment, Julia savored that look. Then sanity returned, and she began her inspection of the next volume on her stack.

"This is a curious book."

"How so?" He raised his brows in inquiry.

"For one thing, it is a journal. For another, I believe portions of it to be in a type of cipher." Living with her unusual family that dipped into spying and what not, Julia had learned a fair amount about codes and ciphers. "It seems a fairly simple substitution type, I believe. Look." She pointed a finger at the page before her.

He had strolled around the desk to join her, now peering over her shoulder with frowning intent. "Hm."

"From the date in this book, I rather suspect it is written by the son of your ancestor who originally built this house. I wonder why he found it necessary to conceal what he wrote!"

"Why, indeed. His name was William Blackford, and by all accounts suffered a fair bit from his rather wicked stepmother. Look here—a peculiar sentence inserted in a quite ordinary paragraph. 'B dews dns ly jbis.' Makes no sense at all."

"It would seem to be monalphabetic, and if we are fortu-

nate, he will have concealed a copy of his cipher somewhere in the book. It is very helpful for the one who writes
it down to have the cipher before him to aid in arrangement."

"You know," he turned that warm, dark gaze upon her
with the usual shattering effect, "I had no idea I would ob-
tain the talents of a cipher expert when I engaged the services of a gifted artist.

"It comes from being a Dancy, I fear." Her eyes met his
gaze, brave and innocent of coquetry. Annoyed with herself
for being so susceptible to his charm, she ran a nervous
tongue over her dry lips, thinking she ought to head for her
rooms if she had an ounce of brains.

His look intensified, and he held out a hand for the slim
volume they had been studying. "Come, it is time this
lovely lady secured a bit of sleep. I shall keep this safe until
we may examine it by day. I suspect this is the book our
ghost wished us to find."

Julia accepted his proffered hand to assist her from the
chair where she had more or less curled up while paging
through the books. One of her legs had become stiff, and
she faltered when she attempted to walk to the door. Immediately his arm wrapped about her waist, helping her until
she steadied herself, regaining the full use of her somewhat
sleepy limb.

"Thank you, sir. How foolish of me to think I might
draw up like that without sad results." Sadder yet were the
feelings stirred within her at his touch.

Julia tensed when her gaze became entangled with his.
They paused by the door for a long moment. She wondered
what went on in his mind. While she had come to terms
with her past, she wondered if he had managed the same.
What feelings for Margaret survived in him?

"Had we but world enough, and time, this coyness, lady
were no crime," he quoted from Marvell's poem in a soft,
rich voice that sent trembling up Julia's spine.

She shook her head, but whether to deny what he implied
or better understand him, she couldn't say. Where was her
sensible heart?

"Best get to our rooms, before we succumb to desires

more fitting at another time and place." He released her, standing back to see if she might manage her leg with no further difficulty.

That he wanted her, Julia knew immediately. That he handsomely dismissed his longings relieved her greatly. Yet a part of her was sorry, for she suspected he would take care to avoid being alone with her again.

Blushing, she hurried from the room with only one backward glance to imprint on her memory the scene just past and the man who stood by the door.

Tiptoeing up the stairs, she scolded herself for her contrary heart. She had claimed no interest in men, yet deep in her heart she was attracted to a pair of beautiful dark eyes, not to mention the man who possessed them. Why were those eyes so remarkable? Dark beauty, rich pools of color that drew one deeper and deeper; they held mystery, knowledge of wonders she might only guess, and sensuous enticement. Small surprise that she found him irresistible. Had Mary Blackford felt the same for Sir Henry?

"Well, it seems the family ghost has returned to its sleep. We have heard naught of it for days," Lady Pamela gaily declared as she joined the others in the morning room.

Edythe Sanders looked up from the pile of baskets she endeavored to tie ribbons on and gave a superior smile. "You are late this morning. If we are to find the best quality nuts, Lady Temple said we ought to get an early start."

Turning from where she contemplated the beginnings of a fine autumn day, Julia said with great patience, "There is no set time to depart. Indeed, Lord Temple is closeted with his steward, so it would be impossible. I have decided to bring the twins along to give Anne a bit of company. It will slow me down, but the rest of you may proceed as you wish."

Julia took note of the satisfied smile Lady Temple gave her tatting.

"How thoughtful you are, Lady Winton," Lady Pamela replied. It was well that the men did not hear the waspish note in Lady Pamela's usually dulcet voice. It hinted of the shrew, a woman most men avoided like the plague.

"What ho?" Reggie demanded as he followed Lady Pamela into the room. "Baskets at the ready, I do believe." He joined Edythe on the sofa, admiring her latest effort. "I see you are one who believes in being prepared. A good organizer, I vow. Admirable," he concluded, his eyes meeting her gaze with a boyish charm.

Lady Pamela was prevented from making a nasty aside by the entrance of Dick Vansittart. She had no doubt learned through her maid that Mr. Vansittart, whilst not a peer, was possessed of a tidy fortune, and no sensible young miss turned her back on such. After all, her host had been most neglectful of her, from what Julia had observed. What with her annoyed glances and sniffs of aggravation, Lady Pamela did not feel as confident as her hostess that Lord Temple might be brought to heel.

Violet brought the twins to Julia just as the group was about to depart, if you might call the straggling that went on a departure.

Anne held tightly to Rosemary while Julia took Tansy's little hand. The girls were all dressed in suitable sturdy muslin frocks topped with proper pelisses and perky bonnets. Anne giggled, a sound Julia hadn't heard for days, when Rosemary insisted she be allowed to ride the donkey that pulled the little cart for them. Violet trailed behind, encumbered with all deemed necessary for infants.

"You are good for Anne," Lord Temple observed as he assisted Julia into the cart.

"Time is a great healer. You have spoken to Nanny Gray? Or perhaps made a few arrangements on her behalf?"

"You refer to the meeting with my steward, I gather. I did mention she would be leaving before long. And I established the wages for Miss Gilpin."

Julia gave him a shrewd look, then commented, "I fancy Miss Gilpin is a fortunate woman. Poor Nanny Gray, she will have to retire, for she is too old to be accepted by another family."

"I have considered that, you may be certain."

"I suspected you would, for you appear to be a fair man."

"Such encomiums go to my head, Lady Winton."

Julia failed to reply to that wry jest. She had been excruciatingly aware of his proximity, desired nothing more than to touch his cheek with her fingers, and gaze her fill at his handsome face. There existed a tension between them that any astute observer could have caught.

However, Lady Charlotte entertained Lady Temple in the morning room, Lord Lacey had gone riding, and the others were far too engrossed in arranging themselves to best advantage in the other carriage to notice anything unusual.

Clearing her constricted throat, Julia said, "And when does the estimable Miss Gilpin arrive, sir?"

"I am not certain. She begged leave to pause at her home on the way here so as to visit her ailing mother. Naturally, I gave permission."

"Most proper of you," Julia replied, an admonishing glint in her eyes. He had not done what Julia felt urgent, prepare Nanny for her coming retirement and departure. What sort of trouble the nanny might present, Julia didn't know, but she felt in her bones that the woman wouldn't leave easily.

He joined Anne, facing Julia, Tansy, and the maid, holding Rosemary on his lap and delighting his daughter with silly tales of nutting expeditions of days past.

When they stopped, Julia glanced about in bewilderment, for they were merely at a wide spot in the road. An apple orchard to one side displayed the crimson and yellow of ripe rennets and russets that awaited picking. In briar rose hedges bright red hips danced in the slight breeze. Brambles and woodbine wove through the roses with delicate abandon, their leaves a colorful accent. Overhead, stately elms and oaks stretched their autumn embellished branches to the heavens. Sunlight splashed its golden blessing over them all, warming and cheerful.

"How quaint, harebells still blooming," Lady Pamela exclaimed, thus exhausting, Julia suspected, her knowledge of wildflowers.

"The golden blooms of the furze rivals the sunshine," Julia said with mischief in her eyes, for she doubted if Edythe or Pamela were sure of that plant.

"If the blooms that covered the hazels last March were anything to go by, we ought to have a goodly crop of nuts this autumn," Lord Temple said, only his eyes reproving Julia, and that with a hint of mirth.

"Where are these worthy nuts, my lord?" Julia caught Tansy's little hand, watching while Anne secured Rosemary's hand in her clasp.

"You must know that nutting is a scrambling affair. We walk down that path over there," he ignored Julia's gasp of dismay at the rough track, "to near the water's edge. They like to grow down by a creek." He offered an arm, which Julia accepted without a qualm. While her jean half boots were sturdy enough, she did not relish tripping on a tree root, of which there appeared to be an abundance.

In the nearby fields, turnips, potatoes, and carrots were in harvest. Close by, she noted crab apples and elderberries in profusion. Tangles of bittersweet displayed bright orange berries, attractive with their rich color. Ripe brambleberries tempted, and before long a deep purplish color stained Julia's lips, the others succumbing as well to the enticement offered.

Julia thought that the day seemed about as perfect as might be with the gentle sun, the smell of autumn in the air, remnants of summer in delicate pink campion forgotten in the passing of the season, and in the distance the spectacular display of the wild service tree with its gorgeous leaves of crimson and scarlet, blending to orange below. Most satisfying. Particularly with Lord Temple at her side.

That, of course, did not last. When the stream came into view, the others gathered about with faintly perplexed looks.

"What ho?" Reggie demanded. "I do believe I see the little beggars down there. How do we pick them?"

Lord Temple stripped off his coat and tossed it over a branch. Then he took one of the baskets that Edythe had decorated in one hand while he forged ahead into the thicket of hazel stalks. "This is the way it is done." He soon demonstrated the simple means of retrieval.

Julia intended to pick nuts as well. She was no pansy, to sit on the sidelines sighing with admiration while a man had all the fun. How fortunate she wore a serviceable jade pelisse, along with a narrow brimmed cottage bonnet firmly tied beneath her chin with a neat jade bow.

Turning to Anne, she admonished, "Take care that the girls do not wander off. I trust you to be watchful." With a cautioning glance at Violet, Julia also picked up a basket and plunged into the thicket with a girlish spirit she thought had gone forever.

The protesting squeals from Edythe and Lady Pamela could scarcely be missed, yet Julia ignored them. She sought the little brown nuts, plucking them from their husk with ease, for they were fully ripe. A glance at his lordship revealed dark eyes dancing with amusement at her attack on the hazelnuts.

Several nuts fairly leaped from their nesting place, and Julia stared after them with a vexed compression of her lips. "Dratted little pests," she murmured.

"Ah," said a voice rather close to her ear, "those nuts shall make some squirrel delighted, I'll wager."

She turned her head, finding his face heart stoppingly close to her. "Sir . . . " she said with a cautioning breath.

He nodded in understanding. Still, he dropped a hasty kiss on her surprised lips before moving away. While she stared after him, he turned back, saying, "I cannot resist the irresistible."

"As if that makes it right," Julia mumbled, but unable to be angry, for that kiss tingled on her lips with the delicious tang of the forbidden.

The twins tumbled about in the leaves, giggling and holding up prize specimens (which was anything they could find) for Anne to admire.

"Leaf," Anne instructed patiently.

"Leaf," Rosemary repeated obediently. Not to be outdone, Tansey also echoed the new word.

Julia heard this and, nutting forgotten, returned to the glade where the children played. The others had moved along up the creek, finding the abundance of nuts easy picking. Shrieks of laughter, cautions from the gentlemen drifted back through the woods.

Heedless of her pelisse, Julia knelt on the ground, picked

up a particularly fine oak leaf, then held it out. "Leaf," she repeated.

The twins, thinking this a lovely sort of game, echoed her as well, and Julia hugged them both in thankful pride, looking over their heads to Anne with gratitude. "You are a fine teacher, my girl."

"I'm proud of you, my dear," Lord Temple said to his little girl, bringing pink roses to her cheeks. Then he turned to Julia and added, "I almost forgot, I paged through that book this morning and found a thin slip of paper stuck into the binding at the back. You were correct, there was another alphabet, rearranged. The word 'wicked' was at the beginning of the line. The cipher read, "'fear for my life.'"

"Who else should he fear but his stepmother?" Julia wondered aloud.

"And if he feared her, would not Mary have as well?"

"So what do you suppose happened all those many years ago?" Julia said softly so that the children would not overhear. "Did Catherine do her worst?"

"We shall try to find out, my dear."

9

"I DO believe Lord Temple has gathered the most," Lady Pamela declared with a sharp look at Julia.

Reggie wandered over to where his friend stood by the little cart to inspect the contents of his basket. "By Jove, I believe he has. Experience is what it takes, I'll wager."

"I suspect he has a great deal of that," Lady Pamela replied in a soft buttery voice.

"Er, yes," Dick agreed, looking amused. "Been nutting in this spot for ages, I daresay."

Julia glanced at his lordship, noted the amused gleam in his eyes, and remained silent. Lady Pamela's little barbs couldn't hurt, but they rankled.

"Well," Lord Temple said in a hearty voice, "shall we all pop into the vehicles? Time for our reward for a job well-done. A picnic."

"Picnic!" repeated an ecstatic Tansy, much to everyone's amusement. Rosemary clapped her hands, echoing the new word to her intense delight. She continued to repeat the new word, practicing, no doubt.

"I begin to see merit in silence," Julia commented as they all resumed the places occupied on the drive to the nutting spot.

"I thought you might, " Lord Temple replied with a grin.

The donkeys jogged along while the adult occupants of the cart remained lost in their respective thoughts. The children chattered quietly, Anne most proud of her work with the twins. She encouraged Rosemary to try a different word, to Julia's relief.

At the picnic site, they all straggled from the carriage and cart, assembling in a cluster for Lord Temple to lead the way, for obviously the picnic site was to be a surprise. Julia hoped the path would not be quite as hazardous. Although she admitted that she had enjoyed the hazelnuts.

Lady Pamela suspected something. Could it be that she envied Julia? Or did she merely wish a little experience of her own? What a blessing none of the others knew about the midnight tryst in the attic, then later the library. That would most assuredly cause a complication or two.

A sylvan glade with a pretty stream wandering through the center held a low table with an array of food, more than enough for hungry nut gatherers. Inviting cushions were heaped here and there, while discreet servants hovered in the background, waiting to assist should they be needed.

"Delightful!"Edythe Sanders pronounced.

At her side, Reggie looked down at her eager face and agreed. "Most delightful."

Julia wondered if she had ever blushed like that, then recalled last evening, and decided she was not as old as she had believed.

"Walk with me a little, if you please?" Lord Temple said to Julia while the others gathered about the table to sample the offerings.

"The children . . . " She looked to where Violet and a footman assisted the twins and Anne.

"They are fine. Come. I want to talk. I am pleased you have reached a rapport with the family ghost regarding your leaving the house. I would not have wished to leave you behind again." His dark eyes held a hint of amusement in them, which she refused to encourage.

"Oh," Julia answered with a wave of her hand, "I bargained with her. It is well that the hazelnuts and the picnic are near the house, for you recall I promised I'd not go farther than the village, and in return I'd help her with what she desired. Whatever that is. It is a pity she cannot tell me." Julia sighed, then glanced up at him. "You still have not seen her?"

"One of these nights I am going up there with you. I should like to meet my ancestress, as it were."

Thinking of last night and the hazards in such a rendezvous, Julia said, "Oh, but she will come to you elsewhere. I saw her in the great hall."

"That is relatively unchanged from when she would have been here, I suppose." He tucked Julia's arm in his, continuing their stroll in the other direction, always within sight of the group, yet out of their hearing. He gestured as though pointing out something in interest, and Julia appreciated this consideration.

"I have also seen her in the corridor outside my room."

"I hope you have not mentioned that particular spot to Miss Sanders. I should hate to find it necessary to restore her following a swoon."

"I daresay Reggie would be most pleased to make the effort. He fair dotes on her." Julia half turned to look back at the group. The prospect of a confidential chat with Lord Temple outweighed the promise of delectable food, she thought. Yet the array appeared most appetizing, and she wondered how long they would be, for she was far too sensible to believe that anything might come from the interest she could feel between them.

"Yes, he does, doesn't he. I frankly had not anticipated things working out as well as they have."

What he meant by that remark Julia couldn't tell. She wondered if he meant his unseemly attraction to herself, for as a widow of no great inheritance, she would not meet his mother's exacting standards.

"I have been observing Anne today. She enjoys your girls very much. I suppose I ought to have married long ago, so she would not have been so alone."

"I expect most people would agree."

"But you do not?" He raised his brows in evident surprise at her reply. "I thought most women were of the opinion that the only good man was a well-married man."

Julia chuckled. "Not if a girl is single, sirrah." Then sobering, she said, "I do not believe one ought to marry for the sake of children. At one time I felt I must, then I realized I simply could not condemn myself to possible grief, just to provide a home for my twins. We do well enough on our own. They are showered with love from my sisters and I. When they are older, I shall have them attend a suitable school for young ladies, so they may make friends and learn to get along with others their age and station."

"Is that a subtle criticism for my keeping Anne at home?"

Julia could sense him stiffening, and she was sorry she had intruded this note on what had been an agreeable conversation. Yet she must say what she felt needed to be voiced. "I realize your mother believes Anne to be of delicate health. I fear I do not see that. Are you certain she is so fragile?"

They paused on the side of the slight rise, looking down on the assembled company clustered about the table. The adults were laughing and eating with apparent pleasure. Anne sat cross-legged on a wool rug by the twins, her clear sweet laughter softly floating up the hill. She held out her hands to welcome Tansy onto her lap, rosy cheeks evident even at this distance.

"I hope this expedition will not be too much for her. Nanny Gray said something about her fragile health only this morning." His clasp on Julia's elbow tightened until she winced and eased away from his side a trifle.

She turned to stare at him with a considering look while she digested what he had said. "I strongly suspect that Nanny Gray wants to retain control over her charge. How better to achieve this than to fabricate the business of poor health? Are you feeling guilty because Anne does not have her mother? Or do you possibly feel you must offer a substitute to appease the judgment of society?"

The rather awesome frown he gave Julia was quickly followed by harsh words. "What utter rubbish! I had thought you to have more sense than that."

Julia found herself being rapidly walked down the little hill to the table, then offered a plate. Silently, she accepted a selection of the food presented, then strolled off to join the girls, hoping the expression on her face did not give her inner annoyance away.

How like a man to refuse to see what was right in front of his nose. Anne might not be a sturdy child, like Tansy and Rosemary, who had inherited their grandfather's build. But Julia had observed time and again that the sturdy child often grew up to be no more hearty than the willowy, thin one. In fact, it seemed to Julia that the slender women had a much better time of it all the way around. Indeed, the plump ones seemed to expire at an earlier age, which made Julia resolve to remain her somewhat thin self if possible.

"You pick at your food," Lord Temple said from over her shoulder. "I hope our conversation has not killed your appetite. While I may disagree with you, I nevertheless respect your opinion."

A tentative smile settled on Julia's face as she speculated on these words. Lovely. Lady Pamela and Edythe were feted, fancied, and fawned over while she was respected. It must have something to do with her being a mother and a widow. While she felt young inside, she had seen so much more of life that it showed both in her face and demeanor, right down to her proper gowns.

When planning her wardrobe to come to Blackford Hall, Julia had selected clothing she felt unobtrusive and modest. One did not wish to present a frivolous appearance when trying to make a proper impression.

There was that word again. Proper. But, she mused, a proper young lady scarcely would have made the acquaintance of the family ghost, much less sought her company and held one-sided conversations with her. And promised to help her with her problem, whatever it might be. Or have been.

Lord Temple might be tolerant regarding the ghost, but when it came to his inner feelings, he remained quite inscrutable, for the most part. Julia could recall few instances when he revealed something of the inner man.

Then, realizing he awaited a reply while she had been woolgathering, Julia apologized. "I fear I have been reflecting on the conversation and not attending as I ought. I appreciate your esteem, sir." But, she added to herself, she would far rather have a repetition of that kiss, which he most likely deemed a madness of the moment. Perhaps picking hazelnuts did that to one's senses.

"I did not mean to be so abrupt. You have a way of saying the most disconcerting things."

"I suppose it comes with age. I mean, I have served as

chaperon for my sisters so often, that I tend to speak my mind, much as the dowagers do." She offered a rueful smile by way of her rationalization.

"You shall have to do better than that, my girl. When you smile, particularly while chasing after ghosts, you look no more than twenty. I refuse to consider you in the same breath with the dowagers."

Julia sighed, shrugging slightly. "Nevertheless, some people seem to believe I belong in that group."

"What is that building on the far hill?" Lady Pamela cried. Her plate contained the remains of scarcely tasted food (evidence of her ladylike appetite), and she looked about her as though wishing to be doing something more interesting than watching someone else eat.

"The family mausoleum. It has a pleasant view of the surrounding countryside." With a glance at Julia, he added, "I believe one has a rather nice aspect of the nearby village as well."

"Jolly good," Reggie declared with enthusiasm. He offered a hand to Edythe, which she instantly accepted, and they sauntered in the direction of the neat, rather lovely, building of honey-colored stone situated at the summit of the gradual incline.

"It sounds utterly delightful." Lady Pamela bestowed a brilliant smile on Dick Vansittart. He wasn't slow to understand her desires, so he rose as well, gallantly offering his assistance. With a narrow glance at Lord Temple, Lady Pamela strolled along the freshly scythed grass with her attentive swain.

"Would you care to test the restriction placed on you?" Lord Temple inquired in a diffident manner, only his eyes alert and very much aware.

"I should immensely enjoy seeing the view from the top of the rise, my lord," Julia corrected, with the knowledge she must sound like a governess.

Pretending not to see the hand he offered, Julia arranged her most sensible gown, then walked not too close to the man who so often proved her undoing.

The gentle slope proved an easy stroll. Julia arrived at the summit not the least out of breath, and was thankful to

Lady Pamela, for the view was indeed most lovely. She decided she would not attempt to challenge the ghosts limitations in any way, however.

"Well?" demanded a voice close to her ear.

"Lord Temple, you must know it is exceedingly attractive." Julia brought her thoughts to a full stop here, for she was tempted to add a line about her appealing host, and one simply didn't do that sort of thing.

She walked along the pillared terrace, pausing to view the distant prospect every now and again. "Your relative selected a commanding view of the countryside for a burial site." She thought a moment, then added, "It cannot help but make one curious just why one of them would wish to leave such a noble structure." She turned about to gaze up at the perfectly cut and fitted stone, rich honey-gold against the deep blue of the sky. "May we go inside?"

"Certainly." With an aside to Dick, Lord Temple guided Julia along to the entrance, then inside. "I must confess, I had not considered the aspect of choice resting places with regards to a ghost. You never cease to amaze and delight me, Lady Winton." He teased, and she knew it.

Without thinking, Julia shot back, "And provoke, too, I daresay."

His chuckle warmed her heart.

"I am sorry," she said softly. "It seems I have a wayward tongue."

"Not at all."

His gaze grew speculative while Julia chose to ignore him a bit. She stared up at the truly magnificent dome, with its exquisitely carved medallions, then the fluted pillars and arched window. "A true thing of beauty, my lord. Your ancestor chose well."

Her words echoed in the room, and she felt a sudden chill. "We are not alone, sir."

"We aren't?" He glanced about him, quite obviously seeing nothing, then gave Julia a quizzing look.

"Come, I sense we are to inspect the chamber where your family rests in peace." She led him to the door that opened to the flight of stairs, and they walked down rather slowly, searching the shadows. Long, narrow windows gave filtered light. Julia repressed an urge to shiver. It was not that she feared the dead. It was the knowledge that the ghost was here while she was with Lord Temple, and wanted them both to see, or know, something.

"I wonder what she wants?" Noel urged Lady Winton ahead of him so he might inspect the place he had not visited since his father's death. His wife was buried in Italy, thank goodness. He'd not have wished her here with the decent remains of his relatives.

"Where is she?"

"Who?" His mind lingered in Italy with his faithless wife.

"Mary Blackford, of course." Lady Winton have him an odd look, which he quite deserved.

"Let me see, I believe she ought to be on the bottom row over in this corner. There is Sir Henry Blackford, the builder of our family home." He pointed to the first of the elaborately carved vaults. "I confess I've not paid much attention to the early vaults."

"I see the name of Catherine, his second wife, on the vault next to his."

"But where is Mary? She ought to be near Henry." He was genuinely puzzled. No scandal had been attached to Mary Blackford that he knew about, and he had been pouring over those old books for days. There was no reason she could not be here. Now, had she been a suicide . . .

"Perhaps that is why the ghost wished us to come inside and to the crypt? He body is missing!" Lady Winton revealed a rising consternation that Noel also felt.

"That cannot be, my dear lady. Mary must be here. Perhaps she *shares* a vault with Henry." Noel searched the row, reading each name with care, taking note of who was where and next to whom.

"When she would have been buried first? I doubt it." Lady Winton also wandered along the row of vaults, examining each tier, then glanced at the unlabeled vaults, silently waiting for coming generations.

At last Noel stood in the center of the crypt, utterly baffled. "You think Catherine had her put elsewhere?"

"I do not know, but regard this, if Catherine had mur-

dered Mary, then convinced Henry that Mary had committed suicide, would he place her in here?"

"No!" Noel answered with certainty.

"I believe we are supposed to find Mary's body."

"After all this time? Why, it would be nothing but bare
bones at best."

"Perhaps. But unless you want this poor ghost to wander
through your home for generations to come, I suspect that
is what will have to be done."

"I believe you have the right of it," Noel slowly replied,
his respect for Lady Winton growing. It was not a pleasant
prospect, but he suspected Julia Winton had been led here
for a purpose, a dark and portentous mission.

"But where do we look?" Her brow furrowed in speculation.

Before Noel could think of an answer to this question,
they heard the creak of a door, then Reggie's strong voice,
"Halloo, in there, or wherever you are. Lady Pamela is
about to have the vapors. Convinced you've been done in
or some such rubbish. Coming?"

Noel grinned at Lady Winton, then moved to the stairs.
"We shall be up directly. Lady Winton had a notion to see
the vaults." His voice echoed up the stairs and into the central chamber.

Reggie popped his head through the open doorway, looking down at them with a puzzled face. "The vaults? Dashed
peculiar thing to want to see."

"They have exquisite carvings, sir," Lady Winton said,
her rebuke quite lost on Reggie.

"See better stuff on a fireplace surround," Reggie muttered, quickly disappearing from view.

Julia shared an amused glance with his lordship, then
walked up the steps with the knowledge they had a formidable task ahead of them. At the top of the stairs, she paused.
"You *are* going to allow me to help search? I am not a
squeamish soul. And I believe she wishes me to assist you."

"I do not suppose I could try to avoid your help if I
wished, dear lady. I am outnumbered, two to one."

Julia flashed the Dancy smile at him, "Mary Blackford is

with me," she teased. "You must confess that we make an unbeatable pair."

Once they gained the fresh air and had convinced Lady Pamela that nothing unfortunate had occurred—both Lord Temple and Julia remained silent regarding the ghostly guest—the group began to straggle down the slope toward the tables where a festive dessert awaited them.

"Do you mind if I ask you something terribly personal?" Lord Temple said to Julia, careful to keep his voice low enough so that the others could not hear him.

"That all depends, does it not?" Julia gave him a started look. For a man as reserved as he, it seemed strange that he would make a personal inquiry.

"Your husband," his lordship began, "I sense you were not happy with him from little remarks you have made. Is that so?"

Julia drew an uncomfortable breath, then decided her story was not all that rare. It no longer hurt.

"It was an arranged marriage. Our fathers knew one another years before. His father saw fit to honor a long-standing agreement, even though my father had been killed while he and mother were on a trip to France, so not able to demand he comply. I did not object, for I thought my new husband seemed quite dashing and romantic."

"However . . . ?" he urged.

"However, it turned out quite otherwise. I daresay I am not the only female who was wed for duty. Shortly after our wedding, he revealed his true nature with thoughtless remarks, an unfeeling and impersonal attitude toward me. At first I was hurt by his neglect. It did not take long before I grew accustomed to his indifference. The husband I believed so romantic considered himself first before any others. He was quite dedicated to his own interests."

"Go on," he prompted when she paused, beset by memories.

"Then I became in the family way. He left me alone after that, went off to his carousing and buckish friends. Then he took a notion to go off to the Peninsula—in spite of his father's protests—convinced that he had sired an heir. He was wrong there, as in so many things. He was not invincible and was killed. When I bore twin girls, I no longer felt welcome in his home. So, I returned to my family."

"The Wintons forced you to leave?" he said with horror.

"No," she admitted softly. "They merely made it untenable to remain. It was all my fault for producing girls. They wished me gone so they might court the next heir, I suspect. Perhaps they wanted him to marry their daughter. I have not paid the least attention to their doings since." She was silent a few moments, then said, "May I ask of your wife, sir? For I sense you have as happy a past as mine." She wanted to hear the story from him, for his words would reveal the state of his heart.

"You dare to ask? And well you might, after what you have revealed," he concluded, answering his own question.

"So, your wife went to Italy?" she prodded.

"Oh, yes, but only after making an utter fool of me with this Italian she found in some drawing room. Singing, as I recall. He was polished and handsome, I'm told, and fed her a deal of romantic drivel. She was bored, for I had considerately taken her to the country, thinking she needed a rest from the Season's rigors. Quite foolishly, I thought she would enjoy some time with Anne. Instead, she fled with him to the Continent. I heard years later that he abandoned her when the money from the sale of her jewels disappeared. She had taken everything that was hers, you see."

"And she died alone in a far-off country? How sad," Julia said thoughtfully. "She took *all* the jewelry?"

She quite deserved the odd look, and almost affronted reply, "No. Only what she had been given. The family jewels she had declared too heavy and old-fashioned, and she left them behind, fortunately, for they had considerable value, if not family regard. I now keep them safe, I assure you. If I do marry again, I would purchase new baubles at any rate. May I ask why the curiosity?"

"It is difficult to explain. The ghost . . . " Julia began.

She welcomed their arrival at the table, and the presence of the others, for she had to consider what her reply to this question should be. If his wife had absconded with all her jewels, and the family valuables were safely in the vault, whose jewels were stashed in the attic trunk? And why had the ghost wanted Julia to find them?

Ten neat packets in a cache more valuable than Julia could estimate concealed in the bottom of a polished trunk! What a dilemma. And now to locate a missing body, one that had disappeared well over two hundred years ago!

"You have been deep in a discussion for such a lovely day," Lady Pamela observed. " I cannot fathom how you could enter that crypt. I fear my sensibilities would never permit such a thing."

"The dead can do you no harm," Julia said, attempting to soothe those tender emotions.

"I say, I jolly well can do without the blessed bodies," Dick observed. He heaped a plate of tipsy cake for himself after offering a dainty morsel to Lady Pamela.

"This has been a very exciting day," Edythe Sanders observed, casting a shy glance at Reggie Fothingay.

Considering the mass of conflicting emotions she had experienced in the past hours, Julia felt that to be an enormous understatement, but could hardly say so.

Tensy had slipped into an exhausted slumber, her head on Anne's lap, while Rosemary nestled in Violet's arms.

"All tuckered out," Lord Temple observed.

"I vow I envy them," Julia said. "It has been quite a day, one way or the other."

Aware that Lord Temple was giving her a rather searching look, Julia turned away and helped herself to a plate of cake. Her luncheon had been interrupted by Lord Temple's insistence upon a walk. Now she felt she needed something to sustain her after the strain she'd had.

The cider refreshed her, and she drank long from her glass. She darted her tongue out to lick her lips, then sensed his presence close by.

"I am sorry if I intruded earlier. I thought perhaps we might consol one another."

Julia raised her eyes to meet his gaze. Was that what prompted his kiss earlier? He thought she missed a husband's attentions as others had assumed? Well, she did, but she'd not welcome another man into her bed without a wedding ring on her finger from a living husband.

"There is nothing to excuse. You forget, I was so bold as to poke my nose into your past as well."

Nothing more could be said by either, as Reggie claimed Lord Temple's attention, and Julia felt constrained to help with the twins.

She welcomed them into her arms, and held them closely on the way back to Blackford Hall. Lord Temple sat opposite, Anne leaning against him in a tired, but happy way. Violet preserved any propriety not covered by the presence of three children.

In the carriage ahead, the four occupants sang a gay little country air, the music floating back most pleasantly.

"It was a good day," Julia ventured to say.

"Indeed." Lord Temple subsided into a silence unbroken until they reached the hall. He assisted Anne into Nanny Gray's control, then helped Julia with the sleepy twins, taking Tansy while Julia retained Rosemary. Violet trailed behind carrying all the rugs and wraps.

The taunt about to flow back from Reggie as the four entered the house died when he observed the girls sleeping. But his expression said he would tease later.

Julia gave the girls to Violet and Hibbett, then walked to the door of her rooms with his lordship.

"I accused you of improper conduct once. The girls are engaging. And I know better now."

She stood by the open door, wondering how to approach the subject that must be discussed.

"The body. Do you think we might be able to uncover it?"

"I shall study William's journal this evening, and perhaps you might like to go over his father's, in the event I missed something in it. Not the easiest reading."

"They were rather creative in their spelling, were they not?"

"But it is all we have to go on for the present. Will you do that for me?" Those beautiful dark eyes crinkled up, smiling down at Julia with warmth.

When he looked at her like that, Julia thought that she would do almost anything for him. Within reason, that is. She hadn't totally lost her senses. Not yet.

"I would be pleased to help. Surely there must be a clue."

10

WHEN had it happened? she wondered while staring out of the window at the setting sun. Muted peach and mauve flowed across the darkening blue sky, brushed by a master hand. Clouds scudded along, tumbled by an impatient wind. But the beauty of the scene was lost to this particular viewer.

"How could I be such a fool?" Julia whispered to the soft blue draperies. She rested her head against the window for a moment, then straightened as Hibbett entered the room with the plum-colored sarcenet Julia intended to don for the evening. She crossed the room to inspect the gown.

"Depressing thing, is it not, Hibbett?" Julia declared, holding out the limp skirt. "I cannot think what I was about when I ordered it from Madame Clotilde."

"Too true, ma'am," the abigail replied with her usual forthrightness. "As I recall, Madame did not like it above half. Said it made you look like a wilting sloe."

"Hopeless. Quite, quite hopeless."

"Now, I would never say that, my lady. If I had a bit of lace, or trim of some sort, I might contrive to change it the way that Madame suggested. Alter the neckline a trifle, fix the sleeves a bit. Wouldn't be difficult." The abigail studied the garment with zealous eyes.

Julia turned a speculative gaze on her maid. "Could you? I believe I shall make a trip to the village for a few things. Do you suppose there are any other of my gowns you might refurbish?" Julia cast her an encouraging look from beneath dark lashes.

"I shall inquire while at dinner as to the best shop to visit. If I may say so, it will be a pleasure to have you looking more your age for a change, instead of trying to ape some ancient dowager." Hibbett gave an emphatic nod at these words, then set about doing what she could with the admittedly plain gown.

Once dressed, and her hair nicely arranged, Julia dismissed the maid, then sat staring into her mirror, toying with the demure string of pearls that curved around her neck.

"You," she informed her reflection, "are a bloody fool! He desires your help, your talent, but not you. And you will stew over those silly gowns, as though *they* will do you any good. Why, oh, why did you accept this commission when you suspected the dangers involved? Couldn't you have guessed?"

"Because," her reflection replied, "you were already half in love with those beautiful, beautiful eyes. It was but a moment for you to love the entire man."

She shut her eyes against the truth, sighing deeply. She pushed away from the dressing table, then picked up her plain white wool shawl. At the door, she paused, wondering if the ghost sympathized over lost love.

"Simpleton," Julia scolded herself. "Peagoose!"

With those vastly encouraging words, she marched down the hall, ignoring the shadows where Mary Blackford might lurk.

The chandelier that hung above the landing of the grand staircase where it branched to wing up either side of the house from the central hall sparkled brilliantly with candlelight. Julia trailed her hand along the mahogany railing as she descended to the ground floor. Above her on the walls, a number of past Blackfords stared from their frames. Scenes from mythological tales awed the eye with their bold colors and execution. The names of the painters thrilled the artist in Julia. How fortunate for the family that the previous Viscount Temple had been of an acquisitive nature when he took his Grand Tour. Paintings by Canaletto, Titian, Van Dyck, and Rubens caught the knowledgeable eye and brought pleasure.

While it did not precisely intimidate her, she keenly felt the antiquity of the house, not to mention the status Viscount Temple held. Highly esteemed by nearly all she knew in London, he had received Lady Tichbourne's highest accolade, that of being the very best *ton*.

How unfashionable she felt, unexciting as the plainest dowager. Why had she not brought some of her more fashionable garb with her? She owned a number of attractive gowns, pretty shawls, and a smashing pelerine of nile green velvet. Utter stupidity.

She reached up to touch her hair with tentative fingers. Rather than the lace evening cap she had taken to wearing, she left her hair uncovered, with a simple white silk flower tucked in the arrangement Hibbett created.

Tomorrow, without fail, she would go to the village. The ghost willing. Julia devoutly hoped that she would not be forced to halt at the village edge, unable to proceed, and looking like an utter fool. Reaching the bottom of the stairs, she was about to turn to the drawing room when the sound of rapid steps caught her ears.

"Lady Winton," Lord Temple said, striding to greet her from where he had been closeted in his library. "I have found a clue."

"Good!" Forgetting all her doubts and dismay, especially her foolish dreams, Julia held out her hands, giving him a warm smile of delight.

"Actually, it is nothing to cheer about, but I believe you were correct earlier in your assumptions. I found another ciphered line." He accepted one of her hands, tucking it close to his side while they inched toward the drawing room where the others had gathered. "It says, 'Flowers on Mother's grave.' So it would seem that William knew about the business of the so-called suicide, or he'd not have concealed such an innocent-seeming observation."

"But, where would Sir Henry have buried Mary? I know a suicide could be interred in the north side of a churchyard. Could she be there, perhaps?" Julia glanced toward the drawing room, relishing a bit of time with Lord Temple, yet knowing she ought to join the others.

"Possibly." He curved his hand about her elbow, drawing her closer to his side, in order, she was sure, to speak quietly and not be overheard. "The church has stood there

since the twelfth century, with modifications there somewhere in the 1650s. It's a rather charming, if chilly, little
building. It remains to be seen what sort of records were
kept, and how well preserved. I know a few fellows were a
trifle lax at times. I shall look into the matter."

He paused. Julia turned to meet his gaze and in so doing,
those amazing dark eyes that had the power to melt her in-
sides to jelly.

"We have never had a chapel in our house as some other
large homes have, such as Chatsworth and The Vyne. Perhaps we should all make a visit to the village church? I
could check records while the rest of you inspect the inte-
rior. There is a new altar of which the vicar is quite proud."

Julia foolishly felt his voice fraught with meaning, and
tried to imagine what a trip to the village church might possibly involve. Her fancy failed her completely. Yet, she
considered her own needs and hopes for a decent shop that
would have trimmings, and nodded with enthusiasm. But
she felt the topic best left to another time, for they neared
the drawing room door, and she was not certain she wished
the entire group to tag along with her.

"I could hope that Mary's place of interment may be
found. But what then?" Julia faltered in her steps, but her
question remained unanswered.

"I wonder if Chatsworth or The Vyne have a problem
with ghosts?" He guided her into the room as they considered the problem of the missing corpse.

"While I have not visited those places, I understand they
are quite outstanding." Julia took care to separate herself
from his lordship by several degrees after they entered,
aware of Lord Temple's sharp gaze. A woman of uncertain
temper was not one to annoy.

"What? Have you not been to The Vyne?" Reggie studied Julia, apparently finding her somewhat of a puzzle. She
doubted he noticed her omission of her customary cap, or
improved looks. Most likely he wondered why she was not
diligently painting.

"After our parents died, we lived a somewhat retired life,
I fear." Julia gave Reggie a kindly look, suspecting he intended no offense. It would be unlikely for three young

women on their own, without a connection, to attend house parties. Perhaps if their Aunt Bel had seen fit, they might have moved about more in Society. However, they had done well enough. Victoria had married favorably, and it appeared Elizabeth would, too. And, after all, Julia had had her chance, although it was not her fault if her marriage had been a disaster. Well, not totally, for she had the twins, and they were a double blessing.

Dinner was again a rather strained affair, what with Lady Temple trying to manipulate her son's interest. Pity the lady did not see fit to join the daily activities. She would soon learn that he had no affection for either of her two candidates for his hand. Indeed, those young women had sensibly turned their attention to the other gentlemen.

Julia felt no dismay about this, not even when Dick Van-sittart deserted her side for the lovely Lady Pamela. Who could blame him? She not only radiated beauty and charm, she possessed a fine dowry, as Hibbett had gleaned in the servant's hall. Quite a respectable match.

When the women adjourned to the drawing room after dinner, Julia stifled a yawn. Being out of doors much of the day led to sleepiness. That, and pouring over Sir Henry's diary before dinner. She had found some puzzling remarks that possibly had been entered about the time of Mary's death, but had not time to determine what they might mean.

She sat quietly, contemplating the problems she faced. Ignoring the matter of her heart, she must cope with completing the portraits, a willful ghost, a missing body, a strange cache of jewels, and the knowledge that Nanny Gray would be fit to be tied when she found out that she was to leave this house before long. What might she do? Julia considered the possibility of her being mad, then rejected that thought. Yet the woman seemed not quite right in her mind.

Where had the sum appropriated for refurbishment of the nursery gone? And the toys sent down from London? Might they be found in the attic? The nanny had to answer to a number of things, Julia thought. Which she seemed most disinclined to do. As to what might happen to the parrot that had been whisked up to the nursery so that it might not disturb Lady Temple, Julia trembled to think. She was not so optimistic about its longevity as Lord Temple.

In addition, Julia believed she had best inform his lordship of the cache of jewels secreted in the trunk. The responsibility that came with her knowledge seemed too great. Perhaps he had a simple explanation of the hoard? Somehow she doubted it. She had searched her mind time and again, and she couldn't dream up a sensible reason for hiding that fortune in a plain trunk up in the attic, where most anyone who took a mind to poke about could find it. It was bizarre, that's what it was. Most peculiar.

At last, when it appeared the men had wandered off to the billiard room after leaving the dinner table, Julia begged leave to retire. The other women followed suit. At the head of the group, Lady Temple muttered rather nastily all the way up to the next floor. Julia, trailing behind with Lady Charlotte, found herself spared the uncivil words.

While they straggled up the stairs, one of the servants lowered the chandelier by means of a winch, and proceeded to snuff out the many candles. By the time they had reached the next floor, only the wall sconces in the hall remained lit. Shadows danced as a flutter of air moved along the corridor.

Julia paused, but no ghost emerged from the dim recesses.

"I believe an early night would be welcome, for I would enjoy a visit to the local shops. One never knows what one might find," she commented to Lady Charlotte.

"That sounds like a capital notion," the lady responded.

Julia suspected that she would have a companion on her morning venture.

The following morning saw them all bright and early in the breakfast room. At least the ladies appeared animated. The men looked as though they'd had a late night of it. Julia was of the opinion they quite deserved headaches for deserting them last evening.

When the other young ladies heard about the planned expedition to the village, they declared it a lovely notion, and

Julia knew she would have a difficult time to get off by herself.

She found her fears confirmed. Lady Charlotte insisted upon joining her in the little gig. Lord Temple was pressed into escorting the other ladies to the village in the large landau. Reggie and Dick rode their horses, planning to leave them at the Bull and Crown with the carriages.

Julia had gratefully accepted the reins of the gig and lack of a groom, fearing the gossip were she to be stopped at the boundary of the village by the ghost of Mary Blackford. She could envision the scene, her little gig and horse straining to proceed along the road, only to be halted by an invisible wall. Too embarrassing for words.

"My dear," Lady Charlotte said, "you have had the most blue-deviled expression on your face at times. Is there anything I may do for you?" She sat with her hands neatly folded on her lap, her head tilted so she might better study Julia.

Ignoring the matter of a very foolish heart and the multitude of matters pressing upon her, Julia turned her attention to more positive things. "I should be grateful for your advice regarding some lace and trimmings. My gowns are sadly lacking smartness. Hibbett insists she could make them a bit more dashing, if only I may purchase an ell or two of fine lace, or perhaps some silk for embellishment. What do you think? She learned that Gresham's is the place for trimmings here."

"Then, by all means we shall explore this shop to discover what might be found," Lady Charlotte declared with relish. "Pity we are not in London. Harding and Howell has a lovely assortment, and Grafton House is another favorite of mine. Clark and Debenham are noted for fine lace. Hose, too. Oh, my, I do miss the city at times."

After leaving the gig at the Bull and Crown, Julia and Lady Charlotte briskly walked to the pretty little bowfronted shop they had espied on their way into the village. They were some distance ahead of the others, due to Lady Pamela's difficulties with something or other. She had gone to her room, not to appear by the time Julia and Lady Charlotte left.

Julia opened the door of the shop for Lady Charlotte, smiling at her ladyship's rattling monologue.

The next hour was spent in the delightful pastime of perusing an assortment of trimmings that proved amazingly fine. It seemed that Mrs. Gresham went up to the city from time to time to replenish her supply, and possessed excellent taste. She had recently returned from just such a trip so Julia found a generous selection, all she might wish, in fact.

Rouleaus of satin in various colors, tatted lace collars, dainty ribands of every color, and elegant lengths of pleated quilling ready to be sewn down along the edge of a gown were displayed for their admiration. With the list Hibbett had given her, Julia selected various amounts of riband and quilling, an ell of lace, for it was very dear, and a rather pretty lace collar for her blue day dress.

Lady Charlotte succumbed to the temptation of some rather fine cambric handkerchiefs, a length of purple riband the lady called mistake because it had lovely shadings in it, and a dainty reticule made of cut velvet in the same shade of purple.

When the two ladies left the shop, both were well satisfied with their foray into the village. They took a few steps toward the Bull and Crown wondering why the others had been so greatly delayed, although Julia had not missed their company in the least, when the other carriage pulled up before the Gresham shop.

Lady Temple had accompanied the two girls, who left the carriage in a flutter of reticules, shawls, and eyelashes, for Edythe had become quite adept at this clever art. The men remained silent for the most part, murmuring between themselves. They set off promptly in the direction of the Bull and Crown, evidently figuring the ladies could settle things for themselves. In a village this size, it would be of no moment to find one another.

"Is it worthwhile?" asked an eager Edythe, peering in one of the bowfront windows at a pretty display of lace and riband.

"It is not to be missed, in my estimation," Lady Charlotte declared, to Lady Temple's gratification. So often women from the city turned up their noses at village shops.

"Charlotte, I must have your opinion on some trimming I saw here not long ago," Lady Temple asserted. "Do say you will advise me, for you always know just the thing."

With an amused glance at Julia, Lady Charlotte apologized softly, then returned to the shop, chatting comfortably about the various lace patterns and widths to be found.

Left to her own devices, Julia strolled along the street, admiring the stately elms that arched over it, and the late-blooming red roses that nestled up against pretty little cottages of stone and slate. The village church could be seen across the green, its modest spire poling above the trees rather nicely. A fine lych-gate guarded the path to the arched door. Peach-colored roses attempted to climb the walls to either side of the gate, with only partial success. Julia wondered what luck Lord Temple might have at discovering the grave.

She had about reached the Bull and Crown when he appeared around the corner of the inn.

He signaled her to be silent, then led her along to the shade of a large chestnut tree, where he apparently felt free to speak at last.

"What a sensible girl you are. I vow I cannot manage the trip home if it is half as maddening as coming. Why do we not slip away in the gig now, and permit Reggie to drive the ladies home once they finish? He and Dick are enjoying a quiet stroll about the village, and I trust will linger in the Bull and Crown with a little persuasion."

Julia nodded. She failed to see why chattering females should drive him to distraction, since he endured his mother much of the time. Then she decided that might be the very reason he welcomed a respite. Of course, being labeled sensible was not precisely desirable when she could think of any number of more desirable compliments.

Within a brief time, during which he informed the men of the departure, they were seated in the gig and jogging along out the road to Blackford Hall. By clever diversion around the village green, Lord Temple managed to avoid being seen by those in the Gresham shop.

"You, my lord, are very devious," Julia said with a

chuckle once they were safely on the road out of the village.

He tossed her a thoughtful look, then returned his attention to the road ahead, although he knew it well.

"Do you suppose since we are involved in this business up to our necks that we might dispense with the styles and the like, at least between ourselves?"

She repressed a smile at his plaintive note.

"I believe it might be possible."

"I wonder . . . Do you suppose I might be introduced to my family ghost? I should like to see her before we supply her with a resting place."

"No harm in trying, is there? Did you learn anything while in the village?" She gathered her reticule and parcel in one hand while clinging to the side of the gig with the other. His pace might be acceptable, but Julia felt the need of something solid beneath her fingers.

"There are a number of graves on the north side of the church, but no stone to identify Mary. The sexton was not around, but I believe he might allow me to search the records if I can find the fellow. He's in charge of digging the graves as well as the bell ringing."

"And so most likely keeps the records as well," Julia added, wondering just how carefully they would note the burial of a suicide.

"Julia, did you come across anything of interest in Sir Henry's journal? I wanted to ask you last night, but then Reggie wanted to demonstrate a new play to the fellows." Lord Temple allowed the horse to slow to a walk, half turning on the seat to better observe his companion.

With an effort, she controlled the quiver that ran through her at his use of her Christian name. How romantic sounding, when she knew very well that he merely wished to simplify their conversation.

"I did, indeed. Those spectacles you brought me are proving a great help, for his writing is spidery and most creative in spelling. 'Tis a blessing he does not use some sort of code or cipher in *his* book. However, I have yet to figure out the meaning of some of his writing. Perhaps you will read it over, and catch something I have missed."

Noel leaned back against the seat, letting the horse amble on at will. "Fine. I shall do that when we return to the house. I appreciate all you are doing for me. Most kind of you. And the painting? How does it proceed?"

"You must come to see for yourself. I am progressing nicely with Anne. You mother is proving a bit more difficult. She finds it displeasing to pose for very long."

He contemplated these words for a time. They neared the turn to the hall, and he competently maneuvered the little gig onto the avenue leading through the parkland. To either side of the road, deer wandered about, while sheep grazed some distance away. Ahead, the prospect of the meandering stream lured the eye to follow along until reaching a bridge of elaborate design that had graceful willows draping over the far end of it. Tall elms and oaks spread their branches in majestic beauty, and the tranquillity of the scene soothed both occupants of the gig.

"I shall try to help you, but I fear there is little I can achieve with Mother," he said at long last. "She can be very stubborn at times. Do the best that you can."

Julia murmured her assent, wondering how it must be for him to live under the cat's paw, as it were, with his mother instead of a wife acting the shrew. It could not be pleasant, and she could see why he elected to go up to London as often as he did.

"Does Anne enjoy the parrot?" Julia asked. "I expect he annoys Nanny Gray, for she likes to have the last word, and I wonder if the bird will allow that?"

"Anne appears delighted. I really am not concerned with what Nanny has to say in the matter. I did not buy the bird for her," he declared in an annoyed tone.

They neared the bridge, and Julia absently took note of the pretty structure, its grace typical of the improvements made by the previous owners of Blackford Hall. Long grasses peeped from beneath the willows at the far end, and sedge grew thickly along the bank of the stream that wound through the park. Capability Brown had straightened the stream in places, widened it in others, and it presented a lovely aspect as they neared it.

Clouds had run across the sky, and it looked to rain, as so

often it does in autumn. Julia hoped that they might reach the house before the drops fell; she hoped to keep her precious purchases dry.

The wheels touched the masonry of the bridge when it happened. A ghostly shape emerged to hover over the far end, wavering and fluttering in the breeze. The eery howl that next came forth terrified the horse, and he reared up, emitting frightful racket. Then he bolted over the bridge, determined to be quit of the horrid place as fast as he might.

"Hold tight," yelled Lord Temple, hanging onto the reins with a resolute grip.

Heart in her throat, Julia firmly clutched the low sides of the gig, sure that it would fall to pieces before Lord Temple could stop it.

Little by little he brought the horse under control with superb skill Julia could only admire in silence. Her voice had been lost about midway across the bridge.

When they at last reached the front of the hall, he brought the horse to a quivering halt. Julia could not prevent herself from trembling, and the poor animal looked about to have a decline. Her bonnet had been blown off, and dangled by its ribands. Lord Temple's hat had flown away, and his hair tumbled in endearing disarray, although his eyes were stormy with anger.

"What *was* that?" Lord Temple demanded, just sitting still in a sort of shock. "Is that what confronts you in the attic? Heaven's above, my girl, you ought to have a medal if you've faced that more than once."

"Whatever it was, it was *not* our ghost." Julia grabbed at the ribands of her bonnet before it could fall, then absently disentangled them, while sorting out her impressions of the ghost at the bridge.

"But I thought . . . It was white, and wavered about like I suspect a ghost would." He sounded just as confused as he looked.

Julia considered his words, the color slowly creeping back into her face as she spoke. "*Our* ghost is a lady, my lord. She is graceful and genteel. She does not frighten, well, at least she does not jump up and shock the daylights out of a person. Oh, I shall confess to a bit of palpitations when I first glimpsed her. But it was nothing to compare with this, I assure you. Mary is far more bodiless, more transparent."

"Then who . . . What?" He look a good look at Julia's face, then whistled for a groom, who appeared around the corner on the run. Noel helped her from the gig, allowing his hands to linger just a bit at her slim waist before releasing her.

"Come into the house. You need some restoring, my girl." His manner was quite firm, and he offered his hand with the expectation she would obey.

"I am not your girl, I think," Julia said, meekly accepting his arm while they walked up one wing of the front steps. The door swung open, and Biggins stared at their disheveled appearance with horror.

"There has been a slight mishap. I wish someone to inspect the bridge," Lord Temple commanded. He gave a few further instructions, then turned back to Julia.

The butler nodded, then accepted his lordships gloves, raising his brows when he realized that the elegant hat Temple always wore when out was missing.

Once the man had left, Julia followed along to the library, where she was nudged onto a high back chair, then handed a glass of sherry Noel poured her.

Noel leaned against the desk, studying the shaken woman who sat so sedately in the chair. Most women he knew would have had a violent attack of vapors, or strong hysterics, at the very least. Julia Winton had clung to the gig for all she was worth and remained blessedly silent.

"You were exceptionally brave during that terrifying drive. *I've* never seen the likes of it."

She cleared her throat, then said, "I believe I lost my voice, so it is not really so amazing. I doubt I could have screamed for anything." She gave him a bemused look that might have become a smile if she'd tried.

"I fully intend to get to the bottom of this, you may be certain." He took a sip from his glass.

"May I suggest that you also investigate that cache of jewels in the attic?"

He nearly choked on his drink, then stared at her, obviously nonplussed. "What jewels?"

"Oh, dear heavens," Julia replied. "You mean you truly do not know?"

11

HIS lordship cleared his throat, then studied Julia with a gaze that was most disconcerting. "No. I have not the least notion what you are talking about. But I should like to know . . . very much."

Crossing to Julia's side, he took her glass, then refilled it. When he brought the sherry to her, he leaned over so that his face was close to hers. His searching stare would have further unsettled her had she not already been in a state of nerves to the point where she felt dazed.

Julia drew back against the chair, feeling oddly breathless. Somehow, she doubted her pounding heart was totally due to the scare she'd just endured nor curiosity as to how he would accept this information.

"Begin . . . if you please." Upon seeing her withdrawal, Lord Temple retreated slightly, watching her closely from where he leaned against the desk.

Ignoring the mockery in his voice, Julia said, "The ghost led me to it. The jewelry, that is. I asked her what she wished me to learn, and she hovered over a trunk until I opened it. Strangely enough, that was the only object in the attic that was clean, polished, if you like."

When she paused, he advanced upon her, holding her gaze with his. "Continue."

"At the very bottom of the trunk, I found ten neatly wrapped bundles of jewelry. I do believe there is a small fortune up there—rubies, sapphires, diamonds, topaz, quite an array, in fact. There are some exquisite gold chains as well. But who might be responsible for the cache, I cannot imagine. Everyone has access to the attic." Feeling a trifle warm, she slipped from her pelisse, then removed her bonnet to place it on top of her parcel on the table by the chair where she perched uneasily.

"This is incredible!" Lord Temple thrust one lean hand into his windblown hair and began to pace back and forth. "I must see this hoard. Do you feel up to a trip to the attic? Now? After that harrowing drive? I realize it is a great deal to ask at the moment, but you must understand my curiosity?"

"This is all aside from whoever pretended to be a ghost at the bridge," she inserted before that subject was set aside. "Upon reflection, I cannot see that most substantial object as a ghost. It simply was not ethereal enough, you understand."

"Dashed peculiar, all around. Are the things connected?" He rubbed his chin while watching her closely. Julia suspected she failed to conceal her emotions from him.

"I doubt it." She considered her hands, tightly holding the barely touched glass of sherry. "While there is more than one person who would wish me gone, I doubt if *you* have an enemy in the world. Certainly not on your own estate. So, we must conclude I am the one who is the target."

"Egad, what a coil." He studied her with narrowed eyes, as though trying to imagine who it was that wished her gone enough to want to harm her. "Had I not happened upon you in the village, you would have been alone in the gig."

"Or Lady Charlotte might have been with me." But Lady Charlotte had neatly been removed so that Julia was completely alone, and the viscountess could not have suspected that her darling son would drive Julia back to the hall. Yet, Julia dare not accuse his mother of so dastardly a plan. However, it would be a simple enough task to get one of her faithful followers to do her bidding while she spent time in the village shop.

"Could anyone from London wish you ill and have followed you here? Considering your sisters and all?"

"I doubt that, as I was never involved in the actual spying, you see."

"Spying? I knew there were unusual incidents, but spying?" His look of astonishment amused Julia, for she had thought he guessed something of her family's involvement from little things he had said before.

"For the government. Perhaps someday you may learn more, but for now, we had best concentrate on the problem at hand."

Looking utterly bewildered and fascinated at the same time, Lord Temple sank down upon a nearby chair to think. Then he jumped up, holding out his hand. "Come, we shall investigate before the rest return from the village. Fewer people to answer to, if you follow me."

Julia took another fortifying sip of her sherry, then placed the glass on the desk. "Very well. I shall lead the way."

With Lord Temple at her side, Julia quietly slipped up the stairs, then along the corridor until they reached the attic door. The smell of paint reached her nose from the nursery and schoolroom. Nanny Gray and Anne had been moved to the opposite wing, far from this area.

With a stealthy look about to see that no one was in the area, she opened the door and within moments Lord Temple had shut it behind them.

She picked up her skirts to prevent tripping, then tiptoed up the steps, taking care to avoid the one that squeaked. From the top of the stairs, she pointed to the trunk.

It sat in a thin shaft of light from the narrow window. Lord Temple crossed over to it, then lit the candle that had been left behind. "Show me," he commanded in a voice not quite steady.

Julia knelt before the trunk, opened it, then delved into the contents. Pushing aside the tumbled garments, she pointed to the neatly wrapped bundles lined up on the bottom of the trunk. "They are still here." There was considerable relief in her voice. Suddenly, she was extremely glad she'd decided to confide in his lordship.

Lord Temple knelt beside Julia. With a hand that trembled just a little, he reached out to pick up the first rolled packet. Once undone, an exquisite ruby necklace sparkled and glittered where it lay draped across his hand. He gave it to Julia, replaced the linen that had been wrapped around the necklace precisely as it had looked before, then went on to the next little packet. When he opened it, the sapphire pendant winked up at him in blue splendor.

"Most extraordinary!" He also handed this piece of jewelry to Julia, duplicating his refolding of the linen wrapping as before. When each of the ten bundles had been checked, the contents duly removed and the linen replaced, he sighed, exchanging confused looks with Julia.

Across her lap were draped what appeared to be the contents of a jeweler's display case, the multicolored stones winking up at them with magnificent splendor. She touched the ruby necklace with a tentative finger, then peeped up at him with questioning eyes.

"I was right, was I not? They are valuable jewels?"

"They certainly look real enough to me. Not that I am an expert, but if they are fakery, it is amazingly good fakery." He picked up the emerald ring, studying it with obvious puzzlement.

"Do you recognize them?" Julia thought the identity of the jewelry was of first importance. It might offer some sort of clue to who stashed them up here.

"Oddly enough, I do. At least some of them. The sapphire belongs to my mother, although she doesn't care for it, so rarely wears it. This belongs to my mother," he pointed to a topaz set, "a gift from my father. This is a gold chain I gave my wife. I had assumed she took it with her when she left. I have no explanation as to why it is here."

Julia noted the irony in his voice, but made no comment. "But the others?"

"These are family jewels"—he lightly touched the emerald ring as he spoke—"and as such ought not leave our possession. I am remiss, for I believed them to be in the safe downstairs. Why they were bundled up in this trunk is a mystery of staggering proportions. Do you have any notion of the value represented in this cache?"

"I estimated it to be considerable. At first," she confessed, "I did not know if I ought to say anything to you. For all I knew, it might be a unique means of hiding jewelry—you know, the least likely place to look? Then after this morning, and the accident, something prompted me to reveal them. There most likely is no connection, but I wanted you to know that I knew about it, so that if it disappeared, I'd not have a guilty conscience."

"Do you believe that someone has placed this jewelry here with the plan to abscond with them at some future time? But who would have occasion to do such a thing?"

"That is a great problem," Julia admitted. "While I might have a notion or two, nothing appears to fit together. Certainly nothing makes sense." But she figured that Lady Temple might have access to the safe. Would there be anyone else who did as well?

"Let's hope that whoever it is will not return to poke about. I shall figure out some manner of hoaxing whoever it is with a substitute. In the meantime, the real jewelry must be placed somewhere that this person, whoever it might be, cannot get to it. It would seem that the library safe is anything but."

"You have a safe in your room? They will be secure there?" She studied the neat bundles in the bottom of the trunk. No one could tell, merely by looking at them, that the jewels were gone. But, it would be necessary to keep everyone away from the attic. First, they must see the real jewelry to a safe place. She collected the splendor heaped in her lap, using an old shirt from the trunk to serve as a concealment and a means of carrying them. She did not want the emerald ring, for example, to drop on the floor at an inauspicious moment.

"Like most old houses, the master suite has a safe built into the wall. Come, we had best go before the others return. We cannot know how long they intended to remain." He rose from where he had knelt beside the trunk, holding out a hand to help Julia to her feet.

Julia figured that since Lady Pamela shopped, it could take them a long time before leaving the appealing contents of Mrs. Gresham's establishment.

On the far side of the attic, a shimmery figure took shape, drifting across the room to stand before Julia and Lord Temple.

"Do you see her, my lord?" Julia said with commendable calm, considering all that had happened in the last hour.

"By Harry, I do!" he whispered with relish.

The ghost said nothing, as usual, nor did she do anything other than hover above the trunk.

"I believe she approves. If only she might reveal who it is that placed the jewelry up here," Julia murmured as she and Lord Temple moved toward the stairs, conscious of the need to hurry. When she turned again, the ghost had vanished.

"She just appears, then evaporates?" He seemed exhilarated by the sight of his ancestress, albeit in ghostly form.

"That she does, my lord."

"Pity she cannot tell us where her husband buried her."

"Perhaps if we ask her to lead us there, she might?"

"Just not in the middle of the night, please." He curved his hand around Julia's elbow to assist her.

They whisked down the stairs, then along to the door to his suite where Julia sensibly stopped. He threw open the door, then accepted the casually wrapped treasure from her. Most properly, she did not enter, for not only did they risk detection, but more a serious charge of Julia being compromised.

"I cannot begin to thank you sufficiently, Julia." His eyes sent a warm message, gratitude, she reasoned. "I had best put these in hiding immediately. Meet me in the drawing room, will you? We could have an innocent cup of tea while awaiting the others, for I feel sure they will be here shortly."

She nodded, backing away as he retreated. He kicked the door shut with his foot, but not before she observed the restrained masculine style of his elegant sitting room. Small paintings of priceless worth, utterly beautiful furnishings, even more perfect then the public part of the house. The thought crossed her mind that if his rooms were like this, the suite reserved for his viscountess must be indeed something to behold.

Pausing in her room to scoop up the twins, for she had an idea that it would be far more acceptable to Lady Temple were she to find Julia and the twins with her son instead of merely Julia, she proceeded to the drawing room.

Biggins hovered in the hallway as customary for the nosy butler. Julia gave him an odd look, then suggested, "I believe Lady Temple and the others ought to be back soon. Perhaps tea would be in order. Shopping can be such hungry work." Julia bestowed a level look on him that he chose not to ignore. He promptly turned to do her bidding.

Once settled on the sofa, with Tansy and Rosemary playing at her feet, she presented a pleasant picture of domesticity and innocence, she hoped.

Lord Temple paused inside the door upon his somewhat breathless entrance. "Clever," he approved. "No one would think we have been prowling about in the attic this past half hour or more."

"All that matters is that the jewelry is safe from harm and theft. Now we may apply ourselves to other, more difficult matters."

"Do you have any ideas? Any clues at all?" He joined her on the sofa, too close for her composure.

She sat at his side, searching for something to say. She could not reveal her suspicions. Yet her hunch existed, and she presumed that if her ladyship sought to get rid of a woman she felt a danger to her house, Julia remained in jeopardy.

"You must leave here, you know," he said, as though reading her mind. "I'll not have your injury or death on my conscience. It is sheer luck that I was with you to prevent the gig from overturning. You could easily have been killed."

"Possibly," Julia denied. "But, I will not go. I have nearly completed Anne's portrait, and I do not have that much to be done on the one of your mother. We shall say nothing of our worries. Perhaps whoever played that trick by the bridge merely wished to frighten me for some reason."

"I cannot think why. You have not been here long enough to make an enemy."

His appraising look brought a tilt to her chin. "I daresay one can make an enemy merely by being at times."

That most curious remark became lost as Biggins entered the room with the tray of tea things. Behind him the voices of Lady Charlotte and Lady Temple floated into the room.

"Oh," Lady Temple said upon entering the drawing room

to find the twins playing quietly at their mother's feet and the tea tray resting on the table in an ordinary manner with Biggins standing at attention off to one side. Nothing in the scene could be misconstrued to be the least out of line.

Julia smiled at the relief that flashed on her ladyship's face, but demurely turned to watch the twins.

"I thought, that is I heard," Lady Temple began in an abstracted way.

"What Hermoine means to say is that we were told there had been an accident," Lady Charlotte inserted in her usual forthright custom.

"Yes, well, there was, but not a serious one," Julia commenced to say. She was cut off by Lord Temple, who rose from his place on the sofa next to Julia to walk across the room in a distracted fashion.

"Someone played a dastardly trick on us. I shudder to think what might have happened had I not driven Lady Winton back to the hall. She might be dead!"

"Mercy," a shaken Lady Temple dropped onto the delicate chair close to where she stood, her face pale.

"What happened?" Lady Charlotte demanded, crossing to pour a restoring cup of tea, then urge it into Lady Temple's hands. "Drink it, my dear, I believe you have need of it."

"All appeared normal until we reached the bridge over the stream," Julia replied, deciding to lighten the account. "Some silly sort of ghostly looking figure popped up and howled like a banshee. I fear it frightened the poor horse half to death, for he reared up and took off at a dreadful gallop. We arrived somewhat shaken. Had it not been for Lord Temple's confident handling of the animal, I tremble to think what might have occurred."

"It took a far stronger hand than a woman might have, I assure you," his lordship added, more subdued.

"I say," Reggie said, when he found the little group clustered about the tea table with serious faces and Lady Temple looking to swoon. "What's this I hear about an accident."

"Lady Winton," Lady Charlotte threw her a curious

glance, "tells us that some sort of spectral thing spooked the horse, and he near ran off with them."

"Oh, now," Julia began to protest when she was cut off by Lady Pamela.

"Another ghost? I declare, this is too shocking by half. I cannot stay here another night, knowing there is something lurking about the halls. Why, should it enter my room, I should have a spasm!"

Dick Vansittart drew protectively close to her, placing an arm about her slender form as though to ward off all evil. "I shall escort you, my lady. 'Tis a most peculiar incident, I'll admit, but not the thing for gently bred ladies to suffer."

She flashed him a smile of gratitude, then left the room after properly saying, "I do appreciate your hospitality, Lady Temple, but under the circumstances . . . "

"I understand, my dear," her ladyship murmured, her face still somewhat ashen.

"Well," Edythe Sanders declared, "I believe I shan't go quite yet. I do enjoy a touch of mystery."

Julia guessed that the lovely Edythe intended to win a declaration from Reggie, and hoped to achieve it before leaving Blackford Hall.

"We are pleased to have you remain with us," Lord Temple said after observing the relief on his mother's face.

"You are the most affected, since you were in the gig when the apparition appeared, Lady Winton," Lady Charlotte probed. "Do you not wish to flee?"

Unable to refrain from a glance at Lady Temple, Julia strove to reply in a calm voice. "Not in the least. I feel sure there is a simple explanation for it."

"You are very brave, but then, I foresaw danger in your future, did I not?" Lady Charlotte dropped this pebble into the stream of conversation with all the effect of a boulder in a pond.

Her words hung in the silence of the room as all, particularly Julia, tried to recall precisely what that prediction had been.

Accepting a cup of tea from Biggins, who had returned with a tray of biscuits, Lady Charlotte gave him a dagger glance that sent him from the room, then she said in a rec-

ollecting sort of manner, "Edythe was to have a meeting
that would lead to marriage. Financial difficulties would be
overcome. She was to beware of a false friend, as I recall."

Edythe darted a glance at Reggie, then fixed her gaze
upon the woman in command.

The room remained silent, all eyes trained on Lady Charlotte, teaspoons clinking absently in teacups while they
awaited her next words. Even the twins sensed the atmosphere
and were quiet.

Lady Charlotte took a tantalizing sip of tea, then continued, "Lady Pamela is to have a favorable time and a wonderful journey by ship, do you not remember?"

She munched her biscuit before resuming her singular
recital. "And Julia was to face danger before she left this
house, but I foresaw a great love for her ultimately."

Edythe wrinkled her brow, forgetting what her mama
had cautioned about women who frowned too much. "But,
is it to be found here, or elsewhere? I do not understand,
Lady Charlotte."

"Well, the cards do not reveal everything, my dear," her
ladyship replied sedately with a shrug of her shoulders.

"But, danger?" Lady Temple repeated bleakly.

Julia wondered if Lady Temple found this useful, or
merely distressing.

"I thought to persuade Lady Winton that she might be
safer somewhere else. She is determined to complete both
of the paintings." Lord Temple said with a concerned look
in Julia's direction. Rosemary patted his leg in a silent bid
for attention, and he bent down to smile at her, offering her
a biscuit.

"I say," Reggie inserted in his usual drawling fashion,
"that is dashed brave of her."

Not desiring to be discussed like this, Julia set down her
teacup with a decided clink, then rose. "I believe it is time
for the children to have a nap," she said, scooping up
Tansy. Lord Temple earned a worried smile as he handed
Rosemary to her.

At the doorway Julia paused, adding, "I shall see you all
later, I expect."

She marched up the stairs, thinking the twins had become very heavy since they had arrived at Blackford Hall. Of course they grew, she'd not wish it otherwise. But, it served to remind her that the day would come when they would be married and she would be alone. Where would that "great love" Lady Charlotte persisted in foreseeing come from, anyway? It seemed rather hopeless to Julia's way of thinking.

Hibbett opened the door for them when Julia tapped with one free finger. Violet hastened to relieve her of her burden, with Rosemary singing, "Nice man," in a happy little voice all the way into the next room, quite obviously recalling the biscuit.

It was past time to confront the ghost about the burial site. Perhaps if she might solve this one thing, the other mysteries would follow in suit?

"Hibbett, did someone bring up my pelisse and bonnet from the library? Especially my parcel from the village?"

With a nod, the maid produced said parcel. Julia unwrapped it to reveal the lace and other trimming found at the Gresham shop.

"It will do very nicely, milady," the maid said with a deal of satisfaction. "I shall begin at once."

Almost of a mind to tell her not to bother, Julia decided to let her be, as she seemed determined to improve Julia's appearance, and that would in turn restore her spirits.

The thought of which sent Julia to the wardrobe. From its depths, she pulled a plain pelisse and simple green velvet bonnet that tied snugly beneath her chin.

"I have something that must be taken care of, so I shall see you later." Not waiting for some sort of acerbic comment from Hibbett, Julia slipped from her rooms, then along the hall and up to the attic.

"Where are you, my lady?" she demanded at the top of the stairs.

From the shadows of the far side of the attic, the familiar shape took form. It drifted toward Julia until directly before her.

"I believe you wish me to find your grave site. If you do, please lead me to it, for we have thought and thought and cannot imagine where you might be placed. I doubt if you are at the churchyard, and I know you are not up at the mausoleum. So . . . " Julia waited patiently. This ghost was not to be hurried. But then, when one lingered about for centuries, time must acquire a different meaning.

Before long, the spectral shape floated along down the stairs, and the same corridor that Julia had traversed. Following in its wake, Julia hoped that no one would appear to upset the ghost. Oh, Mary Blackford would disappear, she had no doubt of that. But Julia wished to solve this question once and for all. Perhaps Mary would be able to rest in peace when restored to her proper place.

Fortunately, the servants all appeared to be elsewhere. The sound of voices drifted to the hall, but no one elected to leave the drawing room. In the entry were signs of Lady Pamela's imminent departure. Portmanteaus and trunks had been piled neatly by the door, giving evidence of an efficient maid and determination to be quit of a haunted house.

Leaving the hall behind her, Julia slipped out of the door and followed the barely discernible white mist along the path of crushed rock until she reached the rose garden. From there she was led up the gentle slope for some distance. At last, the ghost stopped before a yew tree.

Julia examined the ground. No evidence could be seen of any sort of marker for a grave. Nothing but the tree, that is. She turned about to face the hall. From here she could clearly see the library windows, a room reported to have been a favorite place for Sir Henry, from all accounts.

A figure had left the house and hurried up the slope to where Julia stood.

"What on earth are you doing out here, you foolish girl? Have you not considered that whoever it was that tried to do you injury before might not give up?" Lord Temple reached her side, glaring at her with a furious frown, and looking as though he would enjoy giving her a good shaking.

"The sooner the riddle of the grave is solved, the sooner everything else will fall into place, my lord."

"Noel. You promised to call me Noel when we are alone," he reminded.

Such informality did not come easily to Julia, but she gave him a guarded, and admittedly reserved, nod.

"Why are you out here?" He glanced about, then not seeing any sign of a shimmer of white, he inquired, "Did she send you here?"

"Rather, she led me. Since she does not speak, she can but direct." Julia gestured to the large yew. It was a tree of great antiquity but not unusual, for there were any number of ancient trees on the property. "Could this have been planted by Sir Henry? A sort of memorial to his wife, as it were?"

Noel shrugged, then dug in the ground with the toe of his boot. "I shall have to get someone to dig up this area, I suppose. Can you think of an excuse?"

"Buried treasure?"

He broke forth in a reluctant grin. "The very thing." Their eyes met in shared memory of the cache of jewels.

Then he became serious. "I know you are determined to complete the paintings, but I worry about you. I would feel it a far better thing if you were removed from here to a safer place."

"I intend to finish what I began," she said, thinking that he was in a sad hurry to see her gone. "And, did you forget? I cannot leave this property, or at least, I may go no further than the village. Where should I go? I must remain here until all the mysteries are solved." She raised her gaze to meet his and was pleased to note that Lord Temple did not appear the least dismayed by this knowledge.

"Then we had best begin. I shall go at once to order the digging to commence. You had better ask Mary if there is anything else she wishes done. I would end this business once and for all." He strode off toward the stables with a determined step.

"What else could there possibly be?" Julia wondered aloud. With this disconcerting thought, she headed back to the house. She must bid farewell to Lady Pamela, then return to the attic. Another one-sided conference with the ghost of Mary Blackford just might produce the needed clue.

12

WHEN Julia rounded the corner of the house, she observed three things at once. Lady Pamela and her maid were entering their traveling coach, prepared to depart the haunted house forever. The maid looked particularly happy.

Next, she espied Dick Vansittart astride his horse, leaning down to say something to Lord Temple, who must have dashed up from the gardener's shed next to the stables upon being informed of his guest's intentions. They had not wasted one moment in their hurry to be gone.

Last of all, Julia noted that Lady Temple had not deigned to leave the house to bid her chosen guest farewell. Lady Pamela had failed to attract Lord Temple, and for that, she might be ignored.

Of course, there was a nip in the air; the last of the summer roses nodded in the wind, and fallen leaves tumbled like circus acrobats along the graveled path. Perhaps her ladyship might be forgiven for not leaving the house. Julia acknowledged that she was a trifle biased on the subject, and not in Lady Temple's favor.

Lady Charlotte caught sight of Julia as she approached the front steps, and waved to her before turning to say something to Edythe Sanders.

After pausing to offer a quiet farewell to Lady Pamela, Julia marched up the front steps. It was a relief to see that Pamela did not hold ill feelings toward Julia and her ghostly intimate, for her smile seemed gracious. Most likely, she was happy to be on her way with Mr. Vansittart as her escort. His was a respected family, and his personal fortune as good as he was handsome. Her home only a day's journey distant; her family would no doubt be over-joyed to welcome such an eligible suitor.

"Well, you have pretty roses in your cheeks, my dear. 'Tis a lovely autumn day." Lady Charlotte inhaled deeply, then smiled. "I believe I can smell burning leaves, such a lovely aroma. Most nostalgic."

"Reminds me of my girlhood when we would visit the country every autumn," Julia said. "Did they observe All Hallow's Eve on the last of October in your area? Our little church always had a service for the dead on All Saint's Day."

"We did as well," Lady Charlotte said in reply, nodding thoughtfully. "And the farmers set fires the previous eve to keep away the evil spirits. This autumn smoke reminds me of those protective fires."

Fdythe shivered, which was not surprising since she wore nothing but a shawl over her thin muslin gown. Julia might grimace over her own sensible kerseymere gown be-neath her serviceable pelisse, but she felt comfortable, even exhilarated, following her brisk march down the gentle slope after her meeting with Lord Temple.

Of Mary Blackford, she had seen nothing more. The ghost shied away from being viewed by anyone else. Odd, that. To date, Lord Temple was the only person who had beheld the ghost, other than herself. She wondered if he had found anything more in the journals regarding the various sightings that had occurred over the years. He had promised to tell her, but she suspected he teased.

Perhaps Mary's several appearances were connected with nothing more than her wish to be properly buried. Julia intended to confront her to find out what else might be required. Or did one confront a ghost with a query of that kind? It was terribly difficult to have any sane sort of con-versation with one who could not answer in speech, Julia reflected. That wafting and drifting along might do very well for finding a spot, like the yew tree, for instance. It could be more challenging otherwise.

"I think this house is frightful," Edythe said after a pause during which they all waved to the departing carriage that sped along down the avenue. It was a measure of her anxiety that prompted her to be so outspoken, for as a rule she was the most circumspect of young women.

"There is nothing wrong with the house. It has a few unhappy memories, that is all." Julia watched until she saw the coach pass safely over the bridge, then she turned to enter the house behind Edythe. Lady Charlotte briskly marched up the stairs to find Lady Temple.

"I scarce think it was a memory that frightened your horse," Edythe argued by way of reply as they crossed the entry hall.

"That," Julia said with commendable calm, "has nothing to do with the house, I'll wager. Although I will confess it was not a comfortable thing to have happen, I refuse to rush off as Lady Pamela did. I applaud you for your courage, Miss Sanders. Reggie seems impressed with your fortitude."

On her way down the hall, Edythe paused as though much taken by what Julia had said. "Do you, really? I hope so, for I shall admit to you that I nurture expectations there." Her face bloomed with a shy smile, and she glanced at the floor before turning a hopeful gaze upon Julia.

"I think the prospect of his making an offer is more than good," Julia said in a hushed voice, as might be proper for a subject as personal as an offer of marriage.

"I still say it is a pity your husband died so young, leaving you with the two babies. It cannot have been easy for you to be alone with hostile in-laws." For once, Edythe wore an expression of genuine concern.

Edythe's sympathy caught Julia by surprise. While the proper murmurings of the drawing room might be expected, this compassion was altogether unforeseen. She hoped that Reggie might snap this young woman up, for she thought they would do well together. Neither appeared to be deep thinkers, but there seemed to be a spark of genuine regard beneath their social veneer.

With polite murmurs of their goals, the two women parted ways, each intent on her own plans. Miss Sanders drifted toward the billiard room, where Reggie might conceivably be found. Julia marched up the stairs.

On the landing, Julia could hear Lady Charlotte quizzing

Lady Temple of what might be expected come All Hallow's Eve in these parts, and paused to listen. Eavesdrop, was more like it. Still, it seemed sensible to be prepared for coming events.

From what she could make out, they no longer watched for spirits, which was rather a pity when they had their own at the house. Rather, the locals bobbed for apples. The one who managed to seize the fruit with his teeth was required to peel the apple in an unbroken strip, which was tossed over his shoulder to reveal the initial of his (or her) true love. Utter nonsense, of course, traced back to the pagans who practiced a sort of divination rite at the end of their year. Julia could not quite see Lord Temple, for example, tossing an apple peel over his shoulder. But, she wondered, what might that letter prove to be? Turning aside from that tantalizing contemplation, she listened a minute longer, then continued on her way, prepared to banish thoughts of the approaching All Hallow's Eve celebrations from her mind, much less divinations of any sort.

But then, *they* had the estimable Lady Charlotte to help. Julia smiled all the way up the next flight of stairs when she considered what the expression on Lady Temple's face must have been when Lady Charlotte offered to practice her own sort of soothsaying.

Lady Charlotte had told Lady Temple that the smoke had reminded her of the fires they used to light to keep away evil spirits. Julia wondered if it was intended for good spirits as well, then giggled.

On her landing she found Anne waiting for her with a quizzical expression on her face.

"Hello dear," Julia greeted her with a smile. "What may I do for you?"

"I should like you to finish my portrait, if you please," Anne replied without her previous autocratic manner. "I know you are almost done, for I looked. Please?" She extended a soft little hand in a shy gesture that Julia found appealing.

"I should be delighted." She accepted that thin, small hand, then swung about. There was nothing to do but return to the ground floor and the pleasant salon where her painting things waited. After all, *this* was why Julia was here; to paint, not to investigate ghosts, mysteries, and the like, no matter how fascinating she found them.

Hand in hand, the two walked down to the salon, where Anne perched in breathless anticipation while Julia settled to her painting. If thoughts churned about in her head regarding Lady Mary Blackford's ghost, she wisely kept them to herself.

"How is the parrot coming along?" Julia said absently while stroking on a final touch to Anne's hair.

"Nanny Gray thinks he is evil. She says he'll murder us in our beds one of these nights," Anne solemnly reported.

Startled, Julia glanced up at Anne. "That bird? Evil? What rubbish," Julia snapped, indignant at the very idea that the nanny would plant such a notion in Anne's head.

"Well, he does like to bite sometimes," Anne reflected. "I do not think he likes Nanny. When she calls him a saucy bird, he flaps his wings and makes a terrible racket. *I* think he is very funny. Although," she added in a considering voice, "he does say the most shocking words at times. I do not know precisely what they mean, but Nanny's face turns as red as a beetroot."

The image of the green parrot flapping his large wings and squawking loudly at Nanny Gray was amusing. Julia could not repress a grin. "Naughty girl, I shall wager you made that up." Just what those shocking words might be, Julia hesitated to speculate.

"Cross my heart, 'tis true enough." An impish grin flitted across Anne's face, then she became the sober little girl once again.

"Do you like the bird? What is his name?"

"I call him William because he reminds me of my uncle. He snaps and has a nasty temper when he does not get his way." Anne giggled, then went on, "Nanny did not like to be moved to the other wing so the nursery and schoolroom could be painted. She is very cross these days."

"I believe we all have a relative like William," murmured Julia, loathe to rebuke the child for what was undoubtedly an accurate word picture. "And, better a cross nanny than the smell of paint I think."

"Well," Anne replied, "I like this other room better, for I do not hear the rustlings and spooky noises from the attic."

Julia glanced up at Anne, suspecting that the odd noises had come from Julia's prowling about, for the ghost actually made no noise at all.

"There you are," said a familiar voice from the doorway. "Painting at this hour of the day?"

"Papa, Lady Winton has finished my portrait. Come see!" Anne demanded, running to his side to tug him along so he might inspect the completed portrait.

Julia was far too conscious of his physical being as he leaned over her shoulder to peer at the small ivory oval now covered with the likeness of his child. She awaited his verdict with baited breath, hoping for his approval.

"Fine," he said at last. "I believe that truly is my little girl you have captured so well." He gave Anne a hug when she pulled at his hand.

Julia pushed her chair away from the table where she had worked, watching Lord Temple with his daughter. How good he was with her, seeming to know the right thing to say. Yet he did not appear to spend a great deal of time with Anne. Perhaps parenting was intuitive? Julia somehow doubted that had her husband lived, he would have displayed the same kind of casual affection for the twins. From what Julia had observed, few men appeared to see much of their children until they became ten or twelve, nearly grown.

"I am going to tell Grandmama," Anne cried with delight. "Perhaps she will be willing to let you finish her as well."

"Not today, Anne. But tomorrow, perhaps," her father gently admonished.

When they were alone, he returned to look at the painting again, then faced Julia with a determined expression. "I would still see you safely away from here."

"You had best seek permission from your ancestress, in that case," Julia replied with a touch of asperity. "She holds me captive in this house and on your land. I cannot stay here forever, regardless of what Lady Charlotte says with her fancy cards."

"Surely she's not at them again?" He feigned a look of dismay, shaking his head.

"I overheard her offer to do some divination for All Hallow's Eve, which is next Sunday. Do you suppose . . . " Julia began, then stopped, feeling utterly foolish.

"Do not leave me suspended like this. Finish your thought," he commanded, in a somewhat teasing voice.

"Well," Julia continued, "since that is the night the souls of the dead are supposed to roam, perhaps we could persuade Lady Blackford to seek a final resting place. Have you ordered the removal of her bones?"

"I have. You seem confident they shall be found by the yew tree." He turned to stroll over to the window. The yew tree could not be seen from this room, but he seemed sure that his orders were now in progress.

"I thought about it, and when I consider the odd thing Sir Henry wrote in his journal, it makes sense," she replied. "One entry contains a reference to his sadness of heart when he beholds the yew tree he has planted that he sees every day when at his desk. I went to stand at the desk and, presuming it has remained in the same location these many years, the yew tree we went to today is the one seen from the desk. Now, why would the gentleman be sad merely because he planted a tree . . . unless his first wife was buried beside it?"

"Brilliant deduction, my dear," Noel said with a wry smile. "As far as I know, the desk has always sat in that spot, for it is an ideal place, having such a splendid view of the gardens and beyond."

"Before Anne caught me on the landing upstairs, I had intended to visit Mary to see if she might reveal if there is anything else that she wishes done." Julia supposed she deserved his incredulous look. After all, sane people did not go about revealing plans to consult with a ghost.

But, Julia felt quite normal. Oddly enough, it did not any longer seem queer that she could see the ghost, particularly now that Lord Temple could see it as well. She cleaned her brushes, then walked to the door. He followed her along the hall until they came to the library. He gestured, and they went inside.

"Call her up in here," he ordered, albeit with a pleasant manner.

"Here? Well, I imagine I could try." Julia stood quietly, trying to concentrate on the phantom lady. Within a short time the familiar shimmering form began to take shape. She hovered in the shadows close to the fireplace.

"Ah, success," Lord Temple whispered in Julia's ear.

"Mary," Julia began, ignoring those strange sensations she felt when he stood so close to her, "we should like to know if there is something else we may do to please you."

Julia waited, wondering how the ghost might convey her wish, had she another. It seemed that she knew about the effort to place her in the mausoleum, for she did not go to gaze at the yew tree.

Instead, she wafted across the room to stand before the portrait of Sir Henry. Although she could say not a word, she gestured to him, then to the blank spot on the far side of the room.

"Why does she point to her husband's portrait, then to the far wall?" Lord Temple wondered aloud.

"I wonder if there was ever a picture hanging here?" Julia murmured, strolling along to examine the beautiful old paneling.

"Do you realize that another portrait of him hangs in the long gallery, but there is no portrait of Mary to be seen there or anywhere else? Would you not say that is another odd circumstance in a long string of them?" Julia demanded. She pulled a stool over to the center of the area to scrutinize the paneling.

"What do you hope to find?"

"Nail holes."

"That makes sense; I cannot think why I inquired." He paused a few moments, then said, "You believe a picture of Mary Blackford hung there at one time? But none of the other family portraits have been removed, only that grim one of the old woman who gave us all the shudders. Not even the one of the fellow who murdered his wife's lover was taken down, and you must admit that deed gave a reason."

"What! Do you have such a shocking relative? Dick did

not tell me about him," Julia scolded, half laughing, for she really didn't believe the tale.

"True enough, I fear."

The grim note in his voice stopped Julia from any further teasing. Every family had its loose screws, so she ought not criticize this one. Rather, she ran her hand slowly over the paneling until she found what she hunted.

"What is it?"

"A hole, a substantial one, quite sufficient to support a painting of comparable size to Sir Henry's!" She glanced over her shoulder to toss Noel a triumphant smile. With no response, she turned around, aware of her precarious perch not to mention her feeling for this man, and prepared to get down.

"Allow me, for I cannot have our sleuth further endangered, can I?" He drew nearer as he spoke.

With those softly spoken words, Julia found his strong hands around her waist. He lifted her from the stool, placing her close to where he stood.

"I, er, thank you," she stuttered. How foolish she was, to permit this silly infatuation to overcome her common sense. She backed away from him, moistening her lips with a nervous tongue. "Perhaps I ought to go to the attic. I suspect there is more of interest than that trunk to be found up there."

"Have you heard anything?" He did not move away from her, but remained close, staring down at her with disconcerting intentness. "Or have you seen anyone prowling about that end of the hall, or the attics? I have not thought of a connection between the ghost of Mary Blackford and the concealment of the jewels."

"I am coming to think there is no association between them," she replied, reluctantly edging toward the door. She dropped her gaze under his scrutiny. "Anne says she can hear noises at night while in the nursery. I expect it is my hunting about, or it could be the one who stashed the jewels. I hope we discover who it is soon. 'Tis not the ghost."

"I have been going through one journal after another. A pattern seems to be emerging, although what it is, I'm not prepared to say at this moment." A note in his voice brought her gaze back to his watching face.

"You mean a pattern of ghostly appearances?" Julia forgot her urge to flee Lord Temple in her curiosity.

"In the journals of later gentlemen, yes, a pattern does emerge. Mind you, I have been skimming, looking for certain references. And now I check for known dates."

Her interest definitely piqued, Julia firmed her mouth in annoyance. "I do think you might have the goodness to tell me. After all, I am the one plagued with your family ghost, although why, I certainly do not know."

"I believe I do. Trust me, my dear Julia, if my conjecture is correct, you shall be the first to know."

His eyes lit up with a delightful sparkle, prompting Julia to sniff in further irritation. "You are a most vexatious man."

"Please do not inform my mother of the fact. She believes me perfect, poor soul." He assumed a saintly mien that brought forth a hesitant chuckle from Julia.

"Abominable man." Julia grinned at his expression. Then, she realized this was scarcely the manner in which one spoke to one's employer. When had that original constraint vanished? How had this informal mode of conversation developed? Up in the attics? Or as a result of her being thrust into his family history. She tilted her head, giving him a considering look.

"Now what is in your mind?" He narrowed his eyes while searching her face for a clue.

"Well, you just told me that one of your ancestors committed murder. Is it likely to be a family trait, do you think?" Now Julia affected a saintly expression, hoping to tease a bit.

"Over his wife's lover? Let me say that if I marry again, I shall not tolerate my wife in another's arms or bed."

"A possessive husband? How interesting. I believed they were extinct." Julia thought of Giles, and his total lack of interest in her doings during their brief marriage.

"Not as extinct as you might believe, my dear Julia." His advance upon her was halted when the door opened, and Reggie thrust his head around it.

"I say, are you aware some chaps are digging up your lawn?"

"Under-gardeners. Yes, I ordered it done." Lord Temple withdrew to a discreet distance from Julia to her sorrow. Yet, she knew it was for the best.

"Dashed peculiar place to plant a new garden, old fellow. Hillsides are the very devil to care for, you know." Reggie frowned at such foolishness.

Julia crossed her arms, waiting to see how his lordship would handle the matter. She quite ignored the irritated glance at her from Lord Temple.

"We believe the remains of the person who ultimately became the ghost are to be found there. Julia thinks that if we can reunite those bones with the rest of the family that the hauntings will cease." He gave her a look that said the ball was in her court now.

"I say!" Reggie declared, quite impressed with this bit of logic. "Are they likely to be exceedingly ancient? What an interesting visit this is turning out to be."

Julia tried not to laugh and failed miserably. Placing a hand over her mouth in an attempt to stop her giggles, she at last succumbed and leaned against the wall, helpless with laughter.

"Well," Noel said in somewhat of a huff, "I fail to see the humor of it all." Then his eyes met Julia's and he paused, thinking back on all that had been said, and he chuckled as well.

Julia managed to stifle her amusement, then turned to a bewildered Reggie. "I should say the bones would be over two hundred years old. Does that qualify as ancient? You see, we believe that Mary, Lady Blackford, is the one who has haunted the house all these years. I shall not bother you with all the tedious details, but I do believe she wants to join her husband, even in death. I suspect it is a vindication of sorts."

"Dashed peculiar, I say," Reggie replied, darting his eyes from Noel to Julia and back. "If I didn't know Temple better, I'd say something havey-cavey was going on around here."

"Why, my good fellow, how could you think such a

thing of me?" Noel clapped Reggie on the shoulder, then walked out of the library with him.

Julia stood in the doorway, watching the two men disappear around the corner. They would undoubtedly join the others in the breakfast room for a light repast. Julia had lost her appetite when they had begun to discuss marriage. Aware that she would like nothing better than to remain in this house as his wife, Julia decided it prudent to go elsewhere than in a room where she would confront Noel as well as his formidable mother.

She quietly slipped up the stairs to the top floor, passed by her room, and down the corridor until she reached the door to the attics. Soon at the top of these stairs, she searched the shadows, for once not expecting to see the ghostly form of Mary Blackford.

The first, and quite unexpected, thing she found was a parcel containing a beautiful doll, quite obviously the one ordered from London. It had been tucked behind an old chair. Julia carried it to the top of the stairs, then returned to her search, wondering what else Nanny had stowed up here.

Wandering from one area to the next, she poked and prodded, peeked under coverings, and in general inspected all she found. At last her most thorough hunt was rewarded.

"Aha! So I was correct," Julia cried in soft triumph. There *was* a portrait of Mary in existence. Apparently Catherine hesitated to actually burn the thing, preferring to hide it instead. She must have figured that torching the painting would draw undue attention. Concealing it proved easier, particularly when she selected a dingy, remote corner like this one. "And I'll wager she put this sacking over it as well, to deflect any curiosity over it later," Julia concluded to herself.

Casting a wary glance about the attics, she perceived no wavering white shape, yet she suspected that Mary lurked about not far away. Finding that the sacking disintegrated upon handling, Julia searched for and found a soft white cloth with which to wipe off the portrait. When she had accomplished her task, she sat back on her knees to study the long-dead woman.

"What you must have suffered," Julia murmured in sympathy for a woman who had been murdered by a guest in her home. Particularly when said woman set out to snare the husband of that poor murdered innocent. For Julia had no doubt but what Mary had been lured to her death, one way or another.

Sneezing from the dust that floated about in the air, Julia quickly rose to her feet, then carefully tugged the portrait to where it could be more easily viewed. It was beyond her ability to lug the large painting down to the library, much less the steep stairs from the attics.

Upon hearing the door to the attics open, Julia walked to the top, gazing down at Lord Temple with a smug smile.

"Come, see" was all she said.

He ran lightly up the steps, then came to an abrupt halt at the sight of the painting, now bathed in the shaft of light from that horizontal slit of a window. Without looking at Julia, he walked toward the painting, one slow step at a time. "I gather this is Mary Blackford."

Julia found it pleasing that he stated the question, rather than asked if it might be true.

"Incredible," he murmured.

"I feel it must be her, for I was led to it." Julia did not bother to explain further, for there truly seemed no need. Lord Temple appeared to have no difficulty in understanding what she meant.

"Give me a hand, and we shall return this painting to a place of honor." He half knelt to place his hands beneath one end of the portrait, glancing at Julia as he waited for her to join him.

"In the library, I presume," Julia added, while picking up the other side of the painting. She did not question his reluctance to call a servant to the attics, for it no doubt would result in evasions at best. Ghosts could turn the most obedient servant into a spineless chicken.

"Naturally. After all, Mary clearly indicated that she felt her picture belonged in that room."

"With that of her husband."

They managed the first set of steps with a bit of difficulty, then made their way along the corridor. Julia kept expecting Biggins to pop up like he usually did when she didn't wish to see him, but he was nowhere to be seen when his help might have been welcomed. However, he appeared less than enthusiastic to be in this area anymore, so perhaps that explained his absence.

"Tell me," Noel inquired with a casual air that Julia sensed might be deceptive, "how do you feel about the second wife, that is, her portrait? Ought it be banished to the attics?"

"Because of what she did, you mean?" Julia frowned, thinking not of Catherine Blackford, but of Lord Temple's first wife, the late and seemingly unlamented previous Lady Temple.

"Right."

Julia gave him a troubled look, then turned her attention to the next flight of steps. Once established in a pattern, she said, "If that fellow who murdered his wife's lover is still hanging in the gallery, I think the evil wife should remain." Then she looked into Noel's beautiful eyes and grinned. "Gracious, that does sound a bit frightful, does it not?"

His shoulders shook with silent laughter as he gazed up into her amused face. Catching sight of a footman, he called him, turning the portrait over to him with unflattering speed. Julia thought they had been doing quite nicely.

"The library. Right you are, milord," the fellow said, offering no clue to his feelings regarding the sight of his master and a lady guest struggling down the stairs with an immense painting. He signaled to another footman, and the two headed toward the library, portrait in hand.

Noel dusted off his fingers with an immaculate handkerchief, then took one of Julia's hands into his, studying her face as he cleaned her fingers with a lingering touch. "I owe you a great number of debts. I wonder how best to repay them," he softly mused.

Julia could think of any number of methods he might use, but prudently offered none of them, sparing herself a good many blushes. "I neglected to tell you that I found the London doll in the attic. Anne shall have it before long; I'll fetch it shortly for her."

"Another debt I owe you. It may take a long time to

repay them all," he mused while studying her face. Julia supposed she must have turned several shades of pink under his regard.

"You promised to tell me what you had learned about the infrequent timing of your family ghost's appearances," Julia reminded him, hoping she might be able to breathe normally again someday when he no longer held her hand captive in his.

His answering grin lighted up his remarkable eyes, and Julia felt herself falling deeper beneath his spell.

"Oh, I fully intend to tell you what I have learned. But, not just yet. I await the appropriate moment, my dear."

Julia shivered, but whether with apprehension or anticipation, she could not have said.

13

SOMETIME later Julia gazed up at the fascinating painting of the late Lady Blackford, the ill-fated wife of Sir Henry, and shook her head. Fragile lace framed Mary's pleasant face by means of a picadil, the wire support worn beneath ruffs at the time. Her lace-edged shift peeped above the elaborate stomacher worn over her embroidered silk petticoat. Over all this splendor, a white velvet gown trimmed with gold braid completed Mary's rich appearance. Julia's eyes shifted from the elegant lace at Mary's wrists to her hands.

"Something wrong?" Noel inquired at her side.

"He must have cared for her a little since he showered her with beautiful things. Look at those jewels. That emerald ring seems familiar, somehow." She glanced at Noel, then back to the painting.

"You held it while in the attics. Did I not mention that it is the family betrothal ring? My late wife had an attack of conscience, and left it behind." There was no pain in his voice, merely irony.

Julia gasped. "Why that ring must be priceless! To think that there is someone who is trying to steal it and all those other jewels!" Her suspicions of Lady Temple warred with the knowledge that even *that* lady would not steal the family emerald.

"I suspect the jewelry is the next matter of business for us." Noel leaned back against the desk, studying his accomplice with a disconcerting gaze.

Julia thought a moment, then faced Noel with a frown. "I scarce believe I ought to be involved in this."

"My dear girl, you already are involved . . . right up to

your pretty neck." He touched his own neck with a cutting motion, and Julia had the uncomfortable feeling that she had suddenly plunged into dangerous waters.

"We had best attend to the problem of Mary's collected bones first," she said with her usual common sense following the uneasy moment. "'Tis fortunate they were precisely where expected, beneath the yew tree. You must not allow something like that to lie around, the hounds might find them."

Noel shook his head, then caught the gleam in Julia's eyes and reluctantly smiled. "I believe I did comment more than once that you are a spirited lady. Perhaps your energies had best be set to work."

Ignoring the teasing note in his voice, Julia sensibly turned toward the door. "I shall . . . with your permission . . . attend to the remains of the poor departed Mary before someone takes a notion that they are haunted, or worse."

"What do you propose?" He remained where he was, propped against the desk, an arm crossed before him, with one lean hand rubbing his chin in contemplation.

"Send one of the lads to the village to fetch the vicar in your name. Then we may have a simple interment at the mausoleum. You do intend to place her with Sir Henry, do you not? After all this time, there should be little left to require much space." She edged closer to the door, intent on escaping his presence.

"Have you no sense of delicacy, woman?"

"Without doubt. It is all very well to be softhearted, and I do believe I am that to a degree, but one must be practical. I trust you shall marry to continue the line? If so, all those empty vaults will be required some day in the future." She placed a hand on the open door, glancing at him over her shoulder as she paused in her flight from the room.

Noel waved his hand in defeat. "You are right, of course."

Walking along the hall to search out the youngest footman, Julia scolded herself for the green melancholy that had crept over her when he had so readily agreed that he would remarry. Of course he would. As inclined as she was toward the sensible, she must accept the reality of this. Nevertheless, it did not make the truth more palatable.

Once the young man had been sent on his way with a carefully worded message, Julia threw a shawl over her shoulders, then slipped out the side door. A brisk walk along the pebbled path soon brought her to the site of the excavation on the hill by the yew. The grave had not been all that deep.

The head gardener stood to one side, surveying the crumbled remains of what must have been the coffin. Within was a skeleton, neatly composed with arms crossed in submission.

Not sufficiently experienced in this sort of thing to withstand a lengthy study of the shell that had been Mary, Julia turned aside. So much for the practical.

"My lady," the head gardener said, "do you know what is to be done here?" He seemed more concerned with the ruination of the grassy slope than the disposal of a body.

"I believe his lordship wishes the remains to be wrapped in linen, then taken to the mausoleum. The vicar ought to be here before long, and I trust he may be able to assist us."

Julia offered that statement with more hope then anything else. Actually, even if the vicar received his living from the viscount, it did not naturally lead to his agreeing to bury one believed to have been a suicide. Julia was convinced that Mary had been murdered by the evil Catherine, but this could not be proven. Just because Mary's son was deathly afraid of his wicked stepmother did not turn Catherine into a murderess.

Someone produced an old, but fine quality, linen sheet and within a short time, the bones had been properly wrapped for the trip up the hill. If the under-gardeners felt any loathing to do their job, there was no evidence of it.

Julia felt a vindication of sorts as she observed the two fellows cart their slight burden up the incline to the distant mausoleum. The building appeared a tiny structure so far away.

She recalled the day the group had visited it, and the memory of the nutting expedition and that fleeting kiss returned as well. He merely teased. She wished he would not.

It made it hard, to know what she wished should never be hers.

When the men had disappeared from view, Julia drifted back toward the house. Behind her the head gardener issued orders for the slope to be restored, the sod replaced to his liking. It was quite evident that this business of recovering misplaced bodies did not meet with his approval in the least.

Raising her face, Julia clutched the shawl more tightly about her while she studied the great house at the end of the path. The sun peeped out from behind a cloud, dazzling the eye with the great number of sparkling windows, windows that flashed like jewels in the sun's rays.

Somewhere up there, behind one of those windows was the one who planned to steal those priceless jewels. But . . . where? And which person?

Since she had first discovered the valuable gems, Julia's suspicions had rested with Lady Temple. Yet the disclosure of the emerald as the family betrothal ring had made that conclusion highly doubtful.

Had Noel, Lord Temple managed to find some sort of substitution for the now absent jewelry? Wondering if she ought to remind him, or merely mind her own business, Julia slipped back into the house via the side door.

She paused in the passageway, listening. Voices could be heard in the billiard room down the way. Curious, she walked along the narrow hall on quiet feet.

At the open door to the room, Julia paused, a smile curving her lips at the sight that met her eyes. Edythe was contentedly nestled in Reggie's arms, her face a picture of satisfaction.

When he glanced up to see Julia framed in the doorway, Reggie cleared his throat, turning an interesting shade of red. "Ahem," he managed before being reduced to silence.

"Oh, Julia," Edythe said, clearly startled, but seeming entirely pleased with a witness to the scene. She hastily disentangled herself, but remained close to Reggie's side. He did not move a step, ostensibly rooted to the spot.

"Hello," Julia said, not wishing to jump to unwarranted conclusions based on the little she had seen.

"There is an explanation to this," Edythe began, her manner unsure when Reggie said not a word.

"I feel certain that there are many times when things are not what they appear," Julia said, gathering the shawl in her hands and preparing to leave the two to settle matters to their liking without her interference.

"It was the news, you see, that they had found the body of what once was the ghost buried on that slope beyond the house. I was most overset." Edythe's lashes fluttered to reveal her distress in an affecting way.

Reggie stirred at long last. "Dashed odd thing to do, go about digging up skeletons in a garden. Told Noel it was all havey-cavey business."

"I suspect you have the right of it there, if perhaps a little overdue," Julia murmured.

"At any rate," Edythe continued, determined that Julia hear her tale of woe, "I was most affected by the thought of that poor soul buried in the wrong place all these years. Reggie kindly offered comfort, nothing more." She gave Julia a meaningful look, which she chose to ignore.

"That is quite proper of him. I would never believe Reggie to do anything that was not the thing." Julia gave him a friendly glance, then swept along the hall until she reached the stairs.

Most likely Miss Edythe Sanders would be furious that Julia had not jumped to the conclusion that the two were betrothed. Julia had more sensible notions, like a man offering marriage because he wished, not because he was compelled by circumstances. Not that Reggie and Edythe didn't make an ideal couple. They did. But they would have to reach an accord without Julia's assistance.

When she reached the bottom of the stairs, there was a knocking at the front door. Julia paused, wondering if this might be the vicar. At the faint bow offered by Biggins when the man entered, she surmised she was correct.

"Vicar Brightwell?" Julia glided across the entrance hall, earning a frown from the toplofty Biggins. She held out a hand in greeting.

"Lady Winton? The note sent from Lord Temple was a trifle confusing." The plump gentleman doffed his hat and stood with his halo of dark hair resembling that of a curious monk.

"I believe it would be best were we to join Lord Temple in the library. There has been an event that would benefit from your special knowledge, I believe."

Ignoring Biggins, Julia swept the vicar along with her down the hall to the library, rapping softly, then entering at the welcome from Lord Temple.

The vicar looked to his patron with questioning eyes. "My lord?"

With a resigned air, Lord Temple rose from his desk, where he had apparently been puzzling over more of the journals to greet his vicar.

"I suggest Lady Winton manage the explanations. She does these sort of things so well," Noel said with smooth grace, tossing the problem back into Julia's lap without the least apology.

"Please be seated over here, Vicar Brightwell," Julia said, stalling for time. She ushered the good vicar to where a pair of chairs sat near the fireplace, glared at Lord Temple behind the good vicar's back, then took a seat close to the man while hunting for the right words to explain their dilemma.

"There is a matter of concern that needs my attention?" the vicar said helpfully.

"Precisely," Julia exclaimed with relief. "You see, the under-gardeners have dug up the remains of what we firmly believe is one of his lordship's antecedents. She was buried on the hillside. Perhaps it was before the mausoleum was constructed. After a period of over two hundred years, it is difficult to know the details," Julia apologized prettily.

"That long," Vicar Brightwell said, somewhat dazed by the brilliance of Julia's smile.

"Yes, well, time does have a way of slipping by, you know. I feel certain someone intended to see to the problem long ago, only never did." It was a lame explanation at best, but it seemed to satisfy the vicar.

"And now?" Brightwell turned his attention to the viscount, once again seated behind his desk and looking terribly important.

"Tell him, Lady Winton," Noel prompted, an unholy gleam in his eyes.

"Well, we, that is, his lordship desires to give the body, that is, the remains, a proper burial." Julia managed a frown at Lord Temple, then composed her face as the vicar directed his gaze at her once more.

"I see. And who was this person?"

"Her, that is, Lady Blackford." Julia said with a gesture, then gulped as the vicar turned his attention to the newly restored portrait of Mary Blackford that now graced the wall opposite her husband. Julia watched with anxious eyes as the vicar rose to walk across the room, standing before the painting with hands clasped behind his back.

"Recently uncovered evidence indicates that Lady Blackford was wrongly charged with suicide. We feel," Julia glared again at Lord Temple, defying him to deny his inclusion, "that perhaps the second Lady Blackford unduly influenced that decision."

"Interesting," the vicar mused, rocking back and forth on his feet while he studied the portrait.

Julia also rose from her chair, walking to the vicar's side to add, "What a pity to deny a Christian burial to a fine woman, just because of jealous accusations."

"You appear to have found out a great deal."

Hoping he would not demand the proof, for she doubted he would understand the sort of communications she'd had with the ghost of Mary Blackford, Julia merely nodded in reply.

"Lady Winton and I have done exhaustive searching of the family records. That is what led us to the location of the remains and upon which we base our conviction," Lord Temple said, rising to join the others before the painting. "Naturally, if you wish you could spend several days pouring over the old journals as we have done." At this, Lord Temple indicated a stack of yellowed, tattered volumes. "However, I must warn you that the spelling is most creative and the handwriting takes determination to read."

The vicar glanced at the books, his consternation clear on his face. It appeared that he had no love for deciphering ancient scripts.

"The workmen have taken the, er, remains up to the mausoleum by now. Perhaps we might have a simple ceremony?"

Julia took a step back in surprise. She had heard Lord Temple address others, but never in a voice that carried such command, such authority. There was not a question in her mind but that the burial rite was only a matter of time.

Thus, with the word brought to the others remaining in the house of the original party, Lady Temple joined her son, along with Julia and the Laceys in the ride to the resting place of the Blackford family. Reggie remained behind to lend comfort to the sensitive Edythe.

Julia listened to the simple, yet eloquent ceremony. When the vicar spoke the words, "O death, where is thy sting? O grave, where is thy victory?" she felt as though Mary had indeed received more than a decent burial, but a vindication.

Electing to walk back to the house rather than ride with Lady Temple and the Laceys, Julia promised to see them at tea, then began her lone trek.

"Wait a moment," Lord Temple said in that commanding sort of voice he used earlier. He stood on the portico with the vicar, discussing the replacement of some tiles on the village church roof.

Not about to find out what might happen were she to disobey, Julia paused on the green slope beyond the little temple. The cool wind that had been gentle before increased, and she clutched her pelisse to her. By the time the vicar left, and Lord Temple joined her, Julia felt chilled to the bone.

"Well," he said in a bracing voice quite unlike his lofty manner earlier, "do you believe Mary is pleased at long last?"

"Perhaps," Julia answered with caution.

"What? Only perhaps?"

"I fear the chill I feel is not just the wind."

"You do not mean to tell me she is still hanging about?" he said, sounding quite utterly dismayed.

"There must be something we have forgotten," Julia replied in a thoughtful tone, suddenly recalling the mysterious words uttered by his lordship the evening before. She shivered and not just with the cold.

"Oh" was his marvelous answer to that bit of wisdom.

"Is that all you have to say to the matter?"

"Leave the problem to me. I believe I have the solution. What we need at the moment is a brisk walk to the house, then a restoring cup of tea." He glanced at her face, then amended, "Or perhaps a glass of sherry? You *would* walk," he reminded.

"Tea would be best, I believe. Your mother thinks I am beyond hope as it is." Julia reluctantly grinned as she met his smile of understanding.

"True, I fear. She has not taken well to this business of Mary Blackford."

"I wonder why," Julia murmured. Her words were lost as they hurried on along the path to the house, intent upon seeking warmth from the bite of the rising wind.

The next matter for Julia to concentrate on was the completion of Lady Temple's miniature. After all, as Julia frequently had to remind herself, that was why she was here, not to indulge her fancies.

Biggins held open the door, then accepted Lord Temple's hat and gloves, commenting that the others awaited them in the drawing room and there appeared to be "news" in the air.

Knowing that the nosy butler would learn of events almost as soon as they happened, if not before, Julia wondered what was afoot.

"Well," said Noel in an undertone as the two marched up the stairs in a rush, "what do you imagine is next? I vow this has been anything but what mother and I anticipated when this all began as a simple house party."

Julia shot him a look of consternation, wondering if he was sorry he had invited her to his home to paint the portraits.

They entered the drawing room together, darting glances at the assembled group. Lady Charlotte looked amused, her husband sleepy. Lady Temple seemed vexed. Only Edythe and Reggie wore smiles.

Julia relaxed, suspecting what was to come.

"Well," Lady Charlotte said in a cat-in-the-cream sort of way, "Reggie has requested Edythe's hand in marriage. Of course, they must seek out her father for his permission, but I should say that is predictable. After all, Reggie is a most amiable gentleman. And Edythe is a dear girl," she concluded with a fond smile.

"Quite suitable, in fact," Lady Temple announced in a tone that implied otherwise.

"Lady Charlotte predicted I would have a meeting that would lead to marriage," Edythe said in a sort of breathless delight. Her little heart-shaped face glowed with happiness.

Julia wondered what financial difficulties, also predicted, were to be overcome, then supposed it could be the matter of a modest dowry. Although it seemed to her that Lady Temple would not have selected a young woman with less than adequate financial background, appearances could be deceiving.

Amid the pleased congratulations from Lord Temple to his friend, and Lady Charlotte's declarations that it was bound to happen, prediction or no, Edythe edged over to Julia's side.

"I am glad I remained, even if there was all that unpleasantness over the skeleton the gardeners found. Pamela insisted I ought to leave. I think she believed I intended to lure Lord—well, anyway, she tried ever so hard to get me away from here. But I stayed."

Impressed by the girl's modest determination, Julia said, "Did not Lady Charlotte tell you to beware of a friend, for she might be false?"

Edythe blushed. "I confess that I believed she meant you, not Pamela."

Accepting a rueful grimace as an apology, Julia patted Edythe's dainty hand, then drifted over to where Lady Charlotte sat in pleased dignity.

"Well," Julia began, "I have passed danger of a sort. Do you think I am safe now? And may I leave this benighted place?" All of a sudden Julia wanted nothing more than to go as far away from Blackford Hall as she might.

"Never tell me you have given up?" Lady Charlotte said, looking not the least dismayed.

"I very much doubt if I shall find joy, let alone perfect love in this house." Julia did not have to turn to look at Lord Temple. She could hear him teasing Reggie in a most displeasing jocular manner about his succumbing to the parson's mousetrap.

"Boys will be boys, after all," Lady Charlotte commented with a faint frown directed at his lordship.

He apparently redeemed himself in her sight when he inserted his announcement in the next lull.

"Why not have a ball? Miss Sanders can send word to her parents to join her. We shall invite several people from the local area and have a celebration."

At the thought of other—and perhaps equally eligible— young women present, Lady Temple perked up and smiled. "But, of course."

Lady Charlotte exchanged a look with her husband, then she offered to assist Lady Temple with the arrangements, since everything must be quickly done.

Left alone for the moment, Julia wondered if she were ever to complete that portrait of Lady Temple. She resolved to attempt to do as much as she might without her model present. The lady shifted about so much that she nearly drove Julia to distraction anyway. Resolved, Julia crossed the room to offer her services for the coming party.

Given a list of names, Julia walked to a small desk where she was assured she would find proper paper. After hunting about, she commenced writing and addressing invitations for what would be a comfortable group, if all accepted, and she believed they would. After all, an invitation to an event at Blackford Hall was not to be despised.

"Mother has set you to work, I see."

"Indeed," Julia replied with cool restraint.

"Now, Julia, you must have a bit of patience. I promised you shall know all, and you will. In time. Say, perhaps this coming Saturday when we celebrate All Hallow's Eve."

"I haven't the foggiest notion what you are talking about," Julia said quietly, her anger clear in her voice.

"So the lady has a bit of a temper, does she? Ah, well, I appreciate the sense of humor that creeps out every now and again. More than compensates." With that pithy remark, he strolled off to persuade Reggie to join him in a game of billiards, since Edythe had been persuaded to pen the letter to her loving and hopeful parents.

Since the list of names took little time to invite and address, Julia handed the completed invitations to Biggins along with the instructions she had received from Lady Temple. Feeling she was no longer required in the drawing room, for the preparations were well in hand, Julia continued on to the small salon. First requesting a pot of tea and a sandwich, Julia studied the miniature she had nearly finished.

When the maid brought her little tea to her, Julia absently thanked the girl, then returned to her meditations while she ate and sipped her lemon-enhanced brew.

Selecting a brush, she touched it to the paint, then sat with it in the air while she considered the face in the portrait. The lady had decidedly shifty eyes. It was a thing Julia had noticed from the first sitting, and could not eliminate from the painting, no matter how she tried.

If Lady Temple considered Julia to be a threat to her plans for her son, might she not find a way to eliminate her? There had been violence in this family far in the past. Who was to say it might not surface again? Julia placed the paint-daubed brush on the palette, then wrapped her hands about her as though still chilled.

In spite of the emerald ring, Julia still felt Lady Temple to be the most likely candidate for the thief. Not privy to the arrangements for her should her son wed again, Julia could only speculate what prompted her, but those jewels would provide a comfortable living in London, or perhaps Italy, should the lady desire to travel.

Julia wondered what kind of fortune Lady Charlotte would have for her friend, Hermoine.

"So here you are. Painting without your model?"

"Lord Temple," Julia said with apprehension. "I feel if I am ever to complete this, I had best attempt to paint from memory." She turned her head to face his response.

"You are not to leave this house, I recall Lady Charlotte predicting. What do you say to that?" He strolled into the room at a leisurely pace, pinning her in place merely with his look.

"Nonsense," Julia retorted with spirit.

"You could not leave until you made a bargain with Mary, if you recall, and that was only as far as the village." He stood on the far side of the little salon, hands behind his back, a gleam in his eyes.

"I found her portrait, her bones now rest beside her husband's. What more could she want?" Truly confused, Julia pushed away from the table to pace about the room.

"What if there were another reason that Mary makes her periodic returns? What if all this to do with the portrait, the jewels, and her remains were accidental, because she found one who was sympathetic?"

"Rubbish," Julia declared in an uncertain tone. She paused in her steps to turn her gaze from her clasped hands to Lord Temple. "Is it not?" she begged.

His sly grin ought to have warned her. But it didn't.

Julia continued to search her mind for a possible solution when she found her chin firmly held by Lord Temple's fingers. "What?" she whispered, still confused. How had he managed to get to her side so quickly?

"I promised," he whispered back. Then he kissed her again, and it was not the hasty touch of the nutting party. Rather, Julia found herself enveloped in an embrace of the sort dreams were made of; warm, satisfying, and definitely demanding.

How easy to yield to temptation, she reflected in one sane moment before he continued his onslaught. His hands performed magic; his lips brought forth all the yearnings she had sought to repress. At last, she tore herself, albeit reluctantly, from his arms, backing away from him with wary steps. The flames of passion slowly ebbed from her body as rationality returned.

"I believe you ought not do that, Noel." Julia shook her head to dispel the mood and her emotions, then continued, "Please leave me, for I want to finish the painting."

"*That* will not make any difference. I promised, and I do keep my promises, you know." His lazy grin taunted her, and she longed to throw her palette at him.

He walked from the room, leaving Julia wondering just what he meant. The jewel thief was not the only mystery around this house. Lord Temple was an enigma; a passionate, exciting, sensual enigma with incredibly beautiful eyes. And Julia wondered if she would ever recover from him.

14

"Let us roll all our strength and all
our sweetness up into one ball,
And tear our pleasures with rough strife
through the iron gates of life."

JULIA placed the book of poetry on the table, then wandered to the window while contemplating the sentiments contained in Marvell's poem. She'd not read it for a long time and had forgotten the poet's words to his coy mistress.

Although it was deemed satire by those who knew his background, Julia thought his views of "quaint honor turned to dust" and "into ashes all my lust" had a point. Still, she'd not accept his argument that simply because "the grave's a fine and private place, but none, I think, do there embrace" was reason to abandon one's morals.

No doubt he would agree with Herrick, to "gather ye rosebuds while ye may." They were of a kind, and wrote of the conflict between love and lover. But, wondered Julia, what of the consequences? There could be more than broken hearts involved.

So, where did that place her? Lord Temple's words and actions had left Julia in a confused muddle, not even considering that kiss. He behaved as though he *knew* something, and teased her with her lack of that knowledge, as though it had something to do with her in particular. How vexing! Even more annoying was the thought that the man knew the effect he had upon her and relished it!

Her contemplation of Lord Temple and his peculiar actions, not to mention words, ceased abruptly at a frantic rapping on her door. She had been about to consult with Hibbett

over a gown for the little ball coming up on All Hallow's
Eve, and turned toward her door leading to the hall with a
puzzled frown.

At her call to enter, the door flew open and Anne rushed
into the room, throwing herself into Julia's arms in dis-
traught tears. "Julia!" The child was hastily dressed, her
white muslin all askew, with the ends of the untied blue ribbon trailing behind her.

"What is it, child?" Julia soothed the tousled hair from
Anne's brow, drawing her over to a chair. Julia sat down,
pulling Anne onto her lap while studying the girl's face.
"What has happened to put you in such a pother?"

"The parrot papa brought me is dead!"

"What? Dead?" Julia drew Anne to her bosom, cradling
her close while considering that stark declaration.

"I woke up and wondered that he was not scolding us for
being tardy with his food, for he always wanted feeding
first thing, you see." Anne gulped, then looked up into
Julia's face. "And he lay below his perch, very still. I poked
at him with my slipper, but he would not move. Nanny
came in and said she was glad the nasty bird was dead."

Julia murmured soothing words a few moments, then
Anne continued. "It was the horridest thing. How can she
be so mean? I liked William." The last was said on a sob,
and Julia wrapped her loving arms about the child, wondering at the cruelty of some people, especially one whose job
it was to nurture and care for a motherless girl.

"Now, do not fidget yourself, child," Julia murmured.
"At least you now have that beautiful doll your father ordered for you." And Nanny had hidden.

"She said it is the ghost who did it. She means to tell
papa that you must go, for she is sure that the ghost will
leave if you do. Why does she not like you? I think you are
a very nice lady." Anne reached up to plant a shy kiss on
Julia's cheek.

The sight of tear-drenched eyes stiffened Julia's spine
and her resolve. Something must be done. While it was
strictly none of her business, she had been thrust into the
heart of this situation. She felt compelled to offer her comments to the man in charge.

Then something Lord Temple said the night before returned, words to the effect that the ghost had dual purposes,
and that Julia would not be allowed to leave the property as
yet. It was time she left; the second portrait was nearly
completed. However, with only half of the problems about
them unsolved, she was loathe to depart this house—even if
the ghost would permit, that is. But, if not now, when? And
why would the ghost of Mary Blackford still want her here?

Wondering if her head would ever return to normal, she
first straightened Anne's dress and tied the blue sash. Then
Julia took Anne's dainty hand in her own warm clasp. "Let
us find your papa. He will know what to do."

Anne slid from Julia's lap, turning up a trusting face. "I
shall tell him that the ghost is awful, and I want it to go
away. Ghosts who kill pets and scare away friends are not
welcome in our house."

Julia smiled at the serious little girl, then tugged at her
hand. "Let us find your papa and confide your problem in
his ears. In the meantime, I think it best not to say overmuch to anyone else."

Giving a sage nod of her head, Anne slipped from Julia's
room with her sympathizer in tow.

When informed of the new loss, Lord Temple took Anne
into his arms, offering her precisely the sort of loving support she needed.

Julia edged toward the door, intent upon leaving father
and child together without her presence. She found the
sight of Lord Temple with his little girl wrapped in his
arms most touching, and wished her own children might
know such fatherly affection.

"Wait."

The soft command brought Julia to a halt.

"It passes the bounds of belief that someone would be so
cruel as to kill that parrot—even if it was a tart-tongued
pest," Noel said. His voice might be quiet, but Julia suspected that the nanny would do well to have her belongings
packed in a trice unless she welcomed a tongue-lashing the
likes of which she had never known.

"I believe we agree on the perpetrator of this deed?"
Julia exchanged looks with Noel, then turned her gaze on

Anne. "My dear child, I am persuaded that the ghost has nothing whatever to do with the parrot's death. Rather, I mistrust Nanny Gray. Could she not be the one?"

Instead of rushing to her nanny's defense, Anne considered the words. "Perhaps," she agreed. "Nanny never did like the bird. Nor," Anne added, "did she like Wiggles. I think she is a very bad person."

Tossing Julia a look that said "I-told-you-so," Noel hugged Anne, then said, "I believe we ought to see that Nanny gets some rest. Maybe she is tired. What would you say to her moving to a pretty little cottage somewhere?"

Anne thought seriously on this for a few moments, then nodded. "That," she pronounced in a too-solemn voice, "seems a good idea."

"And I believe your father has plans for a lovely lady to come teach you all manners of interesting things. Would that not be splendid?" Julia added.

Anne did not answer, merely frowned. Julia wondered if the child would prove stubborn, refusing to trust another after the lapse of her ever-present Nanny Gray.

Leaving Anne to Lord Temple's care, Julia whisked herself to the small salon where her nearly finished portrait of Lady Temple awaited her attention. She adjusted the special spectacles Lord Temple had brought her from London on her nose, then proceeded to study the picture. After deciding that it was useless to persuade the lady to sit again, Julia concentrated on the delicate lace of the bodice, trying to capture the rich fabric. She had not resolved the matter of the eyes.

It could not be helped. Julia saw those eyes as devious, not open and honest. Perhaps were she to use Anne's guileless eyes as a model, it might be possible to bring off an alteration? It was worth a try.

Shifting from the fabric to the eyes, Julia compared the worldly knowledge revealed in Lady Temple's eyes with Anne's innocent gaze. Finally, with careful touches of her brush, Julia achieved what she sought. Lady Temple might not look guileless, but she no longer resembled one who plotted the downfall of the world, either. A few more strokes and the lace came to life beneath her brush.

Finished. Julia cleaned her brushes, then tucked all her painting gear into the traveling box especially designed for her. A glance about the room revealed nothing remained but the soiled cloth in her hand, and the two paintings awaiting their final coat of varnish, then a suitable frame.

Setting aside the soiled cloth for the maid to take away, Julia placed the paintings atop her case, then walked to the library where she judged Lord Temple might be this time of day.

"Come in, Julia. What have you there?" Noel crossed the room. He politely held out his hands to take the case, then noticed the two paintings. His hands dropped to his side while he looked at the paintings.

Raising his gaze, he said, "You are finished." He studied the miniatures more closely, then added, "They are very good. You have captured my mother as I remember her from my youth. I do not know how you knew that she did not always carry that expression she wears now, but I'm grateful you did and painted her that way."

Since Julia had but tried to make her ladyship appear less devious, she could say nothing in reply.

"Allow me to arrange payment, for you have more than earned the sum you asked." He turned to the desk where he had been seated when Julia appeared at the door.

She squirmed a trifle, feeling as though she ought not accept the sum, yet suspecting he'd be annoyed were she to decline. "I shall arrange to leave on the morrow, as it is too late to depart today."

"Leave? Are you not forgetting a few things?" He whirled about, his brow acquiring a devilish quirk, sending Julia's heart into a pirouette.

"I cannot accept that the ghost of Mary Blackford will stand in my way now. Her problems are solved." Julia didn't trust the sly grin that crept over Noel's face at her words. Such a provoking man. He teased her, yet sought her help. Well, she had completed her task. Now she intended to leave.

"I shall be excessively displeased if you go. After all, can you bear to wonder who it is that concealed those jewels in the attic trunk? Or who played the ghost by the bridge? Or if Miss Gilpin will take to Anne? and the opposite? And, you simply must stay for our little ball. Yes, particularly the ball." He appeared to savor that idea, which made Julia madly curious.

Julia was about to reply that she longed to know the truth of all those things when Mrs. Crumpton bustled to the doorway, looking at Lord Temple with concerned eyes.

"Yes?" he inquired with quiet patience.

"'Tis Mr. Vansittart, my lord. He's returned. Shall I put him in his old room?"

Noel shared a puzzled look with Julia, then turned to the housekeeper. "Where is he now?"

"Talking with Mr. Fothingay and Lord Lacey in the entry, sir." The housekeeper looked surprisingly calm, considering she had a ball dumped in her lap, and now a guest thought long gone returned out of the blue.

After assuring her that Mr. Vansittart was indeed welcome to stay as long as he pleased, Noel took the case from Julia's hands, placed it on his desk, then drew her with him from the library.

"Come, we must find out what's happened."

Quite as curious as Noel, Julia followed closely behind.

"It seems that the prediction Lady Charlotte gave for Lady Pamela did not include me," Dick said with a wry twist of a smile when Noel and Julia walked up to confront him in the entry hall.

"A brandy, I think," Noel said, tossing a look at Biggins.

"It is chilly out in more ways than one," Dick said by way of reply, exchanging a look with Noel.

"What happened, old chap?" Reggie inserted, his eyes nearly popping from his head in amazement. "The last we saw of you, why, we expected a notice in the *Post* any day. Never say the girl's parents have higher expectations!"

"Not only do they, an offer from Lord Crumbley awaited her upon our arrival at her home. Her parents were quite in alt."

Julia couldn't refrain from a gasp, then failed to prevent a chuckle from escaping. With a glance at Noel, she burst into choked laughter she simply could not stop, although she covered her face with trembling hands.

"Well, dash it all, Lady Winton," exclaimed an affronted Reggie, "Chap's had a blow. No need to cut up like that!"

"Forgive me for my wretched sense of humor. But, you see, Lord Crumbley offered for me some months ago . . . and I refused him. He may be a wealthy peer, but he is so grossly fat that I could not possibly wed him."

Lady Charlotte had slipped up to join the little group, and now said in an amused voice, "You mean to tell me that *he* is the one that had to have the table cut out so he might eat with greater ease?" To the others she added, "He needed a half-moon of mahogany removed to accommodate his stomach. Ha! Will she accept that offer?"

"She did," Dick replied. "And I should be sorry for her, but for thinking I have had a reprieve!"

Upon that wise remark, Biggins was welcomed with a tray of restoring beverages for the entire group, who shortly repaired to the drawing room, where they proceeded to inform Lady Temple and Edythe Sanders of the perfidious Lady Pamela.

"Well, I never!" Lady Temple declared, offering Dick a smile of genuine sympathy. "Dear boy, you are well rid of the chit if that is how she behaves. Not at all the thing, to encourage you as she did, then turn you down for a title and *such* a man!"

Julia thought she could almost like Lady Temple for her caring. Then she recalled the episode by the bridge, and wondered whether or not her ladyship was involved in it. She had motive and helpers, and she provided the opportunity. But, did she do it? If not, then who?

"That was well-done of you to diffuse the situation as you did. Fancy Lady Pamela accepting one you rejected," Noel said quietly, suddenly appearing at Julia's side.

Embarrassed, Julia shook her head. "I ought not have uttered a word, for it is not the thing to spread about a report of a rejection, you know. But I think it is infamous that Lady Pamela, or her parents, more likely, should reject a well-favored man such as Mr. Vansittart and accept a toad like Lord Crumbley. I suspect Lady Pamela will be a young widow, for he is overly fond of his food and does not look at all well."

"Will be no more than she deserves, if that is the case," Noel reflected.

"Odd. She seemed so taken with Mr. Vansittart while here," Julia mused to herself.

"I was thankful that she turned her gaze elsewhere." The wry expression in his eyes amused Julia.

"For shame, Lord Temple. I do most sincerely trust that you shall not have occasion to experience similar feelings." Julia tossed him a bland look while wondering what his inner reaction would be to her departure on the morrow. It was all very well for him to tease her about the conclusion of the various mysteries still lurking about Blackford Hall. But Julia knew that it was best for all concerned if she left.

Particularly herself. Before the ball.

"Every feeling is offended, my dear Julia. You promised to call me Noel."

She suppressed a grin at his soulful expression. "Did I, indeed? Your Christian name was to be reserved for use when alone. We are scarcely that here." She gestured to the group clustered about Dick. "You would provoke a saint, I believe. What a wicked man you are, sir."

"No! Am I?" He smiled down into her eyes, and Julia's resolve slipped more than a few notches. "What a delightful thing for you to say. Reggie is always and forever telling me what a dull dog I am. How nice it is to know there is one who thinks me a gay blade."

Julia's mind flashed to her late husband, who definitely was a gay blade, and she protested, "Not that, assuredly. I should say a pink of the ton, or perhaps a top-sawyer. I suspect my brother would greatly admire your address," she confessed. "You do cut a dash, if I may say so."

"You may, with my pleasure." He executed a slight bow in her direction, while holding her eyes with his intimately warm and intent gaze.

At that, Julia forced herself to turn aside to listen to Lady Charlotte hold forth on the treachery of parents who sell their daughters to the highest bidder.

"What are we to do about the jewels?" he whispered in Julia's ear before long.

Julia flashed him a startled look. "What do you mean, sir?"

He drew her along to the window, ostensibly pointing out something in the distance. "I strongly suspect that things are coming to the point when those jewels will be wanted."

"You have found lengths of chain to substitute for the jewelry?" She clung to the glass of sherry that had been handed her, still half-full, thinking she had best take another sip, for Noel was behaving in a strange manner, although he seemed to do that every now and again. There was a restless glitter in those sensually beautiful eyes, and the times he turned his full attention on her were most unsettling.

He nodded, then continued, "Could we set some sort of trap?"

"Perhaps. But what?" She creased her brow in consideration. She took that restoring sip of sherry, thinking it very necessary indeed.

"I do not know right now. Mull it over. We may compare notes after dinner." With that, he left her side, going over to where Reggie chatted with Dick and Lord Lacey, drawing the men along with him to the billiard room, with talk of some new maneuver he had invented. They strolled from the drawing room in animated conversation, Dick's lost heart seemingly quite healed.

"Men!" Lady Charlotte declared. "What odd creatures they are. You would never suspect from his attitude that poor Dick took quite a battering. I believe Lady Pamela led him on most shamelessly. I wonder if she thinks to take him as a lover, for you must know it will be difficult for any man as obese as Crumbley to take an interest in his wife, if you know what I mean. 'Tis fortunate he has an heir from his first wife, for I doubt if he intends more than to have Lady Pamela do other than grace his table. Like a stuffed swan, beauty and nothing more."

"Perhaps she will be satisfied with that," Julia said thoughtfully. "Not all women desire a family, in spite of what we are taught from early girlhood. I have heard rumblings of discontent from many women."

"Rumble, they might, they will produce a child every year if that is what their husband wishes and their body provides," Lady Charlotte snapped quietly.

Julia felt her cheeks grow warm. Although she knew everything Lady Charlotte said was most likely true, it was not comfortable to listen to such conversation.

Yet, had she not been thinking just this morning that the poet had a point when he wrote of the pleasure of love and the foolishness of ignoring the same. As a widow, Julia was as free to take a lover as Lady Pamela would be, except Julia had no husband to fool. Yet, it was a thing Julia could never do. If she were to give her love to a man, it would be within the bounds of convention. And marriage.

"Shall we have special diversions for the ball, Hermoine?" Lady Charlotte queried as she joined the pair near the fireplace.

Edythe Sanders timidly glanced at her ladyship, then hesitantly offered, "I believe Lady Temple mentioned that they bob for apples hereabouts on All Hallow's Eve. Could we not have a shallow tub of water and sufficient apples?"

"For the devination of a future spouse?" Lady Charlotte replied. "I should think that might prove vastly entertaining."

"But one would get one's hair all wet," Lady Temple complained.

"Let the men do it, then, but I shall wager there are any number of pretty country misses who will jump at the chance to get a mate even if it means getting their face wet. The water need not be *very* deep, you know," Lady Charlotte said comfortably.

"We should require knives to peel the apples," Edythe reminded, leaning forward in her eagerness to help.

"I should think there might be a great deal of giggling and good-natured nonsense," Julia added by way of persuasion. Not that she would dream of putting her face in a tub of water to bite at an apple, merely to discover, so legend would have it, the initial of her future mate. But with so many young women cropping their hair so nothing but ringlets remained, it would be feasible for them. "We had best have a supply of linen towels on hand," Julia added thoughtfully, thinking of silken gowns that might be ruined otherwise.

"Most of the young chits will wear muslin for this sort of a ball. We shall let it be known it will be a diverting entertainment, with dancing but other offerings as well," Lady Temple decided, as though the entire matter had been her making from the beginning.

The others looked at her with polite amazement. Julia compressed her lips so she wouldn't be tempted to smile.

"And Charlotte will read her cards," Lady Temple concluded, to that woman's amusement.

"Let us hope that Mr. Vansittart will find a young lady to amuse him, for I believe he was sadly out of curl upon his return," Julia said.

"Excellent thinking, my dear girl," Lady Temple said with a nod of approval. "I believe the squire's eldest daughter is of an age to capture a man's interest, and she is a comely child. I shall see to it that she wears her prettiest."

Julia fancied that there was no question but what the squire and his pretty daughter would be present.

At this point a footman entered with a small paper for Julia. She apologized to the others, then scanned the few words. Excusing herself, she went down to the central hall where she found Noel awaiting her.

"The little wooden box is ready, and I've had the bird put in it. Will you join us as before?" He stood where she came to a halt at the bottom of the stairs.

Even as Julia nodded, Anne hurried down the stairs to where they waited. Behind her Hibbett followed with Julia's pretty green pelisse.

"You were quite certain, my lord," Julia murmured as she drew on her gloves, eyeing Hibbett's stiff back as the maid marched up the stairs after helping Julia into her outdoor garment.

"I knew you would not disappoint me," he said simply in reply, then ushered both Julia and Anne from the house. This time no others came along, for as Julia had told Anne, the fewer who knew of the parrot's demise, the better.

The respectful glances from the Blackford staff eased Julia's qualms. They did not think a funeral for a bird com-

plete nonsense. Anne listened soberly as proper sentiments
were expressed, although from all that Julia had heard, the
bird was a regular Tartar and most likely would not be
missed by anyone but Anne. Certainly, Julia had kept her
distance from the ill-tempered bird.

Soon, the trio had left the two little mounds behind the
stables and sauntered back to the house by a circuitous
route. Gray clouds hovered in the sky, like menacing har-
bingers of unpleasant weather, and a nasty little wind had
whipped the air, bringing a chill to the cheeks, if not bones.

Anne danced along the path, chasing a squirrel who
chanced to hunt this way.

Seeming content to stroll along beside Julia, Noel finally
broke the silence. "Thank you for all you've done. Bad luck
about the bird."

"Luck has nothing whatsoever to do with her loss. Nanny
Gray is responsible, or I'll eat my new straw bonnet."

"That sure, are you? As I recall, that bonnet is particularly fetching on you." At her incredulous glance, he added,
"It *is* the one you wore when we went nutting, is it not?"

Murmuring in agreement, Julia thought he was a most
surprising man to have recalled her bonnet after this time.

"We have yet to devise a trap, you know," he continued
in that confidential tone and manner he had adopted as soon
as Anne had run ahead of them.

"I have scarcely had a moment in which to reflect, my
lord," Julia reproved, then repressed a grin when he turned
a wounded look at her. "Noel," she amended.

Then she grew pensive, considering that if her initial belief that Lady Temple were responsible for the transfer of
the jewels to the attic trunk proved correct, things might become a shade uncomfortable. Noel would scarcely wish to
challenge his own mother, for pity's sake. Unless . . . Julia
found herself hoping that someone else was responsible for
those diverted jewels. She hesitated to use the word stolen,
even in her thoughts, particularly were Lady Temple involved.

"Are you looking forward to the ball?" Noel said, completely surprising Julia from her gloomy speculations.

"Of course. Do you think all invited will attend?"

"Indeed. With the local people and our present guests, there should be above a hundred, I feel sure. I hope the weather cooperates."

In the city a hundred guests would be a small gathering. Julia surmised that in the country it would be a welcome addition to a quiet life.

"You brought clothing that will be suitable? I'd not see you uncomfortable," Noel said, pausing in his steps to study her as though to determine whether or not she revealed the truth.

"With the aid of that trimmings I found in the village, Hibbett has performed small miracles with a few of my things. I shall do well enough." Julia smiled at the memory of the caustic comments that had poured forth from her maid as she altered the prim garments Julia had deemed proper for her visit.

"Good." He tucked her arm close to his side, then continued along the gravel path, watching Anne pick a few stray flowers that yet bloomed. "Save me the first of the dances, and the supper dance as well. I'll not tolerate the company of the square's eldest daughter for more than a country-dance. She is pretty, but a bit of a widgeon," he concluded by way of explanation.

Warmed by his regard, Julia was struck by an idea. "About the trap, why do we not employ Mary Blackford? Could I not try to persuade her to stand guard over the trunk, thus frightening whoever it is half out of her wits?"

"You are convinced it is a woman?"

Surprised, Julia stopped, gazing at Noel with troubled eyes. "I'll confess I am. You are not?"

Noel stared down at Julia's pink cheeks, drawing her closer than was strictly proper. "It is possible."

Precisely what that meant he didn't elaborate, to Julia's utter frustration.

15

JULIA paused before the attic door, then seeing that there was not a soul in the vicinity, slipped inside and up the stairs before she could lose heart for her task.

Once at the top of the stairs, she searched the area, hunting for that familiar glimmer of white. Did, perchance, the ghost now settle cozily in her vault next to her late husband? For once, Julia hoped she might be visited by the lady, for she had a proposition to make her. Or did one offer propositions to ghosts? That remained to be seen.

Walking over to the trunk that had lately acquired a proper layer of dust atop it—proper, that is, for an attic infrequently visited—Julia seated herself, then waited.

"Are you around, my lady? I do wish to talk with you, if you please." It would be the usual one-sided conversation, of course. Were there ghosts who communicated? Not being an authority on the subject, although she certainly could qualify somewhat after she left this house, Julia could not say.

"Psst." Julia turned her head, aware of the creaking of the one step that always failed. When his head appeared above the level of the floor, she gave a vexed sigh.

"Lord Temple, that is, Noel, you ought not be here. I do not mean to seem impertinent, but what if she wants to see me, but not you?"

"Relax," he murmured with a devilish lift of an eyebrow. "I think she will accept me."

Julia made the error of gazing into those magnificent eyes and forgot what her objection was. She remembered to swallow, then said, "I do want to please. Her, that is," seeing that there might be another interpretation upon her words.

"I feel certain you will. Please, that is." He strolled over to stand close to where she sat, and Julia wondered if she would have the presence of mind to inform the white lady, as she had first thought of Mary Blackford, of their request. Or perhaps the ghost might send a substitute?

"I wonder if she would," Julia whispered to herself.

"Would what?"

His voice, Julia decided, could best be described as having the utterly sensual quality of velvet, and that of the finest grade. It rippled along her nerves like the draping of luscious fabric across skin sensitively waiting for its touch. Combined with his eyes, Lord Temple possessed an unfair advantage over susceptible women, of which she most definitely was one.

Her reflections on Lord Temple's attributes ceased when the familiar glimmering began in the shadows of the attic, across from where she sat, with Lord Temple now directly behind her.

"Lady Blackford," Julia said with relief. "I hoped you would come. We are here to ask a favor of you."

The figure swayed closer. She raised a filmy hand as though to indicate Julia ought to proceed.

Encouraged, Julia strove for calm, and continued. "The jewels that were in this trunk have been placed in a safe spot, but we should like to nab the one who attempted to gather them up for whatever purpose one can only guess. I think she intended to take them for support in her later years," Julia concluded, thinking of Lady Temple and her love for beautiful clothes. The velvet dragon, as Julia had continued to consider her ladyship, would probably need a good deal of money to keep her happy.

Unless the villainess was someone else. Or a man. Julia didn't think so, for some reason. The bundles had been quite neat, a thing a woman would do, not a man.

Still, her ladyship had softened as of late. She had been warmly kind to Dick Vansittart, properly castigating that foolish Lady Pamela for accepting the obese, yet titled, Crumbley rather than the prosperous and handsome Dick.

Sitting straighter, Julia made their proposal. "We," and she gestured to Lord Temple, "would like you to keep watch up here. If someone does appear to take the jewels—which aren't here any longer, but shall seem to be if you follow me—we want you to frighten the daylights out of her."

The figure drifted across the room to stand in another shadow, as though considering the request.

"Will you? Please?"

"She can't begin to compare to you," Noel murmured naughtily behind Julia's rigid back.

"How do you know?" Julia daringly whispered back at him.

"Instinct. You are flesh and blood." Even his whisper seemed dangerous at this point. Julia knew that the sooner she left this house, the safer she would be from this far-too-attractive man. She tore her attention from Noel to the glimmer of white across the attics.

The shimmering figure swayed again, this time to the top of the stairs. Her regal nod brought a sigh of relief to the pair hoping for compliance.

"Good!" Julia declared with satisfaction. She carefully rose from the trunk, dusting off the back of her gown with an absent brush of her hand. Then, with a friendly nod at the ghost of Mary Blackford, she walked over to join her. "We cannot shake hands, but I do appreciate your help." Julia suspected that anyone else who overheard this chat would consign Julia to Bedlam immediately. One did not have polite exchanges with a ghost.

The ghost nodded, then disappeared from sight.

"Interesting how she does that trick," Noel murmured at Julia's side, his hand sliding possessively around her.

"Let us hope that this works," Julia said by way of reply. She avoided the squeaking step, then paused at the door, peeping out to see if the corridor remained empty.

"All clear?"

"No, Lady Charlotte is coming this way. I hope she goes into her room," Julia whispered.

They waited, Noel pressed closely to Julia's back while they both peered through the crack. Julia held tightly to the heavy oak door, praying that Lady Charlotte came up to change her gown, or required something in her room that would take time. A lot of time. The lady walked along in an absent reflection, as though pondering her day.

Noel seemed totally unaware of the effect the crush of his body against Julia had upon her. The scent of costmary could be faintly detected from his linens, and he had used a spicy lotion on his skin. In the confines of the stairwell, its scent teased Julia, making her exceedingly aware of him and her longings.

He was all that was masculine, only more vivid than any man she had met before. She had once heard a man described as being larger than life, and now she suspected this well described Noel. She would always, to her dying day, recall the moments she had shared with him, particularly the nutting party and this closeness in the attic. His kisses she ignored for the moment. They were only to be taken out on rare occasions to be reviewed with regret for what might have been. She turned her head a tiny bit so she could see his profile from the corner of her eyes. It was a mistake.

It was a pity that a lady could not blatantly seek the attentions of a gentleman. And truly, she did not know if she was prepared to carry any invitation beyond a kiss. Offering the most faint of sighs, she reluctantly turned again, watching to see what Lady Charlotte would do.

The dear lady obeyed Julia's unwilling wish and shortly disappeared from view, shutting her door with a decisive snap.

"She is gone," Julia said, again turning slightly so her words would reach Noel without effort.

That was another mistake.

His face was frightfully close to hers, and those sensuous eyes gazed down into hers with bone-melting result. Julia froze, unable to open the door and sensibly walk down the hall to her room. All she desired was to dissolve into his arms and let the entire world go mad. Did anything else matter? He lightly touched her lips with his.

"Very soon, my spirited lady," Noel said in the most inscrutable of voices, his words hitting Julia like a cold bath. She longed to punch him with her fist. Hard.

"Ohhhh," she exploded in a hiss, then threw open the door and slipped down to her room, horridly aware that behind her a man was softly chuckling to himself, and he knew she could hear every sound.

Did he also know she had wanted his kiss? Wretched man! She would have been embarrassed had she not been so annoyed with him. Why that air of secrecy? That dratted man knew something that she ought to know, and kept it from her! Her very bones felt it. But what could it be?

Once in her room, she sought the comfort of the twins and the gentle ramblings of Hibbett.

"You have dust on your gown, milady," the maid scolded. "Not my place to be wondering what you are up to, but you had best not let her ladyship see you like that, all starry-eyed and rosy-cheeked."

Julia suspected that Hibbett did not refer to Lady Charlotte. And, what did the maid mean by saying Julia was starry-eyed? Rosy cheeks were no doubt a sign of her indignation. That man was enough to try the patience of a saint. And Julia admitted readily that she did not qualify for sainthood.

"Nonsense. You are imagining things. Oh, not the dust, but the other business." Julia turned to offer Tansy a little wooden dog, and the subject was closed.

However, she also sensed the maid kept a watch on her mistress that was far too knowing.

"Well, milady, 'tis a good thing you found those trimmings, for I've managed to do a credible job on this gown, if I do say so." Hibbett held up a simple gown fashioned of a misty green crape. It now boasted a low, ruffled neckline and tiny puffed sleeves. Creamy satin riband wound around the high waist, held in place by a pretty cameo brooch.

Julia lamented the absence of fashionable flounces or rouleaux at the hem, not to mention silk flowers and leaves, or pretty vandyked borders. But if she was so foolish as to venture to the country with naught but plain gowns, she must pay the price.

"It is lovely, Hibbett. You are truly a treasure. Thank you ever so much for all your efforts to improve your mistress,"

Julia said with genuine warmth. In truth, Hibbett had worked wonders.

"Well," Hibbett said with a sniff, greatly mollified by this handsome compliment, "it would reflect on me were you not dressed to the nines, what with Miss Sanders wearing an ice-blue satin under patent net and pink silk roses bunched around the hem."

"How nice," Julia murmured, reserving comment on the picture presented.

"And Lady Temple's to be garbed in orange blossom sarcenet with two rows of flounces and a drapery of silk blossoms down the front. I believe she intends to wear the Blackford diamonds as well, milady. Her dresser implied they are of uncommon magnificence." Hibbett raised an eyebrow at this revelation.

Fascinated by the maid's disclosures, Julia inquired, "Do you know what anyone else is wearing?"

"Lady Charlotte cannot decide whether to don her red silk trimmed in ermine or her blue velvet with the draped tunic and turban to match." Hibbett gave no indication as to what she thought of either gown.

"Oh, Hibbett, I fear I will be greatly outshone in my simple gown, no matter that you have done your best." Julia eyed the dress again, then decided she was being silly and vain. It had an understated elegance she need not be ashamed of in the least.

"But then, it is only a simple country ball. After all, a ball may have as few as ten couples. This will have a few more, that is all." Sending a warm, somewhat rueful look at Hibbett, Julia sensibly turned her attention to the toy Rosemary thrust at her.

A gentle tap on the door brought Anne rushing into the room when Hibbett went to answer it.

"How are you, dear?" Julia said, welcoming Anne into the little group, inviting her to sit with the girls. The child carried her precious doll, never far from her side.

"My grandmama was looking for you. She couldn't find Papa, either. She said it was very vexing," Anne reported as she helped Rosemary construct a tower of wooden blocks.

Avoiding Hibbett's knowing gaze, Julia rose to her feet.

"Perhaps I had best seek out her ladyship. She may wish me to help her with something. After all, the ball will be an additional burden for her, and it is tomorrow."

Ignoring the maid's sniff of disbelief, Julia left the girls playing happily under the watchful eyes of Violet and Hibbett.

The corridor was empty, with not even the disapproving Biggins to plague her. It certainly spoke well of Lord Temple's forbearance that he tolerated the at-times insolent butler.

Julia discovered Lady Temple in the small conservatory located at the far end of the formal drawing room that would be pressed into use for the ball. Already the footman had begun rearranging the chairs and sofas, removing unnecessary tables, and the like. Julia whisked through the room, avoiding a sofa with ease.

The glass room offered a warm and flowerful contrast to the autumn sparsity of blooms in the gardens. Lady Temple hovered over several pots of carnations, a pretty pink-and-white-striped variety. She did not appear to appreciate their beauty, for she frowned at them.

"A problem, my lady?" Julia inquired. She wondered why such fragrant blooms could be a difficulty.

"I wish for flowers that would flatter my gown. But," she sighed, "I had best accept what we have. 'Tis not like London, where one can send to a florist for any blossom one desires." Lady Temple held up a pot to sniff at one bloom.

"I understand you were looking for me a while ago." Julia decided she had best get to the heart of whatever Lady Temple had to say to her. Not knowing would drive Julia mad.

"I wished to have a chat." Lady Temple gestured to a pretty wrought-iron bench placed by a pot of exotic purple blooms.

Julia perched on the bench, clasping her hands before her so Lady Temple would not know that they trembled.

"I liked the portrait you did of Anne," her ladyship began.

"Thank you. I completed yours as well. Your son seemed

most pleased with it." Julia wondered if Lady Temple would notice the modification of her portrait.

"You altered my eyes."

Startled, Julia's gaze flew to meet a guileful look.

"Never mind, there is nothing you might say to that remark." Lady Temple gave an abrupt laugh. "Noel said the painting reminded him of the way I looked when younger. I suppose he is right. One changes with the years. I suppose I have been overly concerned with the family honor. That shows in the eyes, that sense of pride. It has brought little but misfortune for me."

"I beg your pardon," Julia said, utterly confused.

"You needn't. I was so full of arrogance that I thought I could arrange my son's marriage, even though I suspected he might have problems with the gel. Headstrong and perverse, she was. If Noel wished her to rest in the country, she intended to flout his wishes in every way possible. You know, I suppose, for everyone seems to, that she waltzed off to Italy on the arm of that tenor."

"I heard something to that effect," Julia said softly, beginning to feel sorry for the woman at her side.

"I wish to thank you for deflecting Lady Pamela from Noel. I felt certain that she would be an admirable choice for a second wife. How wrong could a mother be!"

Impulsively, Julia reached out to cover a restless hand with her own warm clasp. "I assure you that I did not come here with the intention of luring your son into an unwelcome alliance. He asked me to paint two portraits. That was all I planned. He kindly invited my two babies along, knowing a mother would not wish to part with her darlings. He is an exceedingly kind man." Not to mention sensuous, devilishly handsome, and a maddening tease who tormented Julia merely by standing near her.

"Margaret left here without saying good-bye to Anne. Not so much as a parting hug or a toy. Heartless wench. I cannot say I grieved when word of her death came to us. But I was wrong to intrude on my son's life again. Fortunately, he paid no attention to either of the latest crop of girls I've inflicted upon him, preferring your delightful company."

Taken aback at this sentiment, Julia searched for a reply. "He was merely being kind to me, for I believe he noticed the three of us did not precisely mesh."

"Is that what you think? You were not married long, I take it? Nor were you much in society before your arranged marriage took place?" At Julia's murmur of agreement, Lady Temple nodded thoughtfully. "You have a good deal to learn about men like my son. First of all, he might be polite to a lady for a bit, but never seek out her company as he has yours without reason."

"Well, there are mitigating circumstances there, my lady." Then Julia clamped her lips shut, unwilling to reveal more of the clever plan Noel had concocted with her help.

"And it is none of my business? Good."

"What?" A startled Julia could not prevent herself from exclaiming.

"There is nothing like shared secrets to bind a woman and man together. You are not at all what I would have chosen, but that is not so important, is it? I shan't put up obstacles, my dear. Not anymore."

With that, Lady Temple rose, checked another pot of flowers, then nodded absently to Julia as she left the conservatory, her mind already on something else.

Stunned at the little interview, Julia sat on the bench, inhaling the exquisitely scented air while she contemplated what had been said and implied.

Certainly her ladyship must be mistaken. Noel merely teased and flirted. Nothing more. Not that Julia didn't long for more. Oh, how she longed for more. From the little she knew of the marriage bed, she sensed that lovemaking with Noel would be vastly different than it had been with Giles. Like night from day.

In somewhat of a daze, Julia left the conservatory to be instantly assailed by Lady Charlotte.

"Dear girl, we ought to have a table for my card reading, do you not agree?"

"I suppose so," Julia said, admittedly like one awakening from a sleep.

"I thought perhaps in that little anteroom just off the top of the stairs. Then, there ought to be a tub for bobbing apples. Or do you feel like Hermoine, that bobbing for apples is too wet and messy?"

"Well," Julia temporized, "why not have a tub for those who wish to bob, and hang other apples from strings for those who wish to attempt the feat of biting an apple with hands behind their backs?"

"Clever girl," Lady Charlotte said with beaming approval. "How fortunate we are to have your resourceful head among ours."

Edythe approached, obviously hesitant to intrude, but intent upon talking with the two.

Quite able to be gracious to the lovely girl, Julia rose and held out a hand, drawing her close. "Do you have any ideas to share?"

"At home we hollow out mangel-wurzels and place a candle in them. Could we not have a few for decoration?" Her beautiful face lit up with girlish anticipation.

"Splendid idea. Do they all look the same?" Julia asked, trying to envision how they might appear.

"Not at all. Each is different, with designs of a face, an animal, or even flowers carved into the skin."

"Well," Lady Charlotte declared, "that is a superb notion. I feel certain an under-gardener might be spared to help you. Ask Lord Temple. Most men will let a pretty gel have anything she wishes. And take Reggie with you. Anything to get the men from underfoot," she added quietly to Julia.

Blushing a fiery pink, Edythe whisked herself off to find Lord Temple and Reggie, while Julia rounded on Lady Charlotte with a minatory look in her eyes.

"That was not kind," she scolded.

"No, it wasn't, was it? I wished to talk with you, and she is far happier doing her mangel-wurzel thing in the gardens with Reggie. Although I cannot fathom how one can carve up a vegetable that looks nothing more than a giant beetroot, and as ugly as may be, to have it turn out pretty!"

Julia gave a reluctant nod, then laughed. "You are a terrible lady, you know."

"I am," Lady Charlotte declared with satisfaction. "It is much more agreeable than being a pattern card." She tucked a stray bit of brown curl beneath her cambric day cap and preened like a miss.

At that Julia giggled, then drew her ladyship to a sofa, where they sat close together while having a comfortable coze.

With a pause for a makeshift nuncheon in the breakfast room, for the dining room was under transformation at Lady Temple's direction, they all bustled about the house, having a glorious time decorating and turning the place upside down.

The mangel-wurzels turned out quite charming, as even Lady Charlotte had to admit.

"I really am surprised," she confided to Julia. "I thought the girl was talking through her hat, so to speak, when she said those ugly things might be pretty. But, with a lit candle inside, they are. Amazing."

Julia smiled at Lady Charlotte, then complimented Edythe on her clever bit of decorating. Lady Temple insisted upon nesting each one in an arrangement of pretty colored leaves, and before long the rooms were gaily bedecked with bright autumnal hues.

When Julia went up to her room following dinner, she was tired, but oddly satisfied. Lord Temple had watched her with a peculiar expression that Julia attributed to the plan involving the ghost and the attic trunk. Surely it could be nothing else.

Once Hibbett had removed her mull gown, helped her into her prettiest cambric nightdress and cap, Julia settled down upon her bed, her velvet robe and slippers handy in case the twins fussed in the night. Although they were much better lately, both occasionally woke in the night.

She had barely dozed off when she heard a piercing scream. Sitting up, Julia threw off her covers, grabbed her robe, and thrust her arms into the sleeves with more haste than care, then pulled on her slippers. Within moments she flew into the corridor.

Lady Charlotte peeped around the corner of her door at Julia, an alarmed expression on her face. Of Lord Lacey, nothing was seen, and Julia surmised he was one of those who could sleep through a storm.

The others were in the opposite wing of the house and most likely couldn't hear a thing.

Julia advanced upon the door to the attic, suspecting what lay on the other side.

"Do not go up there," begged Lady Charlotte in a loud whisper.

"It is all right. Do not worry," Julia soothed, marching to the door and flinging it open.

Beyond the top of the stairs the stout figure of Nanny Gray cringed in utter terror. Not realizing that Julia stood at the bottom of the stairs, she pleaded with the ghost.

"Leave me alone, I say. Leave me be. I've come to get what's mine, I have. You leave me be." It seemed the nanny found few words at her command in her horror, for she kept repeating herself over and over, almost like a litany.

"Nanny Gray," Julia said in a soft, menacing voice, "what do you seek?" She began to slowly walk up the stairs, hoping that the candle Nanny held would not go out, for Julia had forgotten to bring hers.

"You!" the old woman shouted when she turned her head, heedless that others might hear her. "All was fine 'til you came here. Then trouble, nothing but trouble. You want to take Miss Anne from me, dismiss me—I know. Force me into the cruel world with not a roof over my head."

Julia held up a hand when she got to the top of the stairs. Could it be that the *nanny* truly was the one who had stolen the jewels? Julia felt relief after the puzzling chat that morning to know that Lady Temple was innocent.

"That is not true, although I feel certain you would welcome a rest in a little cottage after your long years of service."

The woman ceased her moaning and peered at Julia with suspicion. "Can't you see it?" she demanded, pointing at the ghost of Mary Blackford. "It's real, this time. I see it!" Nanny Gray whispered as she tried to get close to the trunk and the ghost barred her way.

"I do," Julia calmly replied, "but I seek nothing from that trunk. Why do you?"

The terrified woman fell on her knees before the trunk, scrabbling at the lid while shrinking from the figure of the ghost that hovered close by. She was exceedingly determined, Julia reflected. Neither she nor Noel had expected the nanny to actually get past the ghost.

"I come to get my things. I know my days are numbered as long as you are here."

"Things?" Julia pursued. "What things?"

"Mine. I found them, so I claim them."

The woman had gone mad, Julia decided, for some of those jewels had been filched from the safe in the library, others from Lady Temple's room.

"I somehow doubt you 'found' them, Nanny. Tell me, you poisoned the puppy and the parrot, did you not?"

"So what if I did? Nasty, dirty things, they were, too. I did him a favor, getting rid of them."

"How fortunate Miss Anne stays so clean," Julia murmured. "I should hate to think you'd feel a need to get rid of her as well."

The nanny ignored that bit of reflection and dared to lift the trunk lid. She set the candle on the rim of the trunk, a precariously foolish thing to do. Pushing the jumbled clothing aside, she delved to the bottom, then grabbed the ten rolls, dropping them into a canvas satchel in a rush. With a wild look in her eyes, she whirled about to challenge Julia. With candle once again in hand, she advanced.

Realizing that she had quite foolishly remained at the top of the stairs, and thus offered an easy target—a very vulnerable one, Julia attempted to move out of the nanny's way. She failed when her robe caught on a broken chair arm, preventing her evasion.

"Ye'll not stop me, my fine lady," Nanny threatened, moving toward Julia with the most menacing gleam in her eyes that Julia had ever seen. "I got my freedom here. All I need to set me for life. Ain't nobody going to stop me from leaving. Got the gig hitched and waiting, and I'm off at once."

"You will never get away with this, you know," Julia offered, hearing a quaver in her voice.

"But I will. You'll walk ahead of me, and if you don't

open them doors, I'll push you down the stairs. People will think you tripped on your fancy bedgown. All that frippery. You'll never attract his lordship, even with that. Too plain by half, you are. Not like my lady."

Julia sensed Nanny referred to Margaret, the first wife, and wondered that the woman knew her, for had she not come later?

"She was mine, too, many years ago, until she wed Lord Temple. Then I got her girl. Now you want to spoil it all. Yes, I'll push you down the stairs anyway. Just for the fun of it."

Now, quite terrified herself, Julia freed her robe from the chair arm, and slowly negotiated the stairs, hoping to keep far enough in front of the madwoman to avoid a shove in the back.

In the corridor, Julia moved forward with great caution, observing that Lady Charlotte's door was now closed. Dare Julia call out? Would anyone come to her rescue?

They reached the grand staircase, and Julia gazed down the long flight of steps with a shuddering breath. Her mouth was dry, and she knew she trembled.

"Move."

Julia placed her foot on the first step, then felt a fat finger stab into her back. Fear lent wings to her feet. Grabbing up her robe and gown, Julia dashed down the stairs like a flash of lightning.

Behind a stupefied Nanny, the still-dressed figure of Lord Temple appeared.

"I suggest you leave this house at once," said a cold voice, hard and implacable. "I shall see to it myself."

16

JULIA huddled against the newel post at the bottom of the stairs, one hand clutching at the solid oak post, obviously stunned at Noel's sudden appearance. Her face was a pale oval with huge green eyes; the cambric and lace of her nightcap emphasized her fragility. Folds of her dainty sheer cambric bedgown peeped from beneath the shimmering velvet of her robe. She looked utterly terrified.

"Move along," Noel prodded ungently. He followed the grim-faced nanny down the stairs. His candle combined with hers to offer meager light. Shadows danced menacingly about the hall, turning the corners into murky caverns.

Once on the firm floor of the hall, Nanny whirled about, clutching the satchel with the bundles in one hand, holding the candle in her other. Darting a wild glance at Julia, then turning a malevolent gaze on Noel, she snarled, "I'm going. Pity I couldn't give this interfering female a shove. You'd marry her an' shame the memory of my lady!"

She backed another step toward the front door. "I have the gig awaiting me, an' I'll be gone from here. Now. I packed long ago. Had this all planned, you see. All I needed was my bundles." She clutched the satchel with the all-important parcels more tightly, still backing toward the door. "Leave me go, or I'll toss this candle at that woman. She'd burn right nice, I figure."

With a cautionary glance at Julia, Noel took a step toward Nanny. While wicked, for she had murdered a pup and a bird, she had actually harmed no human. She believed the bundles in her satchel to be jewels, only they were naught but the chains he had found and placed there after removing the gems. She deserved punishment for even thinking of pushing Julia to her death, for he very much doubted if anyone might have survived a fall down those stairs. Perhaps finding what she believed to be a fortune was no more than copper chain would be justice enough.

He dared not risk an injury to Julia. The wisps of cambric flowing out from under her velvet robe would burn in a flash. She was far too precious to make punishing that evil woman worth the gamble.

"Very well," Noel said at last when he saw the woman had her back to the door. "Go. I dare not chance a fire."

Behind him Julia murmured a small protest, but Noel ignored it.

Nanny fumbled behind her for the handle, then inched the door open, keeping a wary eye on the two who silently faced her. She continued to grasp the candle's holder—its light flickering in the draft. It was uncertain what she might do with it—toss it toward them or discard it outside.

Noel might have rushed her at this time, he knew. He felt it better to let the evil woman go, be free of her once and for all. She gained nothing.

All at once, she whisked herself around the door and was gone. The heavy oak door swung shut, closing with a dull thud. The silence that followed was eery in its totality.

A few steps brought Noel to Julia's trembling side. How he welcomed the chance to take her in his arms.

"What a nasty woman," muttered Julia into Noel's fine cambric shirt.

"She is gone. I could almost pity her for her delusion. How fortunate for us that in her haste, she did not bother to examine the bundles from the trunk."

"The ghost prevented that, for Nanny was frantic to escape from the attic. She seemed genuinely terrified at the sight of the ghost by the trunk."

Noel felt the slump of Julia's body as she relaxed against him, and he tightened his hold. Her shock might fade, but she must have been frightened half to death.

"How could she think of setting fire to me, or this magnificent house," Julia declared with more spirit. She drew away from Noel, gazing up into his face with what he'd swear was indignation.

"Hush, she is gone. Forget her." Noel pulled his love close to him, stroking her back in an effort to calm her.

"Mary Blackford was here. I wonder why she came down with us? Do you suppose . . . ."

Julia tore herself from Noel's arms and dashed to the door. She flung it open, then ran out onto the terrace that stretched across the front of the house. From there she searched the avenue that led toward the main road. A three-quarter moon peeped from behind a cloud to reveal a strange scene.

"Something's happening at the bridge. I can see a white figure—it must be Mary. What can be going on?" Clutching her robe tightly about her, Julia hurried down one wing of the front stairs with Noel thundering behind her. She could hear him sputtering at her, fussing.

"Woman, you ought not be here. Get back to the house. This is something for me to handle." He caught up with her, and Julia held out one hand, hoping for contact, comfort, closeness, or all three. He must have sensed her determination, for he ceased nattering at her about going back to the house, and helped her along in their mad dash through the night.

They were both breathless by the time they reached the bridge. The overturned gig lay to the far side, a wheel still spinning slowly. Off to one side the ghost of Mary Blackford stood by the rushes, watching, her hands folded before her.

"Do you think Nanny survived such a disaster?" Julia said in a small voice. She did not relish what such an accident might bring. No matter how evil the old nanny had been, or what she had done, Julia didn't wish death for her.

Noel pulled Julia to a halt. She could see his frowning face in the moonlight. He looked fierce, his anger felt in the grip of his hand. She willingly remained when he ordered her to stay put. There had been not a sound or movement from the smashed vehicle.

After a glance at the still figure on the ground, he released the horse. He hastily checked it over, then sent the only slightly-bruised animal back to the stables with a pat. Following that, he turned his attention to the carriage and what he suspected he'd find.

"She's dead," he announced at long last when he climbed around the wreckage of the gig. "Neck must have broken when the gig went over, or else her heart failed her. My guess is that Mary suddenly appeared at the far end of the bridge, and the horse was spooked at the sight of the shimmering ghost. Nanny most likely panicked as well. I doubt she was a good driver, so she lost control quite easily."

"She never found out that her attempt was unnecessary, for the fortune she believed hers was in reality mere copper chain. How sad," Julia said, shivering with the cold.

She found herself scooped up in Noel's arms and carried back to the house in a none too hasty pace.

"I do not see how you can have compassion for a woman who doubtless intended to kill you. Do you not realize that she must have been the one who pretended to be a ghost at the bridge when we made that trip back from the village? There could be no one else who wished you harm. She certainly did."

Recalling her unkind thoughts about Lady Temple and her possible motives, Julia was grateful that the moon offered poor visibility so he could not see the blush that stained her cheeks.

"She was undoubtedly mad, and worried that she would be let go with little or no pension," Julia offered by way of explanation.

"Listen, my dear, those jewels must have disappeared over several years. I have not checked that safe in ages, so I can't say precisely when, but it was not a recent theft. She carefully planned this," Noel growled.

"How horrible. All that's been planned for tomorrow night . . . will her death force cancellation of the ball?"

"I think it best if we say nothing. Mother will need to know, and Lady Charlotte, for it was she who came to warn me what was afoot."

"I owe her a great deal, in that case. She peeped from her room just before I went up to see who had screamed. When we came down from the attic, there was no one about, and the bedroom door was closed tight."

"Poor little love. You have had a hard night of it." He carried Julia up the stairs to the front entrance, then set her carefully on her feet, not completely releasing her while he opened the door. Once inside, the door swung shut while Noel again swept Julia into his arms.

"You best put me down," she said firmly.

He seemed surprised, although it was difficult to tell in the light from the one remaining candle.

"But, you must return to bed," he protested, holding her closer for a moment.

"Sir," she snapped, pretending to be shocked.

He chuckled at this, then stood waiting for her to explain. He did not set her on her feet.

"I am no featherweight, and you have done yeoman's duty as it is, carrying me all the way from the bridge. I believe I am able to make my way to my bed, in spite of a fright." She suspected her smile was a bit strained around the edges, but she was determined he do no more.

At this she found herself placed gently on the floor, but not totally released from his protecting arm.

Julia cleared her throat. "This will not seem as frightening by day, I suspect."

"If you could have seen your face when I appeared."

"I saw yours, which was quite enough. You looked most formidable. It's a wonder her heart didn't fail her then. Mine would have, had you glared at me that way."

Julia slipped away from him, intent upon reaching the safety of her room before she did something utterly foolish. He followed at her side, his hand slipping under her elbow, seeming reluctant to lose touch with her completely.

Julia smiled at her fanciful notion. Girlish dreams. That's all she had, in spite of those strange utterings from Lady Temple this morning.

At the top of the stairs, Noel insisted upon escorting her to her room. Since he had the only candle, both of them forgetting the necessity of another, she could see he was right. At her door, Julia paused, exhausted by all that had happened.

"I shall see you in the morning. Sleep well. You are safe, now. Later, I shall order the wreckage cleared away and none shall know of the disaster. I'll put it about that Nanny ran off, and couldn't handle the horse." He touched Julia's cheek with one finger, then left.

Julia was surprised when she woke hours later to the gentle sound of Hibbett murmuring to herself.

"Robe all tangled, slippers wet and black with dirt. What's been going on in the night, I'd like to know."

"Nanny Gray had died while attempting to run off with some jewels," Julia announced, knowing Hibbett wouldn't repeat anything revealed in confidence. "No one is supposed to know about it. Actually, they weren't jewels, but it's a long story." Julia told the maid all that was needful, then went to reassure herself that the twins were safe and happy. At the sight of their scrubbed pink faces beaming with delight at Violet's chatter, Julia felt that come what may, her world still continued.

Once dressed she made her way downstairs, wondering what she would find.

Servants bustled about the house. The pretty decorations supervised by Lady Temple brought lovely color to each room.

In the breakfast room, Julia discovered Lady Charlotte.

"My dear, I am all atwitter." She glanced about in a furtive way. "No one but Hermoine and I know what truly happened last night. Fortunately, the others slept soundly. How providential that there is no trace remaining of last night's business." She took a breath, then said with careful emphasis, "Miss Gilpin arrived. She has gone up to see Anne. From all reports, Anne is enchanted with the lady," Lady Charlotte said with delight.

"What a blessing. The poor child has endured quite enough." Julia selected a modest meal, then joined the other woman at the table.

"Nanny was quite mad, you know," Lady Charlotte confided over her teacup. "Noel told me that she had been pilfering jewelry for some time. Scandalous goings on. Had it been anyone of a less generous nature, he'd have brought her before the magistrate. She'd have been hanged for certain."

"Perhaps her death at the bridge was fortuitous. Who knows what she might have done next?" Julia offered, with a shiver at the images Lady Charlotte produced.

"Now, enough of that. Noel said to tell you the wreckage has been cleared away, the horse suffered no harm, and the incident shall be as though it never happened."

"But it did. But for the ghost, things might have turned out vastly different." Julia well knew the futility of playing it might have been, so she deliberately diverted her attention to the ball that evening.

"No more reflections, my dear," Lady Charlotte said.

"It seems shocking to make merry when someone has died," Julia said before leaving the subject.

"She was but a servant," Lady Charlotte declared, dismissing the woman with the customary response of one of the upper class.

Knowing she was being foolish for her sensitivity over the matter, Julia finished her little breakfast, then joined Lady Charlotte in a tour of the rooms to be used that evening.

There was a shallow wooden tub for the bobbing, and long lengths of cord awaited crisp apples, so that shy girls might not get their curls wet, yet still try the fun. A table awaited Lady Charlotte, her pack of special cards displayed faceup.

"I intend to drape a scarf over my head, like a Gypsy, for the fun of it," Lady Charlotte explained with a smile.

Edythe's mangel-wurzels would shine prettily from each nesting place once lit. Although, Julia had to admit they looked less than pretty by day, their ugly, beetroot shape seeming an unlikely choice for decoration.

"Charming, is it not?" Lady Charlotte said enthusiastically.

"Quite charming." Julia looked about while crossing the room to the large window that overlooked the rear of the house down to the stables. From here she could see the forlorn wreckage of the gig, and the cluster of stable hands that worked to take it apart. Nothing was ever wasted on a

well-run estate. The wheels would be removed and stored
for future use. Anything else useful would be repaired, the
leather seat set aside to grace another vehicle. Little would
be consigned to the heap, and that would most likely be
used as fuel.

Of Noel, there was no sign. In the distance the mausoleum could be glimpsed through the trees. Julia hoped
that by now the ghost of Mary Blackford was at rest forever.

Wrapping arms about a suddenly chilled body, Julia continued her stroll through the rooms, listening to Lady Charlotte chatter on about anything and everything. Before long
Edythe and Lady Temple joined them. Edythe seemed unaware of any undercurrents in the house, but Lady Temple
cast a number of curious looks at Julia.

It was difficult to face her ladyship after the dreadful
thoughts that had lurked in the back of Julia's mind. How
could she have believed that the elegant lady would go so
far as to eliminate Julia in such a brutal way? It just showed
how the ghost and the other happenings around here could
affect a person.

By the time it became necessary to dress for the ball,
Julia was grateful. She would be glad when the night was
past. She could leave; Noel had promised as much.

A glimpse in the looking glass revealed a tense face
above the low, ruffled neckline of the misty green gown.
Julia frowned, then drew on her long white gloves, reflecting that at any other time she would welcome such a delightful party.

"Now, none of that, milady," Hibbett scolded. "Let me
fuss at your hair. Getting dressed mussed it a trifle." She
motioned to a chair before the dressing table.

Submitting to the soothing ministrations of her maid,
Julia wished she had some pretty jewels besides the modest
pearls her father had given her years ago. Giles had never
bestowed a thing on her. Not so much as a bride gift.

"It will have to be the pearls, Hibbett. And the matching
earrings." Julia sighed with regret.

The maid smiled, then picked up a slender box of dark
velvet. "Maybe not." She opened the box, then drew out the

lovely necklace of topaz stones set in delicate gold filigree. Before Julia could think of an intelligent thing to say, she felt the cool gold against her skin when it was proudly draped around her neck by Hibbett. Matching earrings came next. They looked better than when in the attic.

"Oh, my," Julia said in an impressed whisper. In the looking glass, the well-cut gems glittered back at her. The light of several candles revealed the twinkling beauty of the fragile gold spun around the stones. "But, I cannot . . . ."

"Her ladyship sent these along to you, in appreciation for all you have done," Hibbett reported with a smile.

"Lady Temple?" To Julia, this was a final blow.

"I suspect Lord Temple had a hand, milady, for it was he that gave me the box." The maid wore a disgustingly smug look.

Julia acquiesced at that point, for not only had she performed a service of sorts, but a wistful look told her that nothing had ever become her half so well as the pretty topaz set. She set off down the hall with a few hopes.

Rather than a formal dinner, Lady Temple had elected to have a sumptuous buffet, spread with the fruits of the harvest. Julia had seen harvest buffets before. This topped them all.

People began to arrive. Members of the local gentry drifted through the rooms. Some were tempted by the buffet, others conversed in animated groups. Pretty muslin-clad girls giggled and flirted with their fans at handsome, and some not-so-handsome, young gentlemen. It was an autumn rainbow of color, and Julia felt pleasure in her own appearance, especially after seeing one or two envious glances directed her way.

She heard nothing of the tragedy that occurred during the night while she wound a path through the increasing throng of people.

"There you are," Noel murmured in her ear, coming upon her when she returned to the central hall.

"Oh," replied a startled Julia. Then she touched the necklace, blushing prettily. "Thank you for the jewels, sir."

"But for you, they all would have been stolen. Mother agreed with me that you deserve a reward. May I say they look lovely on you?" He drew closer to Julia, reaching out to flick a finger at the necklace. "Come, we are to begin the dancing. It shall be a fast contra-dance, so I hope you are prepared for a rousing good time of it."

She allowed him to usher her up the stairs and into the drawing room. They were soon at the head of the first set. When the fiddler picked up the tune, the man at the pianoforte joined in with the flutist. It was foot-tapping music, the sort that makes it impossible to stand still.

Before long Julia was breathless, happily whirling along with Noel, laughing up into his handsome face.

She danced with Reggie, then with Dick before retiring to snatch a respite where Lady Charlotte enviously watched the young people.

"Not at all the way we danced when I was a gel," the dear lady reminisced. "The minuet is a far prettier dance, to my way of thinking. More graceful."

"Most likely," Julia agreed, wondering what had become of Noel, then espied him across the room, performing a dance with Edythe Sanders. Dick evidently found the squire's eldest daughter a charming armful, for he remained at her side when not partnering her in a dance.

The room grew warm, and Julia longed for a dash of fresh air. Although it most likely would be a trifle chilly out, if she wrapped herself in a warm cloak she would be comfortable enough. The moon beamed brightly tonight, few clouds to dim the scene, the night cool, but not frosty.

Her mind made up, she whisked herself from the drawing room when Lady Charlotte turned her attention to her cards. A hasty dash found the fur-lined cloak that had been her mother's. Julia slipped quietly down the great stairs and along to the terrace. From here it was but a short distance to the Tudor knot garden.

Pretty paths bordered with herbs and low-growing annuals wound around in a pattern of a lover's knot. Stone benches along the sides proved a welcome spot in the summer. Julia slowly paced along the paths, planning her trip on the morrow.

"So, here you are. I wondered what had happened to you. Biggins suggested I look this way."

Julia whirled about, peering from under the hood of her warm cloak at the man who walked up to her, a quizzical look on his face.

"I sought a breath of air," she said softly.

In the moonlight his handsome dark looks stood out in sharp relief. His black coat of superfine over black breeches and striped silk hose, with a fine white marcella waistcoat above which his immaculate white cravat was tied seemed most appropriate for the light from the moon. Everything around them complimented him in sharp contrast.

She looked up into his eyes, noting they were darkest of all. "Thank you for insisting I remain for this party. Your mother is a marvelous hostess. As you are a host."

"You disappeared. I wanted to talk with you."

She edged away from him, sensing his power over her too keenly to dare remain close to his side.

"Thank you again for the gift. It is far too much, and I know I ought to return it. I shall treasure it all my days." She paused, glancing back at him, wondering what he wished to say to her.

"You never did find out why else the ghost of Mary Blackford returned," he mused aloud. "Did it not strike you as odd that she comes periodically?"

"I did ask you about it. You promised to tell me later. Is it later now?" Julia said in a teasing voice.

"Perhaps. Did it ever occur to you that there are times when you are governed by events not of your own making? That another controls your destiny?"

Julia paused in her steps, her face growing thoughtful. She turned to face him. "I suppose you might say so, although we do not suspect it at the moment. Why do you say that? What brought on such a philosophical mood?"

She found herself drawn to a halt. She searched his face for a clue to his behavior and words, and was puzzled to find what she considered a merry gleam in his eyes. Or was it merely a trick of the light?

"Do you recall all those dusty volumes through which I searched? The journals of those many ancestors of mine who enjoyed compiling their days and events?" His voice sounded amused, too.

"I read a few of them myself." Julia frowned slightly. He teased her. Or did he? She waited with impatience for him to reveal whatever was on his mind.

"I discovered that the ghost appeared with an amazing irregularity, or perhaps I ought to say at predictable times." He moved closer, gazing down at Julia with a warmth that left her almost breathless. Certainly, her heart was waltzing at a furious pace.

"Now, you definitely tease," she said, shaking her head while a chuckle escaped. "What an utter beast you are . . . sir."

"Noel, my love." He gave her a little shake, a fond thing, not at all minatory.

"You ought not say such things, you know," she said, her voice a thread of sound, for his words teased, yet she treasured them so much. If they were but true.

Rather than argue with her, he simply drew her to him with exquisite tenderness, and bestowed the sort of kiss that she had longed for since the last time their lips had met. She felt that same bone-melting languor creep over her. What a blessing she need not move at the moment, she'd be quite incapable of anything other than wrapping her arms more tightly about his neck.

Proceeding to do precisely that, she sighed with deep contentment when he at last released her. Most willing to snuggle her head against his shoulder, for he was such a lovely comfort against the chill of the night, she waited for him to speak. Pray he said words she longed to hear.

"We, you and I, are fated to wed," he said, that deep, rich, velvety voice uttering the words in a very prosaic manner.

Her head flew up, and she gave him a startled look.

"You are as surprised as I was, I see."

"Explain yourself," she said, taking a swift step away from him.

He refused to allow her to leave her snug spot, and pulled her against him. Julia hadn't the will to try again.

"I noticed while paging through each volume, a pattern for the ghostly appearances emerged. Since they were spaced so far apart, people came and went in the interim, and few could recall the events that followed. Indeed, they may have made no connection. Had there been a longtime resident of the house, he might have made that particular link."

"Noel, I swear that if you do not get to the point, I shall do violence!" Julia declared with asperity.

"Remember when Lady Charlotte predicted that you would not leave this house?"

"Yes, indeed I do. That silly ghost would not allow me to go through the doorway."

"Ah, my love, there is more to it than that."

"Noel," she whispered in a warning tone, placing a dainty fist against his chest.

"Quite simply, the ghost of Mary Blackford visits this house—normally—before the marriage of the heir, or the birth of an heir."

"Normally? How may one say a ghostly visit is normal?" Then the content of his words hit her, and she reeled with the meaning. "And you feel she came because you are to marry?" A curious little glow began to grow deep within her along with a seed of hope.

"Twofold, my love. I would not be the least surprised if the two were one." He tilted up her face so to better look into her eyes.

"And?" she boldly queried, trying to search his dark eyes in return, finding it difficult. But she'd swear his gleamed with that merriment she noticed earlier.

"To make it come true, it means that we most likely had better take advantage of that license I obtained when in London. I should hate to have the wrong event first, and I'll confess to the greatest impatience, my dearest love."

His chuckle dissolved when Julia punched him lightly on the chest.

"Say, I do, Julia. I will—I shall—I love you, say any of those, only put me out of my misery, for I have never before proposed to one I love as I love you."

"Oh, Noel, I shall marry you, my dearest, dearest love, and never part from you. There is no one on earth with the peculiar sense of the absurd we share. If nothing else, we shall know much joy through our remaining years."

That understanding settled, Noel proceeded with Julia's wholehearted cooperation to seal their pact with the most devoted of kisses.

In the shadows, a shimmer of white appeared for a brief spell, just long enough to satisfy herself that all went well. Then Mary Blackford drifted up the hill to the little building set on the very top where her own love awaited her. Until the next time.